Shalom

Shalom

A Collection of
Australian Jewish Stories

Compiled by NANCY KEESING

Collins
Sydney · London

This collection © WILLIAM COLLINS 1978
First published 1978 by William Collins Publishers Pty Ltd, Sydney
Type set by Filmset Limited, Hong Kong
Printed by Colorcraft Limited, Hong Kong

ISBN 0 00 221596 9

National Library of Australia
Cataloguing in publication data
Shalom.
I. Keesing, Nancy, ed.
A823'.3

Acknowledgements

I thank all the authors who gave permission for their stories to be included in this book, and also those descendants and/or copyright holders who gave permission for the use of copyright stories by deceased authors.

Stories which have appeared elsewhere are: 'The Boarding House' by Hertz Bergner and 'Café in Carlton' by Pinchas Goldhar in *Southern Stories*, Melbourne, n.d.; 'Doris and the other Fräuleins' by David Martin in *Quadrant*; 'Going Back' by David Martin from his novel *Where a Man Belongs*, published by Cassell Australia Limited; 'Music a Terror' by John Lang in *Botany Bay*; 'Who Then Was Alice's Evil Fairy?' and 'Middle Eastern Questions' in *Southerly*; 'Mr Bronstein Learns His Lesson' in *Two Ways Meet: Stories of Migrants in Australia*, E.L. Rorabacher (Ed.), published by Cheshire; 'Original Anzac' in *The Messenger*; 'Well, What Do You Say to My Boy?' by Judah Waten in *A Century of Australian Short Stories*, C. Hadgraft and R. Wilson (Eds.), published by Heinemann Educational; 'Hostages' by Fay Zwicky in *Coast to Coast 1973*, F. Moorhouse (Ed.), published by Angus & Robertson; 'My Greatest Ambition' by Morris Lurie in *Happy Times*, published by Hodder & Stoughton (UK), and 'Messiah in Fatherland' by Morris Lurie in *Australia/Israel Review*, and in his new novel, *Flying Home*, published by Outback Press.

Contents

INTRODUCTION	9
Part I EUROPE	15
A Man *Lilian Barnea*	17
The Boarding House *Hertz Bergner*	37
My Grandfather *Lilian Barnea*	45
Café in Carlton *Pinchas Goldhar*	60
Doris and the Other Fräuleins *David Martin*	76
Going Back *David Martin*	86
Part II AUSTRALIA	95
Music a Terror *John Lang*	96
Who Then Was Alice's Evil Fairy? *Nancy Keesing*	107
Mr Bronstein Learns His Lesson *Nathan Spielvogel*	124
Original Anzac *Lysbeth Rose Cohen*	130
'Well, What Do You Say to My Boy?' *Judah Waten*	137
A Peaceful Life? *Judah Waten*	154
Made in Czechoslovakia *June Factor*	164
Hostages *Fay Zwicky*	171
My Greatest Ambition *Morris Lurie*	178
Bailey's Pine *Len Fox*	189
The Fat Girl *Harry Marks*	199
Part III AUSTRALIA-ISRAEL	211
Middle Eastern Questions *Nancy Keesing*	213
Messiah in Fatherland *Morris Lurie*	221
BIOGRAPHICAL NOTES	235

INTRODUCTION

THIS ANTHOLOGY offers a representative selection of fiction by Australian Jewish writers for the first time in Australian publishing history.

For a long while I have thought a book like this would be interesting and valuable for two chief reasons: by collecting works of varying kinds and from different eras it could yield insights about Australian Jewish life and thought, and, in a wider and more general way, about migrant experience. I believe *Shalom* does fulfil these expectations.

It is appropriate that this book will appear during the Jubilee year of the Sydney Great Synagogue. Among the convicts who arrived by the First Fleet were nine Jews—arguably the oldest 'ethnic' group in this country. The Jewish congregation in Sydney, from which grew the Great Synagogue, itself developed from a burial society established in 1817.

It is also appropriate for this book to appear during an historic year for another reason: John George Lang (1816–64), who was Australia's first native-born writer of fiction, was descended from one of those First Fleet Jewish convicts; indeed he had the rather rare distinction of being born, at Parramatta, near Sydney, a second-generation Australian in 1816. Lord Casey (also an author), who was Governor General from 1965 to 1969, was a descendant of Lang's convict grandfather, John Harris.

There is not, and never has been, an identifiable school or group of Jewish writers of fiction in Australia. For that matter there are not, and never have been, many Australian Jewish writers of fiction. This may not seem surprising if one considers the small numbers of Australian Jews in relation to the total population. On the other hand that small minority has produced remarkable numbers of eminent people in the professions, in commerce, the armed forces, the performing arts (especially music), and to the office of Governor General—two out of nineteen since 1900.

As to writers the explanation is chiefly historical and essentially linked with language; the raw material of any author. The Jewish population, a few thousand people scattered throughout a huge country, often in communities too small to muster the ten adult men necessary for congregational prayers and rites, remote from centres of Jewish life, thought and religion, and, throughout its history in Australia, eroded by intermarriage and assimilation, has always and only maintained or increased its numbers through immigration.

The earliest Jewish convicts, mostly of English origin, were augmented by a handful of energetic free settlers, also mostly from England, until and during the 1830s. The Hungry Forties accounted for further modest migration, but it was the gold rushes after 1850 which attracted fairly large immigrations of Jews, predominantly from England and Western Europe. Later in the nineteenth century people fleeing the partitions of Poland and Germany and the compulsory military service of certain European countries, which imposed impossible conditions on young men practising orthodox Jewish religion, arrived. (The families of Sir John Monash and Sir Isaac Isaacs were among the wave of immigrants from the Polish corridor.) Towards the turn of the century Jews escaping pogroms in Eastern Europe swelled the Australian population (Judah Waten's family were among these).

No doubt because Australia is so much more distant from Europe than is America there were no mass migrations to this country, nor did the populations of whole villages arrive here, as happened in America. Consequently, in Australia, Eastern European Jewish culture—writing and publication in the Yiddish language, self-renewing Yiddish drama—had a tenuous existence. A few Yiddish writers wrote stories in Australia, the most accomplished being Pinchas Goldhar and Hertz Bergner, represented in this book in Judah Waten's sympathetic translations.

Large numbers of German and Austrian Jewish refugees ('reffos' as Australians and even, to our shame, some Jewish Australians, referred to them) came to Australia during and after the 1930s; followed by Jews from Central and Eastern Europe, chiefly Hungary and Russia, and from Mediterranean and Arab countries, a migration which continues at present together with increasing numbers of South African families.

In other words, the Australian Jewish community has always contained a high proportion of first and second generation migrants. If good writers are rare in any population, they are rare indeed (or so the American experience suggests) before a third migrant generation.

One interesting thing about the authors represented in this book is that six of them (Barnea, Bergner, Factor, Goldhar, Martin and Waten) were born in Europe. Of these, Barnea, Factor and Waten were chiefly educated in English speaking countries. At the other end of the scale are Harry Marks, Len Fox, Lysbeth Cohen and myself from families settled in Australia generations ago, with many forebears who were Anglo-Jewish and/or Western European before that. Such families are usually long divorced from any Yiddish speaking or Yiddish cultural tradition. Some strict traditionalists may dispute Fox's inclusion since his Jewish descent is on his father's side, from a family whose members have included the distinguished Australian literary critic A. A. Phillips, the British parliamentarian Dr Marion Phillips, and Emanuel Phillips Fox, a pioneer of impressionist painting notable in the history of Australian art. Len Fox says that increasingly he thinks back to his family and their background and his fine recent story, 'Bailey's Pine' justifies his inclusion.

Given writers of such varied eras and backgrounds I wondered, at the outset, whether any pattern for the anthology might or could emerge. As a last resort one can always arrange a compilation chronologically, or alphabetically by contributors; but my preference, both as reader and editor, is for anthologies which have architecture, logic and force in their own right. In the first place I wrote or spoke to most of the present-day contributors explaining the project and was delighted that every writer I approached agreed, and with enthusiasm, to submit stories. Several asked whether Jewish themes and/or Australian backgrounds were preferred. I declined to offer guidelines. In the event all but one of the items selected have some Jewish reference. As to background an interesting pattern emerged.

The book opens with a fine story by Lilian Barnea, a new writer of great power, which, together with the other stories in the section called 'Europe', most movingly and precisely typifies the kinds of fear and persecution that drove the Wandering Jew to these shores in this century. Another story in this group, 'Café in Carlton' by Pinchas Goldhar, also typifies the Australian distrust of 'foreigners' (and not only Jewish 'foreigners'). Mr Mandel sadly represents only one of those hordes of migrants who have broken down under the stresses of misunderstanding and unkindness—unfortunately there are too many unhappy 'Mr Mandels' be they Italian, Greek, Turkish, Lebanese, Jewish or whatever, and be they male or female, among our migrant population in Australian cities, towns and countryside here and now.

By contrast 'Going Back', an excerpt from David Martin's fine novel *Where a Man Belongs* is to some extent the other side of that tarnished coin—the return to a country of origin; the distress and strain of matching ideals of forgiveness to personal realities and memories of hate.

The stories wholly set in Australia cover the span of European settlement here. John Lang's tales are all based on actual people and events. His auctioneer, though his accent is disguised as cockney, was very likely Lang's kinsman, James Larra, a French Jew who arrived at Sydney as a convict with the Second Fleet in 1790. My story, 'Who Then Was Alice's Evil Fairy?' is really a combined account of several of my own relatives. 'Alice' embodies both an aunt of my mother and a step-grandmother of my father, but I also traced in the story a general historical pattern. Nathan Spielvogel was best known for his local histories of Ballarat. 'Mr Bronstein Learns His Lesson' speaks of and for the many 'foreigners' who suffered from misguided Australian patriotism during World War I. I regret that, to balance this tale, I could not find any fictional account of the many Australian Jews who have served in the armed services in two world wars, but Lysbeth Cohen's story 'Original Anzac' contributes a balance of feeling if not of theme.

Judah Waten's 'Well, What Do You Say to My Boy' recalls migrant experiences of the earlier 1900s; his 'A Peaceful Life', June Factor's 'Made in Czechoslovakia' and Fay Zwicky's 'Hostages' speak for the refugees of the 1930s but also link with Morris Lurie's wholly Australian 'My Greatest Ambition'. 'Bailey's Pine' by Len Fox and the very different 'Fat Girl' by Harry Marks are nevertheless linked in exploring that particular and peculiar awareness of blood ties and tradition that, somehow, tugs at the heartstrings of part-Jewish people or assimilated people, reminding them of their inheritance often when they least expect it.

At least two of the authors here, Lilian Barnea and David Martin, have lived and worked in Israel. Some of the authors represented are Zionist sympathizers; some are not and one is opposed to Zionism. But Jerusalem is a part of the blood inheritance I spoke of and, to keep this in mind, the book ends with two stories which refer to Israel as well as Australia, one of mine and a fine chapter, 'Messiah in Fatherland' from Morris Lurie's new novel, *Flying Home*.

NOVEMBER 1977

Europe

There were Jewish settlements in the Old World long before the Spanish Inquisition drove the Jews from Spain. Recurrent persecutions continued to force Jews from town to town and country to country in Eastern and Western Europe. Many eventually sought refuge in Asia, Africa, the Americas and other New World countries. The stories in this section are as old as anti-Semitic ignorance and prejudice, but as recent as our own times.

LILIAN BARNEA

A Man

IT WAS SNOWING quite heavily now. 'Brrr...' said the droshky driver abruptly stopping the horses. He turned to Wisniewski. 'Mister. No use going any further. They are fixing the gas mains round the corner on Marszalkowska.' Wisniewski had almost dozed off. 'Gas mains?' he asked stupidly. He stared ahead into the swirling snowflakes—traffic seemed to be proceeding normally. 'They are fixing the gas mains. The road is opened up.' The man's bearing was insolent; his voice mocked with a kind of gleeful cruelty. Wisniewski felt the sudden, familiar pull of fear at his bowels—in a split of a second he was icily awake. Tall, blond, blue-eyed, (though his profile was a little too Grecian, perhaps?) Wisniewski knew without doubt: he knows. He stiffened—a hunted animal. Some part of his mind, that was not frozen with fear, cautioned: behave naturally. But, under the circumstances, it would be natural to make a scene, for the droshky had only gone several blocks. And a scene was out of the question. 'Well,' said Wisniewski, trying to sound nonchalant, breezy, cheerful even—a devil-may-care sort of fellow, an old Warsaw pro. 'That's too bad, isn't it? We'll have to give the old feet a workout!' And wished he could take the words back, as soon as he said them. They jarred, they rang desperately false—their effect was not softened by the wet curtain of snowflakes that mercifully blurred the sharpness of visual contact between himself and the man. The driver, half turned in his seat, hovered above him like some threatening bird of prey. 'Thirty zlotys,' he said. Wisniewski had thirty-five. He took the sweaty, crumpled roll of banknotes out of his pocket, wordlessly detached thirty zlotys and handed them over. His hands shook ever so slightly, he could not control them. He scurried down the droshky step to the pavement and walked very fast in the direction opposite to his destination.

He walked blindly, trying to moderate his steps. Must not run. People, obscured by the wet snowflakes, jostled him indifferently and after a while this indifference helped him to regain a semblance of calm. He was grateful for the womb-like safety of the snow. Please, let it snow forever, let it snow till the end of the war! Now that he had relaxed a bit, he became painfully aware of the pressure in his bladder. He hadn't relieved himself for hours. And the nearest public lavatory was in the main railway station on Marszalkowska and Chmielna. Well, in order to get home he had to turn back anyway. Wisniewski turned abruptly, simulating the annoyed air of one who reminds himself suddenly of something he has forgotten to take or do. He even mumbled and lightly struck his forehead with his fingertips. An actor, that Wisniewski. Acting, always acting —for in order to survive he had to assume that he was being constantly watched by some hostile, furtive stranger. Only in his sleep, in his dreams, did Wisniewski stop acting; then Kirshbaum took over, and Wisniewski would wake up in cold sweat lest Kirshbaum had inadvertently betrayed him.

The snowflakes were beginning to thin out. Now and then a passerby glanced at Wisniewski with curiosity; his shabbiness was eye-catching even in poverty-stricken Warsaw. Wisniewski had eaten nothing for almost twenty-four hours, but hunger was now completely eclipsed by the intolerable pressure in his bladder. To piss! He hesitated at a massive house entrance—its dark inside beckoned invitingly. Just one minute in some corner! He walked in.

Boys were pelting each other with snowballs in the well-like courtyard beyond the corridor. But they seemed absorbed in their play. A tantalizing smell of boiling cabbage wafted from somewhere. Most likely from the janitor's room. Wisniewski could see it clearly with his mind's eye—the puffy featherbeds, the holy pictures on the wall with Christ's bleeding heart in the centre, everything saturated, enveloped in the thick steam of boiling cabbage. He stood in the corner formed by the heavy door and the left-side wall and fumbled with his buttons. Courage! But somebody might walk in, somebody might pass through, and surely any minute now the janitor would come out. And him Wisniewski knew as well as he knew his room. The man was an institution, always true to type, an illiterate lump of meanness stuffed with cabbage. 'Mister,' he would surely say in his janitor's voice. 'Mister, what do you think you are doing here?' And Wisniewski, if he hadn't lacked that little piece of skin, Wisniewski could have answered in the same tone of voice, as he daintily held his fearlessly exposed member and directed an insolent stream at the other's feet: 'I am pissing, can't you see?' But Wisniewski was in no position to answer anything. So he took the only way out left to him—the coward's way out—he buttoned up his brimming need and walked out into the street.

At once he realized that it had stopped snowing. A fresh wind had sprung up; the sun shone fitfully, retreating every other minute behind dirty clouds that seemed to race across the sky in order to bump into each other violently. A war in the sky—a war on the ground. Wisniewski took this change of weather very personally. Once, in his student days, long before the war, he had been to England. With longing, he suddenly remembered the fogs. If one could spend the war walking around in a dense, soupy fog, one would surely survive. If only the Lord would visit a plague on Poland: fog. That it may cover the land, and seep into their dwellings, and under their skins, and into their nostrils, and into their food and into.... Like in the ten plagues visited upon Egypt. Darkness, blood, lice, hail.... Had the Lord visited fog upon Egypt, or hadn't He? Wisniewski couldn't remember. Darkness, blood, hail, frogs, lice.... Anyway, there was no lack of lice in Poland. It was unfortunate that they didn't discriminate and plagued the Jews as much as the Poles. At the thought of lice, Wisniewski felt his scalp crawling. He lifted a hand and scratched vigorously. Darkness, blood, frogs, hail, lice.... Scratching? Hadn't there been scratching in Egypt? Wisniewski scratched.

A man stared at him. Too hard—too long. And, very hesitatingly, started to approach. The past washed over them in an all-engulfing wave and for a second would not be denied. They had been classmates—the only two Jews in a quite exclusive Polish school. Gurewich stared at Kirshbaum, and Kirshbaum stared at Gurewich. A whole gamut of feelings passed between them in the course of that second: tremulous recognition, longing—and fear. The fear won out. The man lowered his eyes and quickly passed on. Wisniewski felt shaken to the very roots of his being. Gurewich—his friend Gurewich! Why hadn't he spoken to him! He looked back urgently, but Gurewich was receding with shuffling little steps, he was no longer within call. And anyway what could Wisniewski have called? Gurewich—Gurewich wait! You fool, he rebuked himself, you bloody fool. Destruction lay that way. And that thinking about the plagues, that, too, was dangerous thinking—it was Kirshbaum thinking. He must stop all this nonsense right away.

He turned into Marszalkowska. As he had expected, the road was closed up—traffic was normal. In spite of the war, the street had retained some of its old elegance. Instinctively, Wisniewski straightened up, squared his shoulders and walked with a lighter step, as though, by so doing, he could obliterate some of his lice-ridden shabbiness. Marszalkowska still held its old magic for him—it was made up of the stuff of dreams. Memories welled up in Wisniewski of youth, love, luxuries large and small purchased here. Even the all-pervading numbness in his bladder no longer seemed to matter. Gurewich. This street had once belonged to him and Gurewich. And the girls: Jana, and Basia, and Hanka Lesinska, and lots of others. He had walked them all here and had boldly whispered sweet nothings. How confident he had been in those days! His confidence inspired and maintained by his student's cap, its arrogant brim set at a jaunty angle, as indispensable to him as the nose on his face. But the nose itself was not very confidence inspiring with its slightly too pronounced downward curve. So, confident in a cocky sort of way—yes. But secure—never. And, come to think of it, the confidence had also been precarious; its shaky balance could be tipped by an unfriendly glance. Still, precarious confidence is better than no confidence at all. Wisniewski passed a café he had used to frequent and looked in eagerly through the steamed-up window. Incredible! The place was full of people. He looked away quickly—someone might recognize him.

And all because of that little piece of skin. His parents had not been observant Jews—they had been atheists and totally assimilated. Why then, had they thought it necessary to mark him for life? Right now, castration would have been preferable to circumcision. A gust of wind pierced Wisniewski's numbness. If he hadn't lacked that little piece of skin, he could now turn back and walk into the café. Though, of course, there would be no need to turn back, because if he hadn't lacked that little piece of skin, he would have walked into the café to begin with. First, he would boldly use the smelly little men's room at the back; then, imperiously, he would order coffee and cakes. And if somebody there knew him, if someone recognized him, if the café owner threatened exposure, or tried to blackmail him, or if some friendly soul sidled up to him furtively and said in a shocked, frightened whisper: 'Kirshbaum, are you crazy, what are you doing here, Kirshbaum!'—he would be able to answer: 'I am not Kirshbaum. Kindly step with me into the back, where I can remove my trousers in privacy, and I shall prove to you that I am not Kirshbaum. I am an adopted orphan, a foundling, a bastard if you like—but I am *not* Kirshbaum.'

A bastard. What a bastard he was. Not by birth, but by nature. Would you deny your own parents, you bastard, you! Would you? Would you deny your own parents? You! Kirshbaum! Would you? Yes, acknowledged Wisniewski sadly but fiercely, and he pulled at the already pulled out collar of his dirty, tattered coat, and he huddled within himself to retain that last bit of warmth that was fast deserting him. Yes! And a thousand times—yes. In order to preserve life, he would deny life itself. And Wisniewski shuddered—this time not with the cold, but with self-loathing. Where was his honour? A Japanese would have committed hara-kiri long ago. He Wisniewski—or rather, he Kirshbaum—would not know how to commit hara-kiri; but how varied the possibilities in death where there were none in life! One could jump off a building; or jump into the river; or hang oneself; or set oneself on fire; or plunge a knife into one's heart; or poison oneself—though obtaining poison might prove somewhat difficult. And surely, if only he exerted his imagination, there were other ways, too. Such *embarras de richesse*! But would Kirshbaum avail himself of any of these? Kirshbaum would not. Because Kirshbaum wanted to live. So Kirshbaum would continue to hold desperately on to the glossy, slippery surface of life, darting hither and thither to avoid capture—the way an insect on the kitchen floor darts to avoid the squashing boot.

And now Wisniewski was almost home. Home was where

A Man

his wife lived—where he had once lived with his wife. Zlota Street. Sunk in thoughts as he was, the name of the street loomed before him suddenly and caused him shock. Zlota Street. Just a few steps and he could be home; but Wisniewski walked on. One did not go to one's beloved wife, one's estranged, beautiful, terribly desirable wife, whom one had not seen for almost a year and then only very briefly; one did not go to that kind of a wife and walk straight into the lavatory. He would go to the main railway station, relieve himself, perhaps even tidy himself up a little —and then go home. But already from afar, he could see that the main railway station was swarming with Germans. People pushed past him to get away from the vicinity of the danger spot as soon as possible. 'You better turn back, Mister,' conspiratorially advised an old woman, who had bumped into him in her haste. 'There's a round-up of some kind.' Wisniewski turned back. For a moment, he felt good. These were the first kind words addressed to him in a long time.

So—home to Maria. Maria might, of course, be out—and he had no key. Come to think of it, what had he done with his key? He had taken the key when he left home almost three years ago to enter the ghetto. And had always carried it on him, had always carefully transferred the key to his new pocket on the rare occasions when he changed his trousers. For, after a while, the key had become a symbol; the key, and a much-handled, slightly faded photograph of Maria on the beach—a tousled, exuberant Maria—were the only tangible proof that the past had been real; and, as time went on, this became increasingly difficult to believe. After he escaped from the train he had, systematically, gone through his pockets; and, among other things, he had torn up the photograph of Maria into little shreds and had scattered the shreds to the wind. In his urgency to live, he felt no qualms about having destroyed the photograph; however treasured, it was only a fragment of the past imprinted on a piece of paper. But the key! Where was his key! Had he thrown away the key? A key was an innocuous, a neutral thing. A key looked the same whether it unlocked a Jewish or a Christian door. And he—the fool that he was—must, in his panic, have needlessly thrown away the key; when, all the while, the incriminating evidence was there, indelibly stamped on his body.

Wisniewski entered Zlota Street. What if Maria were out? Maria was certain to be out. Hadn't she told him, when she last came to see him in the ghetto (how uneasy she had been then, how embarrassed, how eager to be gone); hadn't she told him that she had taken an office job? Of course, Maria had to be working; if Maria wasn't working, what did she live on? I am sure Maria works, Wisniewski reassured himself. But if Maria were out working, how would he get into the flat? Perhaps Maria was not working today. Perhaps she was sick—nothing serious, of course—perhaps she had only stayed at home with a cold.

And how would Maria receive him? Would she be happy, relieved at his escape, would she be glad to see him? 'She could have saved you,' were the last words his mother had said, before being taken away. 'Maria could have saved you,' said his mother, bitterly, scathingly, in a terrible, final indictment of a marriage that she had never approved of. But this Wisniewski would not admit; this truth—if it were the truth—he could not contemplate, lest he lose his sanity. Maria was like a flower; a soft, beautiful flower—an expensive flower—a flower that exuded gentle whiffs of Chanel No. 5, which no vulgar smell of acrid smoke could ever obliterate. Whatever happened around her, Wisniewski felt sure, Maria would remain untouched, uncontaminated; she would always go on gently exuding Chanel No. 5; and this was only right, this was as it should be.

Home, at last. Wisniewski wished he had a hat, which he

could pull down on his sweating forehead to obscure his face. As it was, he could only hope. Hope that the janitor was in his cabbage-permeated cubby hole; hope that he would not encounter any of his old neighbours on the stairs. Because what he was doing was, of course, sheer madness; it was criminal. The punishment for harbouring a Jew was death; he was exposing Maria to the penalty of death.

The entrance was empty. In the courtyard a little girl— a thumb in her mouth; funny, endearing pigtails sticking out from underneath her bunny-rabbit hat—stared at him trustingly. The staircase, too, was mercifully empty; with a madly pounding heart he took the steps two or three at a time.

She must have sensed the urgency of his knock. The door opened immediately, giving him no chance to compose his features. He stood on the outside, breathless, panting, dirty, exposed in all his vulnerability; and there she was: fresh and fragrant as ever. And for a very long second utterly disbelieving. Then she said, quite clearly, but sort of resignedly: 'You'd better come in.'

As soon as he entered, he understood. He took one step in the narrow, little passage; the kitchen, with its shiny red floor, was to his left. The warmth, the light, and the delicious smell of food assailed him all at once. So did comprehension. The man at the kitchen table looked up in impatient inquiry, steadily holding in mid-air the spoon he had been carrying to his mouth; and a spark of hope was extinguished almost before it had been born. No, this was not a guest. His demeanour proclaimed him master of the house. Two gleaming plates filled with a creamy-textured red liquid in which floated bits of white, steamed invitingly. Tomato soup with rice! Wisniewski was an intruder in a world to which he no longer had any right.

And, in the meantime, Maria had closed the door. 'Come. Come and eat, you must be hungry,' she said hopelessly, but kindly. At these words, ridiculous tears stung Wisniewski's eyes; the numbness in his bladder melted suddenly; abandoning all thought of dignity, he bolted for the lavatory.

The lavatory was at the other end of the flat, next to the bedrooms. There was no need to quiet his noises. But now he found it very hard to urinate; his long-denied bladder would not be coaxed. By the time he had induced a reluctant little trickle that would stop and have to be encouraged again and again, he was in a state of near panic. And all the time, he was aware of their arguing voices—till the front door was slammed angrily; then, there was silence.

'I escaped from the train,' he said, trying to make it sound different than it had been. Trying to convey: *I am a man. What are their trains to me, they won't get me, you know me, don't you Maria?*

But she knew. She may have been like a beautiful, expensive flower, but she was no fool. And anyway, even a fool would have known. It was there for anyone to see: in the way his hands shook, in the way he slurped his soup, greedily, sloppily, in spite of himself; above all, of course, in his eyes. So that embarrassed, guilty, helpless, she could only repeat: 'Eat. Don't talk, eat your soup while it's warm.' And after a minute of impossible silence, which filled the kitchen like another presence: 'I'll go and start your bath—you must want one very much.'

'Wait!' said Kirshbaum. Some of the soup dribbled on his chin; he wiped it away with clumsy fingers. 'You... who...?' he began. The question stayed poised between them, but remained unuttered. It was not a question Kirshbaum could ask in his present state of degradation. 'Tell me how you have been, Maria,' he asked instead. She squirmed—and it afforded him momentary satisfaction. Squirm, you bitch, squirm!

'These are awful times,' said Maria, at last, with quiet

force. Which, of course, summed it all up; and, after that, there was little left to say.

The water came up to his neck. It pervaded every inch of him with a sense of luxurious well-being...aaaaah.... To be able to stay in the bath for ever and ever and ever.... No wonder the Romans cut their wrists in the bath. What a marvellous way to go! A death fit for an emperor! Suddenly Kirshbaum felt elated at the prospect of such a death; it did not frighten him the way the other deaths had. All he had to do was to get out of the bath and take a razor blade out of the little medicine cabinet. The razor blades were kept in the left-hand corner on the top shelf. Maria shaved her legs as soon as the slightest suggestion of fuzz appeared on them; she was never out of razor blades. And the man must shave, of course. At the thought of the man Kirshbaum felt his heart beat violently in his throat; tormented, he sat up in the bath. To end it, end it once and for all! He stood up decisively, making the water spill on to the floor over the rim of the bath. He put out a foot; the deed was almost as good as done; and then it occurred to him that in death, too, he would be an encumbrance. Because of that little piece of skin. Because how would Maria explain that little piece of missing skin! In wartime, it was easy enough to explain a corpse. A friend has been staying with me. He committed suicide in the bath. Take him away, please. Easy as pie. Who cares? But where a corpse was a mere trifle, a corpse with a missing piece of skin became a very grave matter. A matter of life and death. So that, for the moment at least, Kirshbaum was unable to commit suicide.

Shivering with cold (for the bathroom was unheated) and weak with relief, he sat back again in the now tepid water. He released the plug, emptied half of the bath, then turned the hot water on. But the water that came out of the hot water tap was tepid, too. And he hadn't yet washed his lousy hair. Kirshbaum plunged his head into the remaining water and rubbed his head with the yellowish soap. His eyes smarting, he scrubbed very hard. The smell of the soap offended his nostrils; but certain, later knowledge was still being mercifully withheld. These were still the good times when one attached no special significance to a cake of soap; soap was still thought to be soap, albeit of poor, war quality. Kirshbaum rinsed his hair in running water. No longer cold, he felt exhilarated with cleanliness. He had not been this clean for years. When he came out of the bathroom with a large towel tied around his waist, he was feeling good. He was almost on the point of whistling, when he heard them talking. The man had come back.

'Karol will have papers made for you,' Maria said quite energetically, momentarily at ease for the first time since he came, because now they were talking of survival; and such things as sex and marriage paled in comparison with what was at stake. For one fleeting second they were partners again; plotting together, conspiring to outwit death.

'Is there any particular name that you prefer?'

'Wisniewski,' said Kirshbaum. 'Jan Wisniewski.'

'I'll tell him,' said Maria, awkward once more at having to join her lover, who was waiting in the adjoining room. Kirshbaum had not seen the man again—they avoided each other assiduously. As far as he could tell (for the other had been sitting when he saw him), the man was of approximately the same height and build as himself. 'I wonder if he wears my clothes,' thought Kirshbaum, glancing down at the white shirt and the crisp fabric of his suit. 'Probably does, the rat.' Though, to be quite fair, the man had not been wearing anything of his. Kirshbaum stopped his pacing to stand in front of the mirror. His face stared back at him—pale, gaunt—but, considering everything, he did not look too bad. He was still a fine figure of a man. The suit was only a bit too loose—he had been somewhat overweight when he had entered the ghetto. At that time he had left most of his good clothes at home—there had been no point in taking them along to where he was going. His hair was too long; it curled at the base of his neck. Made him look quite interesting, actually. Like an artist, or something. But, of course, it would not do to look interesting; rule No. 1 in the game of survival was: do not attract attention. Don't be conspicuous, blend in with your surroundings. The suit was too good. And he must get a haircut. At the thought of entering a barbershop, Kirshbaum went weak at the knees.

The murmuring voices in the next room had suddenly become louder.

'Yes, yes I know,' the man was saying with impatience. 'No need to write anything down. I'll remember. Wisniew*ski*—Jan Wisniew*ski*,' he said, accentuating the *ski* with derision.

Kirshbaum was all hate. Rage and humiliation overwhelmed him. He wanted to kill. For a brief instant he was indifferent to survival; anger predominated and lent him abnormal strength. He was on the verge of making a clean end to it all: murder that bastard, murder that bitch, kill himself; in that instant, weak and emaciated as he was, he was strong; he was capable of anything. But already the strength was at its peak—already it was waning—already it was gone. The urge to survive reasserted itself. Wisniew*ski*. The *ski* was too aristocratic, too pretentious. A *ski* was what every Jew longed for in the privacy of his heart. The man— may he roast in eternal hell; may his balls fall off, may his hair fall out, may he become scrofulous!—the man was right. *Ski* was wrong. What was needed was something more plebeian, something with more authenticity.

Their voices were receding down the hall; their footsteps echoed on the polished floor. Was the man going out again? 'Maria,' called Kirshbaum. 'Maria!' he bellowed. The footsteps hesitated; stopped. Maria came back.

'Maria,' said Kirshbaum. 'I have changed my mind about that name. Make it Wisniak.'

Did she actually prefer the man to himself? Or was the man there merely because she had to have a man—to earn for her, to escort her, to tell her how beautiful she was. And to make love to her. Karol. Did she say to him (in that slightly affected way she had): 'Hold me, Karol, hold me. Hold me tight.'? Or had she changed her vocabulary with her man? Had the fact that he, Kirshbaum, was Jewish ever really mattered to her, disturbed her? Did she find the man superior because his nose slanted upwards rather than down? (Thus pulling at his upper lip, and giving him a somewhat pinched, foxy look.) And that extra little piece of skin: did his, Kirshbaum's, lack of it detract from his potency, his virility? Did she find the man superior in that department?

Dusk was seeping into the living room. Kirshbaum, legs crossed, reclined in an armchair and turned the screw. Did she? Had she? Would she? He could not ask her, because she had gone out. Shopping, she had said. She had been gone for a long while. How much shopping can one do in wartime? And when she returned he would not be able to ask her, either. For a wall had grown between them, which was sturdier even and more impenetrable than the walls of the ghetto. So that in her presence, as well as in her absence, he could only conjecture. Might she? Will she? Does she? On and on and on. Like a ripe boil filled with pus, so he was filled with pain. One pinprick, and he would burst. The pain would ooze out of him slowly, painfully; there was enough pain in him to flood the world.

It was nearing curfew time. Maria came home just as he was beginning to worry. Tense, he now sat on the very edge of the armchair anticipating her return; nevertheless, the grating of the key in the lock startled him. One of these days his heart would surely explode in his breast, or choke him with its pounding—and that would solve everything. He heard her busily opening and closing the kitchen cupboards, as though to say: see, I have done a lot of shopping. Today he had found her with a lover firmly ensconced in his place; tomorrow, or the day after, or in a few days at most, he would be leaving. Very likely, he would never see her again. It was, therefore, utterly preposterous that it should matter to him how she had spent the afternoon. And yet, it did. It mattered very much.

The ghetto was burning. From where he sat, Kirshbaum could see the red sky. Dusk had deepened to darkness; but both were reluctant to switch on the light—afraid to see each other's face. Despite the war, despite the horror lurking in the streets, the rules of the game were being strenuously observed. The man was absent; they were alone. For this evening, this night, they were once again man and wife; sitting together in the cosy darkness, yet each on his own. The problem was how to fill the screaming silence with words that did not say too much. An impossible situation.

'And Magda and Stach?' asked Kirshbaum, groping for a safe subject. 'What's become of them? Do you ever see them?'

'We see them quite often,' said unthinking Maria, piercing him with the *we*. *We*. *We* see them quite often. How completely the man had replaced him! With his wife. And with his friends. Because Magda and Stach were, or rather had been, *his*, Kirshbaum's, friends—they were people Kirshbaum had known well long before he met Maria. A man, it would seem, is easier to replace than a favourite chair. Once he and Maria had been *we*. Now Maria was being *we* with somebody else. Now Maria was being *we* with Karol.

'Yes...' said Kirshbaum bitterly. 'Yes.'

By now Maria had realized her mistake. She got up abruptly to screen the window. Darkness no longer hid them from each other. 'I am going to make supper,' she said lightly, much too lightly, as she turned on the light. And like everything they said, this trivial little announcement sounded wrong. Words, reflected Kirshbaum, are clumsy things. In themselves they mean little; they take on colour from our thoughts—they take on full meaning from the intent they are spoken with.

'Good,' he lied. 'I am hungry.'

It had been a very long evening. It was going to be an even longer night. Unless.... But Kirshbaum could not, would not ask. And Maria had, wordlessly, made up a bed for herself in the living room. So....

He turned restlessly bothered by dormant desire. This morning he had been hardly human, incapable of any feeling but fear. This afternoon he had been tortured by jealousy and doubts. But, for the moment, his cleanliness, his physical well-being and the relative security of his bed, restored to him some vestige of self-respect and confidence. And with these, inevitably, came the return of desire. Of course, the man might have denounced him, disregarding out of anger the consequences of this denouncement for Maria. Harsh footsteps could resound on the stairs at any minute, and with them would come the dreaded knock; the unspeakable German: Open up! Open up!; but he was too steeped in the unaccustomed comfort to care.

Pyjamas carelessly transferred by Maria on top of a bundle of bedclothes, evoked burning memories. Blue pyjamas with white dots. The trousers almost new—the top worn out with use and faded to a very pale blue (for a reason, which made Kirshbaum toss and turn in an access of desire that changed from dormant to agonizing in the span of a thought). Transparent pyjamas made from some fancy material (organdie? tulle?). Should he go to Maria? Very transparent pyjamas. Pyjamas Maria had used (well, not so much used, as taken along) on their honeymoon. Pyjamas she wore nowadays when she went to bed with Karol. (No, he would not go to Maria.) It was very still in the living room. Was she lying with bated breath, hoping he would come to her? Or was she lying with bated breath, terrified of his coming, waiting for him to fall asleep? Or, worst of all, because that would indicate indifference, was she sleeping?

Toss and turn. Turn and toss. Thinking that he would never fall asleep—Kirshbaum fell asleep. Towards the morning, on half-waking from an erotic dream, he had an ejaculation, which he vainly tried to prevent. The dirtied sheets and the dirtied pyjama trousers (he could not remember having seen the pyjamas before, they probably belonged to the man) worried him terribly. He would have liked to have been spared this final humiliation. He cleaned up the mess with his handkerchief, as best he could; he tossed and turned again. Some time later, he heard her get up. The lavatory chain was pulled; water gurgled in the pipes. A passing truck made the window panes rattle. The wet spot on the sheet was drying out. Soon, the day would have to be faced. Kirshbaum closed his eyes and drifted into a troubled slumber.

At nine o'clock Maria brought him breakfast to bed.

The interminable morning was cut by the shrill ringing of the telephone. 'Your papers are ready,' Maria told him, as soon as the receiver was back in its cradle. 'I'll go and get them.' Ready in record time! The forger must have been paid well, extremely well, he must have stayed up working all night. How eager they are to be rid of me! thought

Kirshbaum. But, he too, was eager to be gone. He realized this with surprise. He could hardly wait to leave this comparative safety, this luxury, and to head for the streets. An irrational feeling, under the circumstances. Or not? Being out in the streets was very bad, but being here was unbearable. And he wanted to exchange the unbearable for the very bad. There was nothing irrational about that. What an expert he had become in misery! The bad, the worse, the worst—the unbearable. He had experienced them all in various degrees. If he survived, a new profession would be born. He would hang up an elegant shingle inscribed:

>Dr Leon Kirshbaum, B.T.I.A.
>(Been Through It All)
>Consultant in Pain

Tell me, Professor Kirshbaum, how bad can the bad get? Well now, son. Well.... Mhmmmm.... Let me see.... The bad can get bad, son. Yes, sir. The bad can get bad. Very bad. So bad, in fact, that it can become worse. And the worse, in its turn, can become very bad, too; so bad, that it, again, becomes the worst. And so on, and so forth. Now, do you see?

Yes, Professor. Yes, I think I see. But Professor Kirshbaum (here the voice would slow in hushed reverence), sir: Do you think you could tell me...that is...do you think I am ready to know...I mean...what is *unbearable*?

Here, Professor Kirshbaum would become very grave. He would fondle his beard, he would tentatively scratch his venerable head. And, finally, he would say: That, son, is a purely personal matter. It depends on you, really. It is, you see, a matter of choice. Hmmmm.... Yes.... It is, indisputably, a matter of choice. What is there, son, that you think you might find unbearable: a death, a rejection, an itch? Purely personal, you see. You can take your time, son. And you can take your pick. The possibilities, you see, are many. As many, in fact, as there are ways to commit suicide. Maybe more.

Maria! Alone in the house, his mask off, Kirshbaum was able to indulge in tears of self-pity. He cried copiously, conscious that this opportunity might not soon repeat itself: it would not do for a Wisniak to cry. Not unless he were drunk, and Kirshbaum had no intention of getting drunk: had never done so. He splashed his face with cold water—just in time.

'Here you are,' said Maria, handing him a very passably forged document. They had used an old photo of his in which he looked—had been—much younger and more handsome. It fitted in well with the date of issue. He now had a passport to life—provided no one ordered him to take off his trousers. 'Thank you. I think I'll go now,' he said. A bright, mottled pink suffused Maria's face. It did not suit her. 'I think you should stay and rest for a few days,' she recited. Punish her. Stay polite to the bitter end, Kirshbaum counselled himself. But he was unable to. 'This is no rest, you whore, this is torture!' he cried brutally, thus breaking his vow of silence and easing the tension. He could have kicked himself. Already his brutality had absolved some of her guilt.

'Yes. Yes, I know,' whispered grateful Maria. 'But what can I do?'

'Let's get going,' said Kirshbaum, still brutal. 'I need some money. I need a different suit, this one is too conspicuous. I want to get out of here. The devil take it all! Let's get going.'

The preparations for his departure did not take long. She insisted on sewing her diamond engagement ring into the lining of his coat. She insisted on giving him much more money than he had asked for. No, he would definitely *not* stay for lunch. He stood in the doorway of the kitchen, impatient fingers drumming on wood; while, over his objections, flustered Maria made up a pile of sandwiches. Finished. She wrapped the sandwiches and put them into the little suitcase she had given him. She had also given him Karol's pyjamas. She closed the lid. Kirshbaum could not look at her. 'Goodbye,' he said. He picked up the suitcase and opened the door. He pulled the brim of the hat (Karol's?) as low down as it would go. He tried to immerse himself in Wisniak, to assume Wisniak's identity, Wisniak's expression; he would—were it feasible—have moulded his features into Wisniak's by a sheer effort of will; so that if he met someone who knew him, that someone would see only Wisniak and think: what amazing resemblance! But he could not concentrate. Behind him Maria was crying—harsh, ugly sobs. Kirshbaum felt a sudden, totally unexpected surge of pity. Poor Maria! He could not leave her so. He closed the door and put down the suitcase. Her nose was very red, she looked ugly with a red nose. With comforting fingers, he touched one of her wet cheeks. 'Maria,' said Kirshbaum very softly. 'And if I survive...? Maria...? Should I come back?'

Almost imperceptibly, Maria nodded her head.

Once again, Kirshbaum picked up his suitcase. Firmly, he closed the door behind him. Lightly, he skipped down the stairs. He met nobody on the way out and he took this to be a good omen. In the street, he hesitated. Left or right? He had absolutely nowhere to go. He had no idea what he was going to do. Yet he felt strangely elated. Happy, one might have called it, were it possible to feel happy in a situation such as this. You fool, he upbraided himself, you cretinous dunce! A woman, passing, looked at him in surprise, and he suddenly realized that he was smiling.

Stop it! Wipe that idiotic grin off your face! he ordered himself sternly.

With ridiculous hope in his heart he finally turned to the left.

HERTZ BERGNER

The Boarding House

Translated by Judah Waten

COVERED with a black coat, the body was still lying on the floor when the conflict started. Wind and noise filled the room and the candle burning at the head of the body leaned to one side. But when everybody had gone and Riva was alone with her son, and the man who watched over the dead slept in the corner, the flame could be heard gathering itself to climb again to the ceiling. Riva could not remember how the conflict had started or what it was that her son's friends had wanted her to do. She was certain only of one thing—she would not give in to them. Now that her son was dead he belonged entirely to her.

She stared searchingly at her son's bed. But it was pulled apart, the cover thrown back, and only the hollowed outline of Hershell's body was there. On a chair nearby lay a nibbled lump of sugar and a half-empty medicine glass.

Riva stretched groping hands towards the black mound on the floor, but suddenly everything swam away from her and the candle flared to a bright light. The man in the corner snored peacefully, his fur cap falling over his thick swollen beard. She woke him up, wondering how any one could sleep so comfortably when such a terrible thing had happened. From little yellow slits his dull gaze wandered around the room and over her face. Then he fell asleep again to snore more loudly than before. She looked towards the window, but daylight streamed in as brightly as on any other day of the year. Outside in the passage the tap was running as on every morning at that time.

Riva wanted to talk with her son, but he lay strangely deaf to her and her troubles. The coat had slipped, showing a foot with transparent yellow nails like those of a waxen doll, lifeless and not at all like Hershell. His long face was set in a terrible grimace as though he smiled at her with the sardonic smile of the dead for the sorrows of the living.

Only yesterday she had come in from the street icy cold and he had held her hands in his and warmed them under the bedclothes. With his pale weak fingers he rubbed her hands until they were warm again. He fell back on the pillow exhausted and his eyes implored her to cool his burning brow. With wide, blazing eyes and tightly set mouth he seemed to ask forgiveness for all the sorrow he had brought her—for not heeding her, for always being away with his friends who boarded with her; above all for that night when he came home late, perspiring, worried and with fear in his eyes. She had overheard him bragging to his comrades about how he had been 'followed'.

'But as soon as I left the house,' he boasted. 'I saw the pimp waiting at the gate across the street. But I led him such a dance that he didn't know where he was—in an alleyway off the Zamenhafe Street I slipped away under his very nose.'

It was on that night that his illness had begun, and it had robbed her of her last penny. She had even borrowed money from her boarders.

No! Now that he was dead she would have him to herself. She would not hand him over to his comrades. She would bury him in the Jewish way, the way of her own people. She would not have him buried under the red flag as his comrades wanted. A fine favour they were doing him. First of all they got him to do their running around for them, and now that they have led him to the grave they still won't let him out of their clutches. Let them leave him alone with his mother! It's no good them telling her any tales; she knows that his illness began that night when he came home sweating and agitated. It was after that he began to cough blood just like his father, and God knows he was no Samson. He had died young too. No! His friends could not have him, she would keep him to herself.

And somehow it had happened quite differently. She hadn't noticed the boys come back, crowding the room and bringing frost and wind. Then Riva felt herself pushed out of the way and it appeared that she was to have no say at all. She stared at the man in the corner as if she was seeing him for the first time. But he slept on, only his thick beard heaving, as the comrades closed around the body.

Later the undertaker came, confidently self-assured, driving his black-covered horses almost blinded by their blinkers. In his black bowler hat, with frost on his beard, he stamped his feet to keep himself warm. He found he was no longer needed and swore loudly, but having no choice, he turned the empty hearse, mumbling rapidly into his beard and followed the slowly moving funeral procession down the frozen street.

Riva felt lonely and neglected as she stumbled behind her son's funeral among the self-possessed figures moving in files as at a parade. Nevertheless she was proud that such respect should be shown to her Hershell and that so many people should follow him. With her shawl over her head, she watched the four pallbearers with their uncovered heads handling the red-draped coffin as though it were a cardboard box. They might even drop it in the snow.

She wanted to run up to them and tell them to treat it more carefully. She was sure she heard the body rattle against the sides of the coffin and she remembered how thin and small it had looked.

She peered at the faces of his comrades marching in

orderly files through the snow with wreaths in their hands, and she hated them.

The funeral moved through the narrow, crooked side streets of Warsaw. Shopkeepers dressed in long coats, once black but now faded to yellow, blew into their hands as they danced from one foot to the other. They stood in doorways which looked like the entrances to dark caves. Inside the shops could be seen oily barrels of frozen herrings and bags of onions and potatoes. Old women wrapped in shawls sat by baskets of pastry and dishes of hot, freshly cooked beans. Their many skirts and jackets made them so big and broad that they looked like bales of cotton. They held in their laps small pots filled with charcoal, and their faces became scarlet as they blew into the charcoal until it glowed red. Pedlars with big caps pulled over their ears to keep the cold out hoarsely shouted their wares as they pushed carts filled with frozen apples and fish coated with ice. Their harsh cries were muffled in the snow as though by cottonwool.

Riva couldn't bear the shouts of the pedlars and the noisy turmoil of the living city. The noise stabbed her ears, and whenever she saw passers-by leave their business and walk a few steps with the hearse she was grateful to them. The procession moved so slowly that it seemed bogged in the snow. But once into Genshe Street the mourners began to hurry, as if tired of the long journey and anxious to be rid of the body. The frost sharpened and the setting sun reddened the sky like blood from an open wound.

It was dark in the cemetery as the final words were spoken into the open grave. The white snow-covered fence echoed the muffled words of the speaker as he farewelled his comrade. He gabbled his last words as a preacher hurries through the last lines of a prayer. The sun had long set, leaving flecks of blood on the frozen sky, when suddenly a soft voice was heard intoning the prayer for the dead. Somebody quickly mumbled the words: *'May his great name be exalted, and sanctified throughout the world, which he hath created according to his will—'*

It was so unexpected that everyone turned to see where these words came from. They saw a broad-shouldered Jew with closed eyes gently rocking backwards and forwards in the snow. Riva stood near him, small and shrunken, greedily watching his mouth to make sure that he said every word for which she had paid him.... The yellow mound of clay sadly looked out from the snow-covered earth as the people hurried from the cemetery, pleased that a well-lit house and a warm bed awaited them.

II

When Riva arrived home from the funeral her boarders had long since returned. They were lying on camp stretchers which squeaked every time they moved. The house had been aired, and smelt of frost; and the kettle was boiling. The black-draped mirror and the empty unmade bed were the only signs that a dead body had been taken from the room.

Before she entered the room, Riva made a sign for a dish of water to be brought to her. She poured it over her hands, as mourners do when they return from a funeral. Still wrapped in her heavy shawls, she sank wearily on to a low box and removed her shoes, as a sign of mourning. The hollowed outline of Hershell's body stared at her from the bed. With trembling hands she touched the hollow, still warm with his body.

And later when Beinish, a boy from the country who had recently shifted into her room, moved into Hershell's bed, she hated him. She could not stand the way he curled up so comfortably and pulled the cover right over his head. All night long she turned from one side to the other, unable to sleep. And even when the frost had left traceries of trees and flowers on the window, blue with the early morning light, she could still hear his heavy breathing.

Beinish always came home later than the others. When she got up and groped among the stretchers to open the door her sleepy voice murmured: 'It's already morning, Hershell.'

Late into the night Beinish would read the worn books and crumpled papers that he pulled from his coat pocket. He never had time to sit down and eat a meal, but he chewed pieces of bread which he kept in his pockets with his books. He was as obstinate as Hershell had been. He knew more than everybody else and he argued over every little thing. His books, his clothes and even his pieces of bread were always scattered all over the room. Sometimes he couldn't pay his rent, and then he came home late so that he wouldn't have to face her. On tip-toe he crept into the room, and she would hear him chewing a piece of bread in the dark. As he undressed and slipped into bed a sleepy voice always grumbled and cursed, demanding to know why Beinish must always wake everyone up.

Each boarder brought the odours of his own factory into the room, so that the forest scent of freshly sawn timber vied with the smell of tanned leather, paint, oil, grease and soldered tin. With all these mingled the strong smell of sweat. As each boarder came in he ate his meal in a hurry and settled down to drink tea made from a big black kettle that boiled merrily in the semi-darkness. Riva listened to their bickerings as she pottered about the room, always addressing a different one as Hershell. Doubled up, muffled in a black shawl, she longed to join in the conversation; but she never understood what they were talking about.

In the morning she was up first before it was light outside. She watched her lodgers while they jostled each other at the tap and dressed hurriedly. The big kettle already sang on the stove, for she had lit the fire long ago. Before the boys left the room she had put away the stretchers and swept up the straw that had fallen from the mattresses.

All day she looked forward to the evening when the

boarders would return. Weary and shrivelled, she waited by the cold stove in the empty room which stretched before her as the day dragged on. In the winter evenings the small kerosene lamp with a smoky glass patched with paper threw a lonely circle of light, while the corners of the room were always dark. The stretchers covered with sacks and tablecloths printed with brightly coloured flowers, were crowded against the dingy walls. Two heavy, old-fashioned beds leaned against each other just as they had when her husband was alive. She had not slept in either of them for a long time, for just after her husband's death she had turned the room into a boarding house and made up a bed for herself near the stove. There she dozed day and night, her eyes half open like a sleepy hen. Nobody came near the place in the daytime, but sometimes a neighbour would knock on the door asking: 'Riva dear, keep an eye on my room, I'm just slipping out to buy something.'

Every now and then an anxious man would call, always in a hurry, to leave a parcel which he had brought from the country for one of her boarders. She would carefully examine the parcel, all bundled up in rags and paper like a child well wrapped up against the cold by a mother. Once when a letter and a parcel had been left for Beinish, brought from his home by the bustling messenger, she could no longer sit calmly by the stove. She turned the grubby letter over and over in her hands peering at the sprawling writing that spoke so warmly to her. With guilty hands she undid the parcel, peeling off the layers of paper, and took out a little jar of butter wrapped in cloth, a small sticky bottle of fruit juice, a few apples and an old warm scarf. Then she quickly put everything back and placed the parcel on Beinish's bed.

That night she listened for Beinish to come in. She heard his quick breathing as he stumbled among the stretchers. He felt the parcel on his bed and lit a candle. She watched his face as he bent over the sprawling letter. His glossy black hair fell into his dark blazing eyes and with nervous fingers he pushed it back. She saw his hands, stained and scarred with cuts and scratches from his work on roofs and drains. She could feel again Hershell's rough fingers as he warmed her hands when she came in frozen from the street.

Now her days were filled with fear as she waited for her boarders, her ears alert for the faintest sound. Each day she feared anew that her boys might not come home again. They might get lost in the strange streets that frightened her so much. She never undressed till late, waiting for Beinish who was the last to creep in. She was always afraid that he would be pursued. Her heart raced at the thought that he might come in perspiring and trembling as her son had done. Only when he had fallen asleep and his even breathing could be heard through the room would she throw off her clothes and try the door to see that it was securely bolted.

She never went to sleep now until all the boys were asleep. She listened to all their arguments to the very end. And even when they fell on to their beds tired out, she still could not sleep. The familiar noise of the strange arguments rang in her ears. Looking over the beds crowded so closely together she saw Beinish kick off his bedclothes. In the darkness she could see his white feet and part of his body. She got up and covered him to the chin. He turned over with a sigh and continued to sleep. For a long time she wandered among the beds, listening to his heavy breathing. Then she lit a candle and from a trunk she took out Hershell's coat and spread it over Beinish.

She went back to her bed again and listened, while the deep breathing of her boys filled the room.

LILIAN BARNEA

My Grandfather

HE IS RECEDING from me down the corridors of time and it is making me sad—every day he becomes a little more indistinct. The more time passes, the less I am able to separate memory from experience, love from knowledge; so that I cannot help disapproving of some of those very qualities which made me love him so much. I want to try to recapture him on paper, while I am still able to.

For documentary purposes, his name was Jozef. To family and friends he was Eusiej. *Eusiej*: very soft, very Russian. At home, spoken of in my presence, he was always referred to as *dziadzius* (little grandpa). I remember that the mere sound of his name, in whatever form, conveyed reassurance; a pleasant, warm, all-enveloping sense of safety.

In Polish, quite incongruously a language of diminutives, *dziadzius* sounds even more diminutive than does 'little grandpa'. But Grandfather was a tall, imposing man. Whenever I think of him, I see him dressed for the street in an elegant, blackcloth coat with a fur collar. His greying hair is smoothly brushed. He carries a cane. His face seems almost young, his blue eyes are commanding, his whole bearing haughty.

An unlikely picture of a Jew in pre-war Warsaw; in Warsaw at any time, for that matter.

Sometimes I ask myself: was he really like that? How I would like to believe that he was! Or was his bearing merely a façade, a pose sustained out of pride at first, and later out of love; for surely he must have been aware of the sense of security and dignity that we all derived from his behaviour.

And, reluctantly, I conclude that it must have been a pose; for though he was born in Kiev, outside the pale, to parents who had been almost totally assimilated, and he went to a good Russian 'Gymnasium' where he was practically the only Jew, yet there must have been barbs, and the fear of insult, and the terrible longing to be the same as the other boys, the deep wish *not* to have been chosen; so that his polite (yes, not arrogant!) self-assurance could not possibly have been the product of such a tortured childhood. And if it was a pose, what an effort it must have cost him, at times, to sustain it!

I never spent as much time with Grandfather as I would have liked. Ours was a formal household, and I was constantly in the care of a governess who adhered to quite a rigid routine. For me, from as far back as I can remember, the day began at eight o'clock. I washed, dressed, and then sat down opposite my governess—a very respectable and mean woman—in the stale stillness of the dining room. She had coffee, while I drank a glass of 'tea'—a drop of tea in a glass of milk, just enough to give it a tinge of pinkness, the degree of that tinge being largely dependent on the mood my governess was in on that particular morning. We each had a sweet bun. Then, weather permitting, out into the courtyard for a ride on my bicycle. The courtyard, enclosed by the house on all sides, was rather like a well; like all Warsaw courtyards it was sunless and gloomy throughout most of the day. In the middle of our courtyard there grew a solitary, pathetic little lilac bush; and round this lilac bush I circled with determination, showing off for the benefit of the little boy on the second floor, until I was called in for my lessons. (Much later it transpired that this little lilac bush had really been very sturdy. Several months after the war, propelled by what I can only very inadequately describe as a feeling of dread-filled anticipation, I went to see the ruins of our house. I was then so awed by the freedom of movement, by the very fact that I was *free* to go back home, that while knowing how utterly impossible it was, I somehow expected my home *to be* there; in spite of this, the bombed-out street, which I found with great difficulty, gave me no particular feeling of shock because of its anonymity—by then all Warsaw streets consisted of identical piles of rubble; I wasn't really sure whether this had been our house, or the one next to it, or the one beyond, so that I had to go to the intersection and start counting: one, two, three, four, five.... And then I saw the lilac bush. It was unbearably unchanged and in full bloom....)

Breakfast was at ten o'clock. Grandfather was away in the mornings; my mother, who liked to get up late, was monosyllabic and still wore her dressing-gown. My recollections of my grandmother are very hazy; I vaguely remember her as being dark and petite—there is a photograph imprinted on my mind in which she stands perpetually poised over a huge soup tureen, a ladle in one hand. But I am sure she was there at the breakfast table, as well as the governess who sat inexorably on my right. On nice days the dining room would be filled with the morning sun, which shone on the highly polished parquet floors and the heavy crystals on the sideboard. The yellow of sliced, boiled eggs, the red of tomatoes, the various browns of the herrings looked extremely colourful and appetizing against the snow-white damask tablecloth. Grandmother's meals were a kind of art—she must have attached tremendous importance to food and to the way it was served. When my mother left my father and came to live with her parents, I had been three years old—a thin, pale child, typically revolted by food. Every mouthful had had to be coaxed or forced down my throat. By the age of five—a feat the women never tired talking of—I had developed into a chubby, rather greedy little eater. I savoured breakfast slowly, reluctant to let it end, already looking forward to dinner; not for the sake of food, now that I was full, but because (unless there was some special treat in store) dinner was the focal point of my day: lessons, as well as excursions into an often hostile world, would be over by dinnertime. And Grandfather would be coming home....

Lessons (which I know took place, but do not actually remember having) were interspersed with various other activities, vivid glimpses of some of which have remained with me: I am skating, and I hate it. I am terrified of falling on the slippery ice, I sweat, my hands are clenched; yet I go on skating, clumsily, doggedly. It never occurred to me to ask to be let off, and I never confided my fear to anyone. Like Grandfather, I preserved a stiff upper lip. Unfortunately, sports played a large part in my curriculum—I suppose it was my family's way of saying: look, we are different.

Or my governess takes me to the park. Some children come up: will I play hide-and-seek with them? I don't feel like it, but I say yes, I will. So I play. I run, I hide, I seek, I shout with the best of them; in fact, I lead the game, after several minutes I am the undisputed leader. Why then do I feel such relief when my governess calls: 'Time to go home!'?

About a year before the war, I began learning to play tennis. Tennis held no terrors for me. I knew how pretty I looked in my white, made-to-order tennis dress; little as I was, its social implications were also not quite lost on me— none of my few friends played tennis, and while until now I had envied them their freedom (none, save one, had a governess), I suddenly became rather conscious of my privileged position. Another very vivid glimpse: a huge, sun-filled tennis court. I am sitting on a bench awaiting my turn. I am filled with a sense of luxurious well-being, which seems to have communicated itself to my governess, for even she is less sour than usual. This is my third or fourth lesson, and I enjoy these lessons immensely. On the way back home we will stop at a marvellous pet shop in the heart of the city to get some food for my goldfish. Suddenly a lady sits down next to me. She beams (what a cute little girl!), she is very friendly. She begins to ask me questions, which I answer coyly, guardedly.

Do I like to play tennis?

Yes, I do.

But I am a little young to be playing tennis, aren't I?

Yes....

Do I go to school?

No.

?!

Here my governess feels obliged to explain. No, I don't go to school, I learn at home. When I turn ten, I will be sent to a boarding school in England. My family prefer that I have an English education. Yes, to a very good English school, one of the best. That's why I am having tennis lessons already, and English lessons too, of course.

The lady seems suitably impressed, but for me the day is ruined. My feeling of well-being drains away to be replaced with unease. Why don't I go to a Polish school? I have never been told, yet I know. I was born with this latent knowledge, it is ingrained in the very pores of my skin. Being shielded from being Jewish only makes matters worse; I suffer the more, for being told so little. This constant camouflage, which I know is expected of me, also without ever having been told, is extremely trying. (As a result, I was a nervous, oversensitive child, too proud for my age, and proud for the wrong reasons.) I want to go home and stay there. I wish I were sick, not terribly sick, just enough so I could stay in bed. When I am sick, my governess disappears and Mother hovers around me anxiously. She takes my temperature, she reads to me and brings me trays of tempting food. How I want to go home to dinner....

In order that we should all be able to get together once

a day (my grandparents and Mother often went out in the evenings), dinner was at the peculiar hour of three. One look at Grandfather; one big, loving hug: 'And how is my little girl today?'; and I would be reassured, I was safe, everything was all right again. And I felt even better when Grandfather started talking. He talked a lot at meals, eating as though the food were incidental, a sort of appendage to conversation. His vibrant talk fascinated and excited me, he rarely spoke of the trivia of everyday life, but liked to discuss world politics, often letting ll names of faraway, exotic places with such intimate ease as though he had just returned from them. He also loved to reminisce and to mention important people: Trotsky, who, he said, had helped him to get out of Russia, when the revolution broke out while Grandfather had been there on business; Pilsudski, Jan Kiepura, Maurice Chevalier; no matter what their political persuasion or their claim to fame, Grandfather had met them all. Indeed, in his study—a small room, almost completely taken up by a piano, two comfortable leather armchairs, and a worn-out sofa on which Grandfather took his after-dinner naps—there was a group photo, taken at the grave of the Unknown Soldier in Paris, in which Pilsudski and Grandfather both stood in the front row, two people apart.

Here I note, with vague disquiet (so that I almost don't write it down, but try to push the memory back into my subconscious), that there were few books in Grandfather's study; and how am I to interpret that? Was he perhaps not very well read, not very studious? I am disturbed by this possibility; somewhere, on the way, I have acquired the notion that there is virtue in studiousness.

After dinner, relaxed, all my unnamed, unspoken fears stilled for the course of the afternoon, I was free to do what I liked during the few hours that remained of my day. Usually I played or read in my room; occasionally I visited or was visited by friends. Grandfather always retired to rest. This routine did not give us a chance to see much of each other; and a visit to Grandfather's room was a rare treat.

I have a peculiar propensity for remembering places. I have retained only the dimmest impression of my father, but I remember well the furnishings of my parents' flat in Sosnowiec, a gloomy Silesian coal town, where I spent the first three years of my life (but where I was *not* born, for my mother made sure that the birth took place in Warsaw).

So now, as in my thoughts I slowly enter my grandparents' bedroom, which was referred to by everyone, including Grandmother, as 'Grandfather's room', I see it before me in vivid detail: the huge, old-fashioned double bed flanked on both sides by marble-topped bedside tables, which matched the marble lamp shade on the ceiling; the enormous wardrobe where, among myriads of other things, Grandmother stored stacks upon meticulously folded stacks of perfumed linen; her dressing table with all its bottles and jars; the blue-green siphon bottle on the window sill; while Grandfather in bed is a dim, obscure figure.

It must have been on this or on a similar occasion, that I perceived on Grandfather's bedside table a set of teeth in a glass of water. It grinned up at me hideously from the depth of the glass; and I was shocked. This was my first encounter with false teeth—an encounter shocking enough in itself; I took a close look at Grandfather: he seemed different, shrunken somehow. A gap yawned when he opened his mouth. His speech sounded funny. I started to cry, and was taken away. This episode, so very clear in my memory, puzzles me. I go over it in my mind, again and again. Grandfather receiving ladies without his teeth in? How utterly unlike him—how improbable! How it disturbs my whole concept of him! I can only surmise that this happened towards the end and that he was feeling (momentarily) defeated.

I say: receiving ladies; for Grandfather treated me like a lady. A little lady, sometimes a naughty little lady, but definitely a lady. He never condescended, never spoke down to me; never demeaned or humiliated me, as the best of grown-ups often did in those pre child-oriented days. In his presence, neither Mother nor Grandmother dared insist that I finish my spinach, or my grated carrots, or the Russian 'spring borsch' which I detested.

Sometimes, Grandfather and I went out together. I have unforgettable memories of the Saxon Gardens or Lazienki on balmy spring days; of sitting on a bench and devouring a large, chocolate 'Eskimo' ice-cream on a stick (strictly against my mother's wishes, because ice-cream in those days in Poland was considered to be a dangerous food; to eat ice-cream was to court a sore throat). In cafés or in restaurants he would hand me the menu, let me choose for myself and abide by my choice. He showed me Marszalkowska at dusk: lights springing up to illuminate the wonders in the windows of Warsaw's finest street; neon signs flashing. He took me to the old city; with him I explored all the beauties of pre-war Warsaw.

I can still hear the measured, rhythmical clip clop of the horses' hooves, as we went by droshky—I, full of joyous anticipation on the way to the city, and sleepy and sated on the way home; Grandfather delighting in my pleasure and conscious, I think, always very conscious of the fine figure he cut. And when we finally got back: 'Here you have a very tired little girl,' he would say. 'But we enjoyed ourselves, didn't we, Lilusia?'

We lived on the ground floor of a large, massive block of flats in the best part of what was later to become a part of the Warsaw ghetto.

The house had been bought by my great-grandfather—my grandmother's father. He had had three daughters; he gave each a flat in the house when he married them off. The remaining flats were also occupied mostly by relatives: uncles, aunts, cousins and their respective families, wealthy or less well off, regardless of their occupation or profession, all lived in the same house. The rooms were large and high-ceilinged, warmed in winter by huge porcelain stoves, which the maids would light very early in the morning; and furnished, for the most part, with solid, dark furniture and heavy crystal and silver objects.

Great-grandfather had invested all the money he had made (he had started out by selling spoons at street corners) in real estate and a lamp factory, one of the largest in Poland. A widower, he left everything to his daughters when he died. It was Grandfather who managed the factory. He had, I understand, brought little into the family except for his good looks and his bearing; and by virtue of these he became the family's spokesman in dealings with the outside world. But not, I think, by unanimous consent. Little as I was, I remember sensing the resentment and jealousy that the other two husbands felt towards him; on one occasion I overheard them talking about 'that *Luft Mensch*' (the then mysterious phrase, or perhaps the derisive intonation of it, went through me like a shaft, and filled me with horror and shame; though no names were mentioned, I knew they were referring to Grandfather).

We also owned a large, sprawling summer villa in Otwock, a holiday resort near Warsaw. Here, the few small children of the family spent their summers accompanied by my governess and a cook. The grown-ups rarely came, preferring, I suppose, more sophisticated places; or perhaps the lack of plumbing had kept them away. It was the magic spot of my childhood—I have never revisited it for fear of spoiling my memories.

The villa was surrounded by a high, wire fence. There was a tall, green iron gate. A path strewn with tiny white stones led up to the first house, in front of which were two well-kept, elaborate flower beds. This was the only 'artificial' part of the villa; the rest was all pine wood. The other two houses were well to the left of the first and hidden from view, as one came in through the gate. Each house consisted of three rooms and a kitchen; there was no running water. We washed our hands and faces in a white enamel bowl, or under the water pump—one child washing, one pumping. Once or twice a week, we were given baths in a large, wooden laundry tub. The place was looked after by a janitor, who lived there all year round with his wife and three children in a small red cottage beside the fruit and vegetable garden in the middle of the wood. They had a fierce, sad, red dog called Canis.

What a blessing those summers were! The vine-covered fence kept out the world; the heady smell of pines and the sounds of the country lulled me to security. Waking early in the morning to the chirping of birds, impatient to start the day, I would lie in bed waiting for the first ray of sunshine to peek through one of the two little hearts in the green shutters. Or, soothed by the patter of rain on the roof, I might drift back into sleep. Later, barefoot, we raced to the lavatory; a wooden shack with a rusty hinge on the door and a heart carved in the wide seat. A fly or two always buzzed around drowsily. I would peer into the smelly depth to frighten myself: what if I fell in? And with a pounding heart I would bounce back into the welcoming safety of the wood.

Day after day we played in that wood, never tiring of it. We climbed trees; we lay on the thick, green moss staring up at the blue sky between the tops of the pines; we tried to catch squirrels; we took turns on the old swing; we picked blueberries off the bushes behind the houses; we ate unwashed, unripe apples from the garden, then pumped water into each other's hands, drank it furtively, and awaited disaster. To drink water, especially unboiled water, after eating unripe apples was certain to result in stomach cramps. But nothing ever happened. About once a week, accompanied by the governess (girdle off—bulges out, and her authority greatly diminished thereby), we ventured out of the villa for a dip in the nearby river.

All the woes of city life were forgotten. Living, as I did, in a state of perpetual contentment, I did not miss Grandfather, nor even pause to think about him; and I can recall only two occasions on which he came down to Otwock. Neither was a happy one. On the first, he was indisposed; he stayed in his room, and Grandmother let none of the children come near him, and I felt very hurt not to be singled out; after all, he was *my* grandfather.

The second time he came, was even less propitious. War broke out on 1 September 1939. Probably because it had been in the air for some time, the family was less scattered than usual. My mother and various aunts and cousins were staying at the villa; in fact, we were quite crowded. The first of September had been a singularly lovely day. The warmth of summer still lingered, but was already merging with the beauty of autumn; and war, though not unexpected, came as a shock in the form of an announcement on the radio. I can see that radio, as I write: a massive, rounded brown box with big knobs, its front covered with rough, beige fabric.

Gas masks were distributed; anti-aircraft ditches were dug; yet, in Otwock, war seemed improbable. But several days later, by some fluke of fate, one of the first bombs of the war fell on the Otwock orphanage, and panic ensued. Everybody, including the janitor and his family, was crowding around the radio when this happened. Magda, the janitor's wife, crossed herself rapidly and with a muttered 'Jesus, Maria, Josef!' gathered her children, dived with them under a bed, and could not be made to come out for some hours. This struck me as extremely funny. In the way of children, I thought the whole thing a lark.

Then Grandfather arrived in a large, black limousine (at that time! when so few people owned cars and transport was being requisitioned by the army!) to take us back to the relative 'safety' of Warsaw, which had not yet been bombed.

I remember the long corridor of our Warsaw flat full of frightened people; the corridor sways; plaster falls from the ceiling; the light goes out. Warsaw is being bombed. I sit on Grandfather's knee. Grandfather holds court. He tells stories of World War I; he encourages; he cracks jokes. Things are bad, but they could be worse. When he was in St Petersburg during the revolution.... The corridor sways. That was a near thing! I am just a little bit frightened, but it is not an unpleasant feeling. It's quite exciting to have my routine disrupted in this unusual manner. I enjoy sitting on Grandfather's knee. Some of his importance, his uniqueness, rubs off on to me—I am his favourite, his only granddaughter, am I not?

I also remember the morning when I looked out of my bedroom window and saw the green uniforms of the first German soldiers.

All of Warsaw 'knew' him, and he 'knew' all of Warsaw. He wheedled, he cajoled, he persuaded, he humoured, he bluffed, he charmed; he could avert nothing.

I wonder at what point he realized that he should have taken us out of Poland before disaster struck. I hate to think how he must have felt then.

The wall encircled us. There were no more treats, no more excursions with Grandfather. Our world shrank and became very limited; but it was still clean, still warm, there was still food; there was still routine. In my eyes, Grandfather stayed unchanged; he became a little more pensive, perhaps.

My Grandfather 57

Increasingly, he talked of his childhood; he quoted poetry. There was a poem by Lermontov that he was especially fond of, a fragment of which has remained with me:

> Skazhi-ka dyadya, ved' ne darom
> Moskva, spalennaya pozharom,
> Frantsuzu oddana....

He still wore the fur-collared coat; he still swung his cane; he still talked big. And he still reassured; he still inspired confidence. In his presence people relaxed; for a brief while the reality seemed unreal. They came to our house in droves to ask his advice: and what did *pan dyrektor* think of the situation? Could *pan dyrektor* help, could he arrange this or that or the other? Here and there, Grandfather was still able to do something for someone; he still had a lot of connections both inside and outside the wall.

I have few coherent memories from that time. An impression persists of utter desolation, in the midst of which Grandfather was the only bright spark. Nothing really bad could happen to us, as long as Grandfather was around. From the blackout, only various shadowy scenes flash on to the screen of my mind.

But I do remember the end very clearly.

We left the ghetto in the summer of 1942. Blood was flowing in the gutters of one of the streets we passed. 'Borsch,' said my mother unconvincingly, tightening her hold on my hand. And, sheltered as I was from the horrors surrounding us, I almost believed her. We walked with a group of people detailed to work outside the wall. Once out, our ways parted. They went on to whatever their miserable destination may have been; ours was a villa in Konstancin, an Otwock-like resort on the opposite side of Warsaw.

Pines again. And squirrels. And breathtaking smells, and sunshine, and birds, and flowers, and the unbelievable wonder of it all. What were the 'connections', which made this possible? I didn't know. I don't want to know. I loved him very much.

The family we stayed with, spoke Russian. The mother was a big-bosomed, black-haired woman, bursting out of her dress—rather beautiful in a creamy kind of way. The two sons wore moustaches and played the guitar. The father was an indeterminate little man. In exchange for our money, they were supposed to obtain for us forged documents and suitable hiding places. They didn't. Eventually, precarious arrangements for survival were made for my mother and myself—my grandparents had to return to the ghetto. I learned all this much later. During the few weeks we spent there (quiet and inconspicuous as mice), I was merely told to play—and leave the worry to the grown-ups.

My play was pervaded with unease. One evening, at suppertime, as I was playing next to the house behind some bushes, the impossible happened: I caught a squirrel. The squirrel and I were both equally startled; I hadn't wanted to catch it—it had simply walked into my hands. Undecided, I crouched in the dusk. Should I keep the squirrel? Or let it go? I could hear the clink of cutlery—the dinner table was being laid on the verandah. 'Where's Lilusia?' I heard my mother ask in sudden panic. For some reason, I said nothing. I heard my mother come down the steps and look for me in the garden; but I crouched there silently, holding the squirrel by its tail. Keep it? Or let it go? My mother returned to the verandah. There was a mutter of anxious voices. I still crouched, clutching the squirming squirrel with both hands, quite worried now by the concern I was causing, when: 'Lala, Lala!' called Grandfather into the pines in a hesitant, quivering voice.

Lala? Why Lala? But in asking myself that question I was playing for time. Another second. Another split of a second. Because, of course, I knew the answer almost before I had formulated the question. Where Lilusia might hint of

My Grandfather

Jewishness to any spying ears lurking around, Lala would not. Camouflage, again. A Jewish girl might be called Lilusia. Lala sounded hard, and crystal clear and very Polish.

I felt very humiliated. Cheeks burning, I let the squirrel go.

For the first time I realized, that Grandfather, too, was vulnerable. Grandfather, too, was helpless and afraid. And in the span of that realization, I stopped being a child.

I let the squirrel go and I got up.

Many years after the war, I met a neighbour from our street. He had, he said, seen Grandfather die.

'How?' I wanted to know.

The man hesitated.

'*How?*'

'He was shot.'

'How?'

'On the street.'

'How?!'

'On the street ... from the back. He knew nothing. I saw him fall.... I don't know...from the back...a stray shot, maybe....'

I let it be. It was the only kind of death to be envisaged for my grandfather, under the circumstances. Nobody would have dared shoot him to his face. And any other kind of death is, of course, unthinkable.

So I asked no more questions. I let it be.

PINCHAS GOLDHAR

Café In Carlton

Translated by Judah Waten

ON THE DOOR of Mandel's Kosher restaurant in Rathdown Street, there is a chalk drawing of a swastika, and in big childish writing is scribbled, *Jew boy Jew, call him five to two*.

The swastika and the scrawl have been almost wiped away, yet whenever Mr Mandel looks at the door they hit him in the eye, but he pretends not to see them. Ever since he opened the restaurant he has been pestered by small boys who keep scrawling these insults on the wall, on the door or on the window. He rubs them out, scrubbing and washing until no trace is left, but all to no avail. As soon as he turns his back the boys are at it again. He lies in wait for them to catch them red-handed, but as soon as they see him they scatter noisily, poking out their tongues at him. Only Georgie doesn't run away. He is a thin bare-footed urchin with straw-coloured hair that stands out from his head like the peak of a cap. As he backs slowly away he screws up his green eyes which peer out at Mandel through stiff white lashes like the hair on a gooseberry. Mandel longs to twist his ear, but George's insolent hairy gaze gets the better of him. He points his finger as he reproves him.

'You bad boy!'

'Bat boy, bat boy,' mimics Georgie wrinkling his freckled nose as he moves away with the slow confident gait of a grown-up man.

Mandel has given up chasing the boys, for he could see that it didn't get him anywhere. He was making a fool of himself; children were leading him by the nose. He stopped taking any notice of the insulting scrawls; what he didn't look at he wouldn't see.

But although he turned his face away he couldn't help seeing the defaced door. As if on purpose, the childish jingle and the crooked cross, although partly wiped away, hit him in the eye. He knew by heart every stroke and twist of the clumsy childish scribble, and it was because he was so well acquainted with it that he couldn't resist looking at it every time he went near the door. In spite of its childishness, it radiated an unholy force which fascinated him. Against his will he found himself staring at it and mumbling the verse, *Jew boy Jew, Jew boy Jew*.

'Just childish pranks—not worth worrying about,' he thought, and he waved it away with his hand. But his low womanish round shoulders, which moved with such easy grace when he was serving his customers, stiffened and flattened like a piece of board at the sight of the scribble. Stealthily he brushed the door with his hand, but drew it back quickly, thinking that Georgie's green eyes were watching him from some hiding place. Involuntarily Mandel turned round, but the street was as usual, quiet and empty. The dilapidated single-storeyed houses were huddled together like a mob of horses that had gone to sleep standing up, their heads resting on each other. The sloping, rusty roofs cut the skyline in every direction. From the hotel on the corner, with its big windows and bright blue tiles half way up the walls, came a constant low humming as from a beehive. A drunk staggered out of the open doors, his clothes all crumpled up as though he had slept in them. He gazed at the street from dull glassy eyes and stamped his feet, walking in a circle like a dog that has found a spot to lie down. He could hardly stand up, and it seemed that when at last he lay down all the tired and neglected houses would lie down with him.

In a deck chair on a verandah across the road, old Henderson dreamed with half-open eyes. As he smiled in his dream his cheeks puffed out, pink with age. A gentle breeze blew apart his fluffy white hair and revealed his rosy scalp. He is a gentle old man who would not hurt a fly on the wall, and he lives on his old-age pension which he collects at the post office every fortnight. On that day he wears a black bowler hat, green with age, and a frayed and shiny suit cut in the old-fashioned way with a shaped waist. Except to collect his pension he never goes anywhere. As regularly as the sun rises he appears on the verandah every morning wearing deep felt slippers and holding in one hand a deck chair and in the other a green cushion as flat as a pancake. He shakes his head as he slowly looks around the empty street, and smiles as though saying good morning to himself. That smile never leaves his face.

But now it seems to Mandel that the old man is watching him with his sleepy eyes and laughing at him for worrying about the scratched door and the childish Jew verse. Even the windows of the sleepy houses seem to Mandel to mock him from beneath their lowered verandah roofs. A herd of smoky white clouds crawl lazily across a sky that is flat and faded. The reflections in the windowpanes stand out moist and milky blue like the whites of a horse's eyes. They watch him with a cold, unfriendly stare. From a side street appear two Jews, walking easily and unconcernedly. Completely absorbed in conversation, they wave their hands and shake their heads. Their gestures disturb Mandel; in the quiet street they look jerky and senseless like those of puppets. He watches them as they pass by, and he is filled with bitterness and self-pity.

'*Oh Yidden, Yidden,*' he sighs, and he shuffles back into the restaurant as though hiding from someone.

Yes, those years that he had spent in Berlin, on the *Grenadierstrasse*, are still in his bones. He had kept a Kosher restaurant there, with a small hotel. On the window was painted in gold the star of David with 'Kosher' in the centre, and in a half-circle around the star 'Hotel Metropole' was inscribed in Gothic letters. But if anyone asked on the *Grenadierstrasse* for the Hotel Metropole he was met with a shrug of the shoulders. But after a while even a German would discover what he meant and answer, 'Ach so, that *chassidic** chapel. Certainly! Certainly!' For that was what Mandel's restaurant was called, because the Polish *chassidim* stayed there when they came to the Berlin specialists for treatment. Day and night there was an uproar in the restaurant as at a fair. Polish Jews bustled in and out, and called to each other in loud voices. They were dressed half in the traditional *chassidic* way and half in the German fashion, and they wore on their heads brand new, black velour hats which sat stiffly and awkwardly as if they were made of tin. They had brushed their beards under their chins so that they would not be so obvious. Sometimes they sat for hours at the tables and told stories of the wonders of the Berlin professors or discussed politics, while they puffed pompously at fat German cigars with gold bands. And if there were ten men together, without any self-consciousness, they stood between the tables and intoned the afternoon prayers. From the kitchen could be heard the loud masculine voice of the wealthy Frau Presament from Kalisz. She had no children, and so year after year she travelled to Berlin to be treated by the most distinguished professors. Special delicacies had to be prepared for her at Mandel's—chicken soup made from capon, dumplings fried in the purest French oil, and compote of peaches. Expensively dressed in a black lace dress, like the guest of honour at a wedding, and wearing an elaborate wig which piously covered her head right to the eyebrows, she looked after the cooking

*Belonging to a pious Jewish sect.

herself. She moved about in the kitchen and poked her fat wrinkled neck in and out like a hen picking at grain as she tasted from each saucepan. She fastidiously screwed up her strained face, and in her sing-song Kalisz dialect she boomed, 'Some bay leaf! The soup begs for some bay leaf!'

Although Mandel was a Polish Jew, he had such respect for German manners that he looked down upon his guests. He couldn't stand their 'Eastern' ways. Behind the high, semi-circular counter piled high with dishes of calf's foot jelly covered with a yellow wrinkled skin, plates of *gefilte* fish surrounded by slippery carrot rings, bowls of giblets and chicken livers, jars of pickled white-bellied herrings, loaves of spiced bread, and egg rolls under glass covers, he was almost hidden. Only his silk skullcap, with its knife-edged crease like newly pressed trousers, rose above the heaped-up jars and dishes. He stroked his pointed golden beard as he watched his noisy, flustered guests; and he shook his head angrily at the greatly revered *chassid*, the pious Reb Reckmiel from Radzin, who strode up and down the crowded restaurant. He was a tall, thin man with a scholarly, deeply lined forehead, and his thick tangled sacred fringes with the prescribed thread of blue wool swayed at every stride. His devout eyes closed in pious meditation and hid the fear of a very sick man. He suffered from a serious heart disease and on several occasions he had collapsed at the court of his revered Rabbi and had barely been revived. There had been a great commotion among the *chassidim*, and even the Rabbi, who was not easily excited, had been gravely perturbed and had declared that his favourite Reckmiel must be put on his feet again. This was a command, and although Reckmiel barely made a living as a timber merchant, a few rich *chassidim* took him at their own expense to Berlin, where they themselves were travelling for treatment. Without counting the cost, they took him to the most famous professors. But Reckmiel didn't like the whole business; he was lost in this great foreign city. He wandered aimlessly about Mandel's restaurant all day; he didn't want to go out in the streets and he was full of complaints.

'Where have they brought me? There isn't a Jewish face to be seen, only clean-shaven ones. One would almost think—God forbid—that there isn't a Jew in the world. God preserve me from the sin of melancholia,' he complained bitterly. Every time he was taken to the professor he had to be persuaded anew to pull himself together. They begged him to wear his trousers pulled out over his high boots and to hide his sacred fringes.

'Don't be so old fashioned, Reb Reckmiel,' they implored him, 'You're not at home now. This is abroad—Berlin! You can't go out in those clothes. You'll make a fool of yourself.'

'You won't make me look like an infidel,' Reb Reckmiel replied irritably.

'Gentlemen, please, not so much noise!' Mandel called from behind the counter. He spoke pompously, and in German, and his sharply creased skullcap quivered indignantly. 'What will the Germans say? It's no wonder the curse grows.'

And the curse certainly grew every day. On the surface little altered; Germany was still Germany, and the Germans still wore pleasant smiles and said 'please' and 'thank you'. But danger lurked in the atmosphere. The Brown Shirts were raising their heads. And every day, windows in the Wertheim and Tietz emporiums were defaced with the word '*Jude*' smeared in whitewash. Passers-by smiled to themselves as they glanced sideways at the crude inscriptions, from which the whitewash had run in little driblets.

Tombstones in the Weissensee cemetery had been desecrated; but when the fine marble tombstones in the very centre of the cemetery were profaned, this was indeed a bad sign. On the *Grenadierstrasse* great excitement was caused when Albert Muhsam opened a letter which he had found under the door of his cigar shop. The letter was short and to the point.

'Albert Muhsam, dirty Jew. Look out! You are on our death list. The revenge of the German people awaits you and all the rest of your accursed tribe. Heil Hitler!'

Muhsam was a man of the old school; a pompous fellow with thick white cotton-wool sideboards, and a yellow-stained grey moustache turned up in the Kaiser Wilhelm fashion. Around the dark panelled walls of his shop stood oak showcases with sliding glass doors. The solemn silence was perfumed with the delicate aromas of expensive tobaccos and cigars from distant countries. To this store came only life-long customers, well-to-do Germans as pompous and as antiquated as he was. They took their time over their purchases, carefully fingering and smelling the cigars from the boxes which lay on the counter, and making their selections like connoisseurs. They puffed the sample cigar, which Muhsam lit with such deference, and blew the smoke in slow lazy rings from their lips.

'It's first rate—perfect.'

They discussed politics and commerce with Muhsam, treating him just like one of themselves. Muhsam thought himself above the other Jews on the *Grenadierstrasse*, and held himself aloof from them. For this reason he was disliked, and it was even said that he was a renegade and an enemy of the Jews. But when the news of the letter spread through the *Grenadierstrasse* this rift was healed, and every now and then some of his Jewish neighbours came in to look at the letter. The imposing quiet of the store was suddenly pervaded by a subdued but fear-stricken tension. The bell above the frosted glass door was never at rest, as Jews came and went. And the dignified Muhsam met each one with a wry and secretive smile as he furtively handed over the letter, so that Fräulein Gertrude at the cash register might not see. She was a dried-up old maid with mousey hair twisted in a tight bun on top of her head. Muhsam nodded his head in an intimate fashion, even to the 'Eastern' Jews, with whom he had not wanted to have any dealings, and he winked familiarly, warning them against Fräulein Gertrude. In half-Hebrew, half-German, he said softly, hardly moving his lips: 'Not so loudly. She's a German.'

Carefully the Jews handled the letter with the tips of their fingers, and read it through once, and again, boiling with indignation.

'This should be reported to the police. These Nazi hooligans should be taught a lesson. It's an unheard-of outrage.'

All this time Muhsam mopped his forehead with a white silk handkerchief which he kept in his breast pocket, his hand trembling.

The police filed a report, covering long sheets of paper. But a few days later Muhsam's window was smashed by a stone. And not only Muhsam's. Stones flew at the magnificent display windows of the Jewish shops on the *Freidrickstrasse* and *Leipzigerstrasse*. It grew worse from day to day. On *Alexanderplatz* pogroms began; heads were split open, knives were stuck into ribs, Jews were maimed with knuckledusters. On the streets appeared mobs of young men wearing swastika armbands and long laced leggings. They marched to music and sang the Horst Wessel song. Every time the marchers passed along the *Grenadierstrasse* the Jews hurriedly closed their shops. For hours afterwards the street breathed fear; an ominous stillness hung in the air. Although nothing actually happened the terrible fear remained. Full of apprehension, the Jews felt that this was indeed the beginning of a dreadful inferno.

But when the ranks of the Nazi marchers were swelled by stolid, middle-aged Germans with fat bellies and well-fed thick necks, which fell softly over their stiff high collars, they grew even more afraid. These men marched in a heavy plodding fashion on legs thick like blocks of wood, trying to march in step with the youngsters; but they constantly mopped their sweaty bald heads with big check handkerchiefs. With hoarse beery voices they shouted.

'When Jewish blood drips from our knives, that will be our lucky day....'

Even Franz Hulka, the quiet harmless, stamp-cutter, who lived next door to Mandel's place, began to rub shoulders with the Brown Shirts. He was a little shrivelled man, with untidy thin hair resting like down on his head, and he wore wire-rimmed spectacles on the tip of his nose. The Jews on *Grenadierstrasse* called him familiarly 'Hulkala' and thought that he couldn't put two and two together. Every day after lunch he came to the door of his mean little shop to get some fresh air. Behind the narrow panes of his window stood an enormous dummy stamp from which the red paint had faded, showing the white wood. With his hands behind his back and the breast pocket of his overalls filled with tools, he stood in the doorway and looked over his glasses at the busy, noisy street. His pale watery eyes were flat and squashed like those of a herring. As he sucked the remains of his lunch from his teeth he obsequiously nodded his head to every passer-by, and grunted, '*Mahlzeit! Mahlzeit!*'

Mandel, like all the other Jews in the street, took Hulka for a simpleton and disregarded him. But every time Hulka greeted him with his polite '*Mahlzeit!*' Mandel felt uneasy, as though he was being put under an obligation. No matter how often he tried to get in first Hulka was always ahead of him with his ingratiating, whining greeting, '*Mahlzeit*, Herr Mandel, my best respects.'

But now that Hulka had become a Nazi he was a different person. He gave himself airs and held himself erect so that his stiff neck made a double chin. He blew himself up and tried to look important. He had shaved the scanty down from his head, and the naked skull between his narrow hunched shoulders looked hard and heavy like a cobblestone. The wire-rimmed glasses had been discarded for pince-nez with big round lenses just like those he had seen Himmler wear in *Der Sturmer*. When he stood in front of his shop he no longer greeted anyone; but with arms folded and a swastika stuck in the lapel of his coat he insolently examined all passers by. Through his Himmler glasses his watery eyes looked twice their normal size. If a Jew passed without keeping at a respectful distance his taut face quivered and he screeched in his cracked voice, 'Keep your distance, Jew! *Donnerwetter!*' And when Hitler came to power he really began to show what he could do. Dressed in a brown shirt, with a Sam Browne belt across his chest, he was quite a somebody among the Nazis. He strutted down the *Grenadierstrasse* with a gang of S.S. hooligans and pointed his bony finger, crooked like a bird's claw, at Jewish shop windows, where stickers were to be put. But the '*Jude*' stickers were not enough for him. He would go from one Jewish shop to another, breaking every window pane. He had developed a special technique for smashing even the thickest plate glass with a single blow from his sharp engraver's hammer. When the owner came running into the street, alarmed by the clatter of broken glass, Hulka would laugh in his face, a shrill neighing laugh, 'He.... He.... He.... He....'

No sooner was a new plate-glass window put in, than the storm troopers arrived again and stuck on new '*Jude*' stickers. And then Hulka had another window to smash. If it occurred to someone to leave the window broken, the Gestapo arrived and took the owner to the Brown House for spreading atrocity propaganda by drawing attention to the broken window.

Mandel was distracted. His hotel was empty, for there

were no more guests from Poland, and he was living on the savings he had managed to accumulate in the good old days. Every few days he had to spend money on a new window, but how long could that last? And after all he would still fall into the hands of the Gestapo. He wandered around the empty rooms of the hotel and a deathly silence shouted from every corner. The tables around the walls of the restaurant were empty and unnecessary, and the corpulent counter stuck out awkwardly. Under its unwashed glass top there were only a few stale egg loaves and a jar in which one herring lay soaking in a mouldy green liquid. Mandel didn't know what to do with himself and he lived in perpetual fear. In the silence he could hear Hulka's laugh; in every shadow that fell on the window he could see him; at every sound he thought Hulka was back again with his little hammer. That laughter constantly rang in his ears and ate into him.

And later, when he was deported with other Jews to Zbonzyn in a sealed freight waggon, he could hear the neighing laugh in every rattle of the wheels and every whistle of the locomotive. He heard that little laugh above the moans and cries of the wives and children packed into dark, stinking wagons, and above the shouts of the storm troopers who drove them with fixed bayonets to the borders of Poland.

That laugh followed him from country to country as far as Shanghai. He was to be found on the doorsteps of numerous refugee committees and he pushed himself into the long queues outside many a consulate. And finally, after great hardship, he obtained a visa to come to Australia.

But even in far-off Australia Hulka's laugh haunted him, and deep within him lived the terror of the *Grenadierstrasse*. When he opened his restaurant in Rathdown Street and saw for the first time the word 'Jew' scribbed in chalk, his heart missed a beat. 'It's started all over again,' he thought,

Café in Carlton

and he bowed his head in resignation. He had worked so hard to arrange the restaurant so that it wouldn't look Jewish. He had put a pot plant in the window and hung out a menu card advertising only Australian dishes: ham and eggs, plum pudding, and roast lamb. The tables were decorated with paper flowers; everything was just as he had seen in Australian cafés. At the door he stood a cardboard figure of a smiling blond waitress, in a white cap and apron, carrying a sign, 'Dinner now ready'. And when the first customer arrived, a tall, long-faced Australian wearing a starched collar without a tie, Mandel was delighted. He had really captured the Australian style. He would be able to work up a sound business not like the one on the *Grenadierstrasse*.

His customer sat down awkwardly at the table and slowly ate every dish that Mandel politely placed before him. At every bite his Adam's apple stood still a while above his naked collar and he cocked his head on one side like a rooster. Mandel, dressed in a white jacket, anxiously watched every gesture. His guest caught his anxious gaze and nodded his head encouragingly.

'Very nice; it's a good dinner.'

But he was never seen in the restaurant again. Somehow Mandel couldn't keep his Australian customers, although he hovered around them in his white jacket and served them with the greatest deference. Instead of the Australians, German refugees began to appear. Dressed in long European overcoats, they carried portfolios under their arms and solemnly ate the English puddings, corned beef and steaks, and spoke English with guttural 'r's' and lisping 'l's'. They were overjoyed at Mandel's deferential treatment, and the regular diners began to drop a German word or two. They even began to order *Wiener schnitzels* and *sauerkraut*, so that the English dishes vanished one by one. Then they began to speak German and to behave at

Mandel's just as they had in the cafés on the other side. The painter, Felix Hindermann, who wore a soft stitched Viennese hat and a loose artistic tie, drew caricatures on the serviettes just as he had in Viennese cafés. The others crowded round his table, full of amazement, and patted his back admiringly. 'Wonderful! Neat work!'

Even the two former cantors, Herr Ashenbuher and Herr Pinkus, who always sat at a table in the far corner of the room, heads bent over their musical manuscripts and quietly chanting to each other subtle passages from the festival prayers, each one conducting with his forefinger, would lift their heads to examine the artist's work.

'The Viennese has talent. He's a real artist,' they said, raising their eyebrows knowingly.

Soon some Eastern European Jews began to appear in the restaurant. At first they shuffled in quietly and held themselves aloof from the Germans. But it didn't take long for them to make themselves at home. They began to drink Russian tea with lemon, and ordered *lockshen* and chicken soup and chopped chicken livers. The German Jews followed their lead, and ate less *schnitzel* and *sauerkraut*. They ordered Jewish dishes too, and often enjoyed a dish of stuffed sausage and sweet carrot. Gradually they discarded their correct German manners and began to take part in the lively discussions about the war. They sighed over the fate of the Jews and the ruin that Hitler had brought to the world. They even dropped everyday Yiddish words into their speech—'*Golos*,' '*Chush Ve Scholem*,' '*Kapoora*,'. As the restaurant became noisier and more homely, the decorations disappeared. There were no more paper flowers on the tables and the tablecloths were no longer as white as they had been. Mandel had had to remove the dummy waitress from the door after some little larrikins had drawn a moustache and beard on her face and an obscene mark on an unmentionable place.... No longer wearing his white jacket, Mandel hovered around the tables with a damp dishcloth over his arm, and he chided his guests just as he had on the *Grenadierstrasse*.

'*Mein Herren*, not so much noise!' he admonished them in German as he waved his damp cloth angrily.

But when the hateful, evil inscriptions began to appear on the door and window, Mandel's spirits fell and he became silent. Slowly and heavily he shuffled around his customers. He never had a word to say in the spirited discussions that raged around the tables, and he hardly took any notice of Sergeant Ben, who was an important personage in the restaurant. The diners were all proud of Ben and they made a great fuss of him whenever he appeared. They listened eagerly to his stories of the war; everyone invited him to sit at their table and a crowd gathered around as soon as he began to tell his tales. They drank in every word. He pushed his Digger's hat with the white puggaree well back on his head, and sprawled at ease in his chair at the head of the table while he talked in a loud voice.

'Yes, the Japs are good fighters all right,' he said in the Australian manner. 'But we taught them a thing or two. We gave them a real hiding in New Guinea. Sure they caught it. When we were up at Buna I was in a patrol sent to reconnoitre the Jap positions. We were stealing through the jungle when I saw a movement in a palm tree. Without wasting any time, I fired. It was a Jap sniper all right! He fell from the tree and lay stretched out on the ground. We ran towards him, but I could see by his eyes that he was still alive, and he had a grenade in his hand. It was too late to take cover, but I kept my head. With one jump I was beside him and kicked him fair in the head. The grenade fell from his hand and exploded with such force that I thought my end had come.

'Here you are,' he added, pulling a metal fragment from

his trouser pocket. 'This is a piece of the grenade. I keep it for a souvenir.'

The fragment was passed from hand to hand and they all shook their heads in astonishment as they examined it. Mandel felt it in his fingers and looked sideways at Ben.

'They're not so wonderful, those Japanese,' and he shrugged his shoulders with contempt, 'Anyone can be a hero against them. You wouldn't be such a hero against the Germans.'

'Don't you believe it, Mr Mandel. We taught the Huns a lesson in Libya. I was at El Alamein too, in the very thick of it. That's where I got my stripes. I was a sapper, and one night a company of us Aussies infiltrated behind Rommel's lines and mined his positions. You should have seen the wreck! When we advanced I saw easily two hundred Germans without head and legs.'

'That's not so wonderful,' said Mandel. 'Against mines no one has a chance. Not such a great feat to use mines! Bah! Tell me, how many Germans you killed with your own hands?'

'What do you mean with your own hands? Don't mines suit you? Eh?' and Ben smiled pityingly to the crowd.

'Mr Mandel doesn't hold with mines. He's a new strategist.'

'Of course I don't hold with mines,' Mandel replied heatedly. 'It's too easy a death for them. They should be slaughtered with knives, skinned alive. They should be made to feel something of what they gave us at Dachau and Lublin.'

Ben waved him away with his hand.

'But you're talking nonsense. We have to win the war; that's the main thing. You can't do that with a knife.'

'No, I want a knife,' persisted Mandel. 'Only a knife! To get hold of a German and plunge a knife into his belly so that his foul, unholy blood spurts over your hands.

That's what I want.' Mandel's voice was thick and hoarse and his mouth was twisted.

'If only I could get a German in my hands I would cut pieces off him and cool my blood.'

Mandel caught his breath and stepped towards Ben to speak right into his face.

'Oh, if only a German fell into my hands...if only a German fell into my hands,' he spoke in a breathless, excited whisper, raising his eyes to the crowd. They sat silent and looked at Mandel, who stood with his mouth open, searching for words. Then unexpectedly Mandel laughed.

'He.... He.... He.... He....'

His laugh was sharp and neighing, just like Hulka's. Horrified, Mandel caught his laughter in his throat, shocked by this terrible sound that had been torn out of him. He stood helpless and bewildered, his eyes blinking, choked by that laughter.

DAVID MARTIN

Doris and the Other Fräuleins

I ONLY REMEMBER that it was on the island of Rügen, in the Baltic, at the little resort of Binz where we had gone for a holiday. I would have been five years old at the time. It was a strange summer, filled with sunshine, sand and nightmares, and all the things that happened to me there have faded together as on a spool of film on which the exposures overlap.

This particular Fräulein had taken us, my brother and me, to see a shadow play at the *Kursaal*. I recall nothing of it, except that it frightened me half to death, but whether it was the play itself, or the dark mystery of jerking silhouettes which brought the fear, I cannot say. In any case it was later, on the way home, that the event took place which has fixed the young woman for ever in my mind.

We had come to a badly lit spot when she bade us stop. Crouching down, she put her arms around me and brought her face close to mine. 'Put out your tongue,' she said, and I obeyed. Then she put out her own, and tongue touched tongue in a long, lingering caress. Finally she pushed hers right into my mouth where, for a few moments, it snaked and slithered.

When it was over she did the same to my twin brother. Then she kissed us and stood up, and we trotted on as before, hand in hand, two small boys and a girl who was charged with their protection.

She was the first Fräulein we had, but there were to be many others. A dim caravan of Fräuleins, moving from their unknown worlds into our bright and known one, a procession of females whom one loved, or tried to love, and who disappeared again into the streets of their private being, leaving behind little more than an uncertain face and, now and then, a name.

There were men too—*Erziehers*—but they belong to a different period. My parents were of the class which entrusts its children to the hands of people paid for it. Perhaps we did not suffer by that, for we also gave our trust, unreluctantly, as a natural surrender. Until Doris arrived, when we were about ten, none of these second-hand mothers stayed with us for very long. I associate them mainly with visits to the dentist, the making of costumes for fancy-dress parties, and with tearful farewells when they packed their trunks. Their entrances and departures seem more important now than their example or their companionship, and to them, no doubt, we were souls soon lost in the transit of their work.

One, however, had a concern for my soul which went beyond the terms of her engagement. Whether it has done me ill or good I do not know, and though I have sometimes resented her zeal I have stopped condemning her for it—she acted as she felt she had to, and who is to say that I did not benefit in some obscure manner?

I had scarlet fever, a serious attack. Having to be isolated from the rest of my family I was moved to my grandmother's small flat, two floors further down in the building where we lived, which she had vacated for the sufferer. The Fräulein went with me. For the best part of a month she was my tender nurse, feeding and washing me and, by and by, superintending my slow convalescence.

She was a Roman Catholic. (All these women were Gentiles: this was common in Jewish homes.) I am not sure whether she really wanted to convert me, or whether she simply thought it a suitable entertainment for a rather sick boy; all I know is that when I still had a high fever she sat down by my side and read me stories from the lives of the saints, until my trembling imagination was overflown by clouds of martyred limbs and holy children, tortured virgins and forgiven sinners. Yes, I believe she may have felt that my earthly passage could be nearing its end and wished to save me from perdition. The atmosphere in the room grew heavy with religious emotion, at least on her part, because I merely lay and accepted what she offered. But it entered my dreams. Dreaming and waking became an undivided existence of hot reds and cooling blues, of blood and soft capes... death and the embrace of a gown, a cloth, to enfold those who are saved. Somewhere in all this was the pierced heart of Jesus on a bookmark which she gave me to hold: it was found under my pillow and led to the abrupt breaking off of the mission. By then I was already on the mend, which I know from the fact that I had learned to recite the Our Father and the beginning of Hail Mary. The poor Fräulein was sent packing of course, but much later my mother told me that she had given her an excellent character, for, never having had scarlet fever herself, she had taken some risk in seeing me through my illness.

A year or two after her dismissal we encountered her in the street. Something unique in my experience of Fräuleins had happened to her: she was married, and the baby in the pram which she was pushing was her own. I wish I could remember whether she asked me if I still knew what she had taught me, but it's all gone. Yet even now, when I look at a picture of St Francis, or a book about Theresa of Avila, my sickness comes back to me and the billowing surge of vibrant colours, and I fancy that I can hear her voice, but that must be an illusion.

Still, I would not say that her sowing was altogether wasted. On the waves of fever one of the minuscule seeds that are beaded on to the necklace of creativity was carried to its destination. She would have been accused of misusing an opportunity but no one can tell how the victim will turn it to advantage. I blame her only for this, that she made me a clasp that bound faith to fever: belief was something not meant for healthy people. She had taken service in a house of muddled conventions, neither religious nor agnostic, where saints—any saints—were welcomed with embarrassment.

It must have been just after this that the last of the nameless governesses was hired by my mother. Once more it is her leaving, and how it came about, which has remained with me, and the rest is limbo. The leaving time would also be limbo but for my mother's recollections, prompted from her not all that long ago.

'What about the Fräulein who looked after us in Dresden—was it in 1923, when we spent the summer at a lodge outside the town? There was an explosion, a tower blowing up; something like that. I have almost forgotten her, but not how I yearned for her when she left us.'

The lodge stood at the edge of a deep forest. Into this she would take us for long walks. We would come to a tower which (did she tell us that?) had been used as a shot-tower or a powder store. She would say that a very good man lived in this tower, her friend, of whom we were not to be afraid. Oh, I think she went in to speak to him, leaving us to play in the vicinity.

Then one night the tower blew up, and next morning our Fräulein had been given the sack. Careless Fräulein, taking your charges where explosives are kept! She wept, and so did we. It was a terror of pine woods and shattered walls, with a male ghost at the centre, and a beautiful girl who loved us and had been wronged.

'Not quite like that,' my mother corrected me. 'The forest is right, and maybe the tower. Even the explosion—but this occurred in our own ménage. She was young, she was pretty, and your father would not leave her alone. One evening I found him kissing her, and that was the end of that episode. I dare say he went after her into the woods. Odd, you remembering her with so much feeling! We didn't have her for more than a few months.'

'Was she fond of us?'

'She was almost in love with you two. Playing with you like a sister. The day she went off you were clinging to her like orphans. There was something fey about the creature. I decided we'd never have one like her again; no more Sleeping Beauties.'

She kept her word. The next to turn up was Miss Jacobsen, English of Scandinavian descent. The idea was that we would learn English from her, as in fact we did, to a moderate extent. There is nothing shadowy about Miss Jacobsen, who could have been invented by Christopher Isherwood. She was about forty; tall, bony and with a face like a gentle horse. She always wore a fox-fur wrap and tartan suits, and when we were alone in the house she would smoke like a chimney. She had lived in Germany since the end of the war, and because she was British our household treated her like a woman of quality.

She was, we were given to understand, a very superior governess who knew how to conduct herself in the best circles. To us, nevertheless, she appeared downright queer, but then we saw more of her than did our elders. She hated being indoors, and dragged us from park to park, from river to lake. She also had a passion for museums, especially the less frequented ones, like the Postal and the Railway Museum. With our parents she was sweetness and light, but to the lower orders she behaved with remarkable coarseness. Her German was indifferent, but she had picked up a lot of indelicate slang which she employed to bully ticket collectors and waiters; especially waiters: she never passed up a chance to eat in a restaurant. The waiters would laugh, and she would laugh back. She was either depressed or gigglingly gay, and her sudden changes of mood never ceased to astonish us.

She was supposed to oversee our homework, but the only thing which interested her was English, a subject not taught at school to children of our age. Her method of teaching was to drill us in nursery rhymes. Eventually we knew literally scores of them, but not necessarily their meanings. I, for instance, did not know what a pail was, though I had an inkling that Jack and Jill's hill was a *Hügel*. England seemed to us a peculiar country, where mice lived in palaces under chairs and blackbirds were baked into pies. But somehow one expected such things to happen in Miss Jacobsen's homeland. She was a complete eccentric, but grown-ups didn't notice it. They probably thought that she had a gift for rhythm and rhyme.

She would rehearse us like a conductor, hour after weary hour. Her work reached its apotheosis when our second, and youngest, sister was born. To honour the occasion she pledged herself to write a poem: we would troop into the room where our mother lay with her new baby and, taking turns verse by verse, spiel it off for her enjoyment.

Alas, it was a shameless piece of plagiarism. 'Where do you come from, baby dear?' We did not know the answer then, in either sense, but it was a great sentimental success. So, our Miss Jacobsen was a poet in her own right—how charming! They should have guessed that there was no more poetry in the old girl than in a bicycle pump. But she was English, you see, and the English never lie.

One day I said to my mother, 'What funny arms Miss Jacobsen has got! They're full of holes!'

'Nonsense. Why should they be full of holes? Anyway, what kind of holes?'

'Little pink ones.'

That day Miss Jacobsen was given the sack. She was a junkie, a morphine addict and suddenly, a *mauvais sujet*. I wonder how she ended up, poor, lonely body. I did not know it then, but I know it now: that Germany between the wars was one of the few refuges for desperate spinsters of her type. In London she could never have found a job.

The last is Doris.

She is (I use the present term, for she is still alive) the daughter of a Prussian *Beamter*, a minor Public Servant. There were eight daughters of whom she is the only survivor. There were boys too, brought up, as she would admit, on the whip, but they are also dead. And there was Mutti, her widowed mother, vegetating somewhere in dingy Moabit, not far from the penitentiary. When we were good Doris would take us to visit Mutti, who would beguile us with a cardboard theatre and snowstorms in paperweights and gave us 'Pavement Stones', which are a sort of gingerbread.

Doris was a Tartar, a bit of a sadist, a frustrate and a woman of character. A theoretical anti-Semite, she had only worked for Jews, and was proud that they had all been people of standing. She was the embodiment of loyalty, whether to the Kaiser or to my father, whom she silently adored. She hated everything she called *schlappig*, everything soft; but I have seen her eyes fill with tears when he gave us a brutal scolding. She was mannish, a sergeant-major in skirts, but utterly fearless when confronted by injustice. She longed for the return of the monarchy, and when the Nazis came to power did not shrink from abusing them in public.

She came to us over forty years ago, and she has never left us. Well into her eighties now, she still flies to London when some of my people need her—or pretend to need her, for nobody actually needs her, the quarrelsome, cantankerous old nuisance. She has simply grown to us like a fungus to a tree, but without its fungus the tree would feel bereft.

How hard it is to make her portrait: how does one paint timelessness? I put my hand into the bag of the past. We are in the Harz Mountains, my brother, my two sisters, and two cousins, and we all have mumps. The doctor who attends us is an old army man, and my father resolves that he is the one for Doris. Meetings are contrived, promenades arranged, and it begins to look promising. In her own way Doris is not a bad-looking girl—a good carriage, glossy black hair wound into a bun, expressive eyes—and they have interests to share: both read *Fredericus*, the nationalist weekly. The affair grows warmer, she takes to staying out late. It is, and she must know it too, her last chance. Finally he proposes.

And she rejects him. My parents reason with her, argue, are furious. Doris remains firm. Her life has belonged to others for so long, it is too late to make a new one for herself.

The Great Depression has come, the children have outgrown governesses and *Erziehers*, there is no job for Doris in our house. Her sisters are dying one by one, and the three who remain, including Doris, shut themselves up in the flat that was once Mutti's. They live—they starve—on pensions, eked out by gifts from former employers, most of whom are preparing to leave Germany. It is the unhappiest period of my life, for I am shoved into the garment trade, for which I have not the least aptitude. Doris sends me a note to come and see her. She says she knows me better than do any of my kin, and not to lose courage: she hasn't much time for literature, but perhaps fate means me to be a writer, or something of that kind.

Heaven forbid that I should soften her harsh, Prussian profile! (But there is also strength and virtue in the Prussian spirit, as in any other.) She often threatens us with the stick, and once or twice she uses it, smiling like a greedy cat. She knows how to rule by terror. Yet, years later, when I say to my brother that I wish there had never been a Doris, he shakes his head.

'Don't you realize that without her we might have landed up in a reformatory? She was the one stable thing in our lives, she alone never changed.'

I left Germany in 1934, and did not return until 1967. When I got to Berlin I wrote to her. Would she come to our hotel and meet my wife?

I am ashamed to say I was nervous, ridden by old guilts. What had we to say to each other, in this city of renovated ruins where I hardly recognized the landmarks? Not a house in which we had dwelt, and she with us, was still standing. She would be doddering and frail. The strain would be insupportable. Was I afraid of her, I who had a marriageable son? How ridiculous!

I waited for her in the street. She arrived punctually, on the dot. Straight like a ramrod. Slowly, unsmiling, she walked up to me. She stopped.

'At last! Now, I do beg you, don't embrace me. Please....'

I did not embrace her, nor did I kiss her hand. (The slightly ironic gesture I reserve for women who are too shy, or too proud, to be kissed.) I understood what Doris wanted me to save her from.

We took her out, gave her a meal. How had she managed during the air-raids? Well, I didn't imagine, did I, that she was scared of bombers? It had taken the whole world to bring Germany to her knees. All those upstart races. Had they told me by the way, that last time she was in London she had walked all the way from Swiss Cottage to Piccadilly Circus? She would have told my childhood secrets to my wife, had I not deflected her. She unwrapped the mouldy family gossip and spread it on the table with cold, sharp gleefulness. She had not altered one iota. I teased her about the Hohenzollerns, and she praised a grandson of the Crown Prince.

The night before we crossed into East Berlin she rang me again. Could she come and see me in the morning, if only for a few minutes? And bring a small present for my wife Richenda?

It was not a small present, and when she handed it over I sensed that it was only an excuse. She wanted to look at me again, that was all.

Mein altes Fräulein.

I have not seen her since, and last Christmas, when I wrote to her, the letter was returned unopened, with a short, abbreviated message on the back. It was hard to decipher, but I interpreted it to mean that the recipient was dead.

But she was not dead. She had flown to England to assist at the wedding of one of my nephews. According to more recent reports, she was carrying on there in so Teutonic a fashion that they would never have her over again.

I detest her style, but may she live for ever! Only when she goes will my youth be dead, dead and unresurrectable.

DAVID MARTIN

Going Back

WE STOPPED in Grünewald by a gate with a carved gable. The house was set far back from the street, hidden behind a row of firs. Walking up to it through the garden I could hear, from across a wall, the cheerful voices of girls and the hard smack of tennis balls. A stone stork, balanced on one red leg, was dripping water from his uplifted beak. It trickled into a rock basin spotted with lichen, to spill into a bed of freesias that were beginning to run wild. A pointing finger indicated the path to a newly painted portico, flanked by two cypresses. At one side of the door, above eye level, was a *Mezuzah*, a little capsule which, on a tiny scroll, contains the Ten Commandments. *Please ring twice.* I rang, and presently there was the sound of a door opening and shutting. Footfalls, a bolt being withdrawn. The head of a young woman in a shaft of light.

'To see Dr Loewe. He's expecting me.'

'I am his secretary. This way, please.'

We went up some stairs, not wide but of marble, or imitation marble. Through a billiard room. The table was shrouded under a white sheet, cues were clamped against the wall in an orderly row as in an armoury. A rubber-plant, a heavy bronze candelabrum, a *prie-dieu* covered with a strip of brocade. A narrow door, arched, faced with embossed leather panels.

'One moment, please.'

The young woman knocked and went in. There was the ringing of a telephone, cut short by the closing of the door. I had time to look round. Between the two high windows hung a good copy of one of Rembrandt's last self-portraits, the sad, wise, disillusioned face beneath the gold-cloth turban. It looked across at another portrait, of a woman dressed in a cascading bustle and holding a lorgnette. A complicated plaster pattern edged in gilt decorated the ceiling. The floor was of parquet, highly polished.

'Welcome!'

In the frame of the door, small but erect, stood an old man. He could have been in his middle seventies. A round head with a fringe of grey, a strong nose above a clipped moustache, grey also, and bushy grey eyebrows.

'Loewe.' He extended his hand: his grip was virile. 'Very honoured! Forgive me for leaving you outside my gate like Emperor Frederick at Canossa. Will you step into my dungeon?'

It was a small square room, white and bare above a line of brown panelling, windowless and lit by a skylight. It was furnished with an antique desk, two high-backed armchairs and some wooden filing cabinets. Cluttering the table were papers, books, ashtrays, a florid ink stand, a battery of photographs. There was another door, of frosted glass, through which came the sound of a typewriter being worked at great speed.

'So, here you are. Sit down. Cigar?'

He took two from a box, one for himself, one for me. He snipped off the ends and produced a mother-of-pearl lighter. 'Allow me.' Through the distorting flame his pupils quivered. My cigar began to glow, he started drawing at his own, his nostrils seeming to trail away into the defoliated hollows of his cheeks. A face like Clemenceau's, or like Bismarck's, the large nose notwithstanding. Bismarck at the close of his reign, without his faithful Alsatian.

He measured me coolly, critically, from the aloofness of age. I had not yet said a word, and he was taking stock of me. His left hand resting on the desk, I expected him to start drumming on it. His plain black tie was looped in a winged collar too wide for the neck.

'I have something to refresh your spirit,' he said, 'if you are tired.' His voice was thin but not feeble. 'One more of your grandfather's bank safes has turned up. In Liechtenstein, to make it more interesting. That's the fourth country where one has been found. We shall put in a claim, but don't be too optimistic. I don't believe there'll be any more share certificates.'

'I have never counted on anything. As I wrote to you, I already feel like a grave robber.'

'That's a tune I have heard before. Money is money. You are only taking what is yours. If you want to re-invest part of it here, my services are at your disposal. Germany is booming as never before.'

The next hour and a half was spent in checking depositions and signing forms. Loewe insisted pedantically on explaining everything down to the smallest detail, giving as his reason that he owed this to a man who had come halfway round the world. While I was studying document after document he was watching me like an invigilator. After the last sheet had been replaced in its folder he got out his statement of account. I glanced at the grand total and was surprised how reasonable it was. I thanked him for all the trouble he had taken, and he replied that what he had done he had done not only for me.

'Your father was my very good friend. I have been sitting here and marvelling how much you are alike.'

'As I grow older I am becoming more and more like him, they say.'

'He loved you very much, made many sacrifices for you.'

'That's undeniable.'

'When he was already struggling, he spent a small fortune so that you should pass your exams. He had great dreams for you.'

'He was ambitious for me.'

'He wanted you to have a full life.' He drew the ashtray nearer. 'Can you blow smoke rings?'

'Not as he could.'

'Yes, his were like doughnuts.' His cigar described two circles in the air. 'The chair you are sitting in, he must have worn bumps in it.'

'I didn't realize you knew him so well.'

'Well? There was hardly anything about him I didn't know. And little about your grandfather that my father did not.'

'Then you must have known my mother too?'

He allowed himself a smile. 'Both your mothers, if we may put it like that, as I think we may. At the first wedding I was a witness, and my father drew up the marriage contract. He also drew up her will, God rest her soul.'

'My mother died when she was twenty. I did not know she left a will.'

'We have a copy, if you wish to see it.'

'Did she know that she was dying?'

'Of course.'

'All I was told was that she died in the great influenza epidemic.'

'She passed away within three weeks of her sister and mother. Your grandfather lost all his women in the space of a single month.'

'That I was aware of.'

'Also that your mother insisted on nursing her sister, your aunt Olga, despite the warnings of the doctors?'

'No. Nobody spoke to me of that.'

'And despite the fact that she had only just weaned a baby, that's to say, you. Your papa and I were discussing it the last time he was in this room, a few days before you all left for England.'

'When did you yourself leave Germany, Herr Loewe, and

what made you come back?'

'We went out on the last train, and came back on the first.'

'And are you happy here?'

He lowered his chin until it almost touched his tie. 'I am a notary and solicitor. A German solicitor. In Sweden I was a clerk in a timber export firm. A clerk with a law degree. What would you have done in my place?'

'The same, I should think.'

'I don't often ask myself if I am happy. I write letters, I attend conferences, I go to Bonn when I have to. I deal with restitution cases, like yours. I try to find out what these bandits did to my friends and my father's friends, and squeeze them until they squeal. I am a widower. I eat well, I don't sleep badly, I smoke my Havanas. I do my work; when the weather is fine I walk in the Grünewald. I wait for someone to insult me, but no one does. Everybody is very polite. As a matter of fact, sometimes I am surprised how polite, and even how generous. Yes, generous. The government isn't at all mean with its reparations, you know, if we want to be fair. I read the *Svenska Tageblad* and the German law magazines. Once a year I go abroad, usually to Bad Ischl.'

'Don't you ever feel like throwing a bomb over your neighbour's fence?'

'My neighbour is the widow of a retired general who died last year. I am clearing up his financial mess. I charge her nothing, because he looked after my antiques when we took off for Sweden. It would be like throwing a bomb at myself.'

'All the same....'

'You should be the last to talk about throwing bombs. Why do you think we never got your grandfather's Böcklin back? Because the house of the Nazi who stole it was burnt down in a fire raid.'

'Do you remember the painting he had, showing a girl

leading blind men into a church?'

'It hangs in my son's dining room, and you can see it whenever you like. It was left to my family. Shall we go out there some time and have a look at it?'

'One of these days.'

'It was by a sheer miracle that your grandfather's will survived. Do you want to know who witnessed it? His *concierge*, the same who found him a few hours later with his head in the gas-stove. If he hadn't kept it safe I could not have done nearly as well for you as I did.'

'He must have been paid in advance, or grandmother Élise may have bribed him with some of her silver.'

'She died months before he got the job. Should you like to thank him, I can let you have his name.'

'He witnessed and kept an old man's will. He only did his duty.'

'Duty, duty. But permit me to show you something you haven't seen yet.'

He pulled out a drawer and took out a white cardboard box, which he opened and placed before me. It contained an unframed photograph, a silver pusher and a baby's bootee, bronzified to make an ashtray.

'It belongs to you. The date is engraved on the sole.'

I picked up the bootee. It was my first shoe, a time-saddened trinket, and the pusher was my half-sister's, the initials traced round with a grimy wreathlet. I sniffed at the ashtray, but there was nothing to tell that it had been used.

The photo seemed to have been preserved in tobacco juice. It showed a woman, one hand lightly resting on her hip, the other hidden behind a cushion which supported the back of an infant. The artist had tried to create the impression that the baby was sitting up unaided, but his ruse had failed, betrayed by the woman's unnatural posture, the way she was holding her body and, instead of down at the child, she was gazing straight at the camera. She had on a loose frock, partly obscured by the cushion. One could have called her handsome: lips well drawn, a round but determined chin, the eyes very large. But she had not yet recovered her figure after pregnancy. There was an odd similarity between how she wore her hair and how the baby's had been brushed, to fall in a wispy lock over its frown-wrinkled forehead. The child was Mäxchen, a Mäxchen asking for the world's sympathy. He was holding up his plump hands as if pleading for forgiveness.

I looked at the photograph for a long time before putting it back into its box. Loewe, who had lit a fresh cigar, explained how the mementos had come into his possession. They had not been in any of my grandfather's safes, but the man, a dentist with a large family, to whom his house had been assigned after his suicide, had found them in a drawer, which he had broken open because there was no key. His wife had kept them until the end of the war and then handed them over. But she had sold most of the rest of my grandparents' movable belongings, and Loewe had seen no point in suing for compensation. The insurance company had found a loophole which allowed it to evade responsibility.

His secretary entered with refreshments. As I was sipping my coffee he enquired whether I would visit my grandfather's grave. He was buried in the cemetery at Weissensee, in the Russian sector. At my hotel they would tell me how to get there. He himself never crossed to the other side; it was outside his *Jagdrevier*, the land he was licensed to hunt over.

'He is interred in the same plot where your mother lies. I will get you the information.'

He went into the next room and came back with a notebook. I jotted the number down, and he asked again if I would not care to see the painting my grandfather had bequeathed to his family. Seeing that I was still reluctant, he said:

'It seems to me that you have brought your body back to Germany, but not your soul. That's understandable, but be careful you don't mislay it altogether. Let us not judge them too harshly. There's a new generation growing up here. It is no more to blame for the past than you and I.'

From *Where a Man Belongs*, published by Cassell Australia Limited, 1969.

Australia

As world history is measured, all Australians, a small number of full-blood Aborigines excepted, are recent migrants. Even after three, four, or five generations many Australian people remember which countries their forebears came from and, in their 'new' country, perpetuate older traditions—Highland Scots their dances; Italian fishermen the annual blessing of their fleets; Irish Catholics St Patrick's Day. To be interested in, and proud of, one's family history is not inconsistent with being a loyal and patriotic citizen of Australia. Australian Jews have a common religion but also a wide range of countries of origin and of tradition. Their Australian lives are a microcosm of migrant experience.

JOHN LANG

Music a Terror

MY RECOLLECTIONS of Australia relate to some years back, long before the colony had a legislative assembly or a free press; long before emigration had carried to its shores shoals of men and women 'unconnected with the crown'; long before gold was discovered in the district of Bathurst, or Sir Thomas Mitchell had explored that vast tract of country called by him 'Australia Felix'. I write, indeed, of those times still spoken of by some as 'those good old times', when the assignment system prevailed, and Government were glad to get rid of their convicts to masters who would feed, clothe, and work them; when 'summary punishments' were the order of the day, and every gentleman was his own magistrate; when the quartern loaf sold for half-a-crown, and beef and mutton for three-halfpence a pound; when the value of a hogshead of rum was £200, and an acre of land five shillings; when money could not be borrowed, even upon good security, for less than thirty per cent per annum.

In those good old times, I had, in partnership with a gentleman who managed it, a cattle station about one hundred and twenty miles from Sydney, at a place called Bong-Bong. My partner had formerly held an ensign's commission in the 73rd regiment of his late Majesty George III; but shortly after his arrival in the colony he had fallen in love with a very handsome girl of humble birth, whom he married, and then retired from the army, took a grant of land, and 'settled' permanently in New South Wales.

My friend and partner, Mr Romer, was blessed with a

numerous offspring—seven sons and four daughters. The eldest was a boy of fourteen, and the youngest a baby in arms. They were all remarkably fine children, strong, healthy, and intelligent; but they were uncultivated, of course—like the wilds in the midst of which they had been born and bred. The only white people whom they had ever seen were their parents, the convict servants (some twenty in number), and sundry stray visitors and stockmen who happened occasionally to pass the station and require shelter for the night. Nor had their children ever seen any buildings beyond the mud and slab house in which they lived, and the bark huts occupied by the servants. Nor had they seen pictures or prints save those to be found in the old-fashioned spelling-books, by the aid of which Mrs Romer, in her few leisure moments, had taught the elder children to read. The only music they had ever heard was that which a very rude fife discoursed, when played upon by a hut-keeper; and the only airs that he could compass were 'God Save the King', 'Rule Britannia', and 'Poor Mary Anne'. Neither Romer nor his wife had much ear for melody, and never did more than *hum* the words of some old song.

It was my wont to visit the cattle station once a year, and upon every occasion I used to take with me a variety of presents for my young friends in the bush. Toys, such as tin-barrelled guns, brass watches, Dutch dolls, various wooden animals in deal boxes, etc.: of these they had grown tired, and it now became with me a matter of great difficulty to get anything likely to please and amuse them. One morning while walking up George Street, Sydney (the houses in George Street were in those days all detached residences, standing in their own grounds), I observed an unusually large crowd in front of the auction mart. Curiosity prompted me to ascertain what was the object of attraction. It was nothing short of 'A piano—to be sold by auction to the highest bidder. Terms, cash; or an approved bill at three months, bearing interest at twenty-five per cent.'

There were not at that time more than five pianos in the colony, and *this* piano was considered by far the best, inasmuch as it had once belonged to Mrs Macquarie, the wife of Major-General Lachlan Macquarie, Governor of New South Wales and its dependencies. At the sale of the General's effects, when he was going home, it had been purchased by the provost marshal, whose necessities subsequently compelled him to part with it to a Jew, who exchanged it with an officer who particularly desired it for an allotment of land containing eleven acres on the Surrey hills, near the old race-course, a part of which allotment of land has since realized upwards of £20,000. To trace the old piano through the different hands into which it afterwards fell would be no easy matter. Let it suffice that it was now the property of a butcher, with whom I had frequent dealings, and who bought periodically the fat bullocks which we reared at the cattle station under Captain Romer's superintendence (I say *Captain*, because everyone called him Captain Romer).

It may be as well to describe the instrument now about to be submitted to public competition. It was three feet two inches long, and two feet wide. Its mahogany case had become almost black, and its once white keys were now as yellow as the claws of a kite. The legs were rather rickety; and constant use and frequent removal had greatly impaired and weakened the tone, which, in the infancy of the instrument, had never been very powerful. However, it was a piano, nevertheless; and there was 'all Sydney' waiting to see it sold, and half of those present ready to bid for it.

An auction room—like love and death—levels all ranks; and on that day were to be seen government officials, merchants who had come out 'free', merchants who had originally come out 'bond' (emancipist), traders, wealthy farmers, Jews, *et hoc genus omne*, straining to get a sight of, and close to, this (in the words of the auctioneer) 'eligible opportunity of introducing 'armony in the buzzim of a family circle'.

Amongst the crowd was a Frenchman, whose ignorance of the English law relating to chattels (he had 'taken' some valuables belonging to another person) had led to his being furnished with a passage to Botany Bay. This Frenchman had been a teacher of music in London, and, at the request of the auctioneer, he 'favoured the company' with a few pieces of music, and thus spared the auctioneer—so he said—the trouble of 'hewlogizing the instrument—since it could speak for itself'. Had pianos been common in New South Wales, silence on the part of this one would have been more prudent, so far as the interests of the owner were concerned.

No sooner did I witness the delight which the cracked tones of that old piano afforded to so many of the bystanders, than I made up my mind—was determined—to become its purchaser. I was certain that I should be vehemently opposed on all sides; but I did not care about that, especially as I knew that my friend, the butcher, would have no objection to be paid in cattle instead of coin. I need scarcely say that it was not for myself that I wanted the old piano, although I could play a little; it was for the children of my friend and partner, Romer—whose surprise I longed to witness, when they saw me touch the keys and produce a sound—that I craved for the ownership of that antique instrument.

After a brief while, when the Frenchman had ceased to edify the throng, the bidding commenced. 'What shall we say, gentlemen, for this elegant instrument?' the auctioneer enquired. 'Start it at what you please: £150 if you like.'

'Fifty!' said a voice in the crowd.

A roar of laughter followed this ridiculous appreciation of an instrument—a piano—that once belonged to Mrs Macquarie, while the auctioneer, with an expression of face which plainly betokened how deeply his feelings had been hurt, remarked, very solemnly: 'Those people who come here to joke had better wait till the sale's over, and not interrupt business.' Eventually, it was 'started' at £100, but it was very soon run up to £130. Here it stopped for a while, and I nodded my head. '£140–£140!' cried the auctioneer, who refused to take any bid under £10. A very brisk competition now ensued between several individuals, and I remained silent, though unshaken in my resolve.

The piano was now 'going for £175—going for £175,—once—twice—third, and the—'. I nodded my head.

'£185—£185!' said the auctioneer.

There was 'no advance' for some minutes, and I was in hopes that I should get it for that last bid of mine, but I was mistaken. A gentleman known as Billy Hatcherson—an expatriated highwayman—a very wealthy man, wanted it for one of his daughters, who was about to be married, and he roared out, in a very defiant manner, '£200—there!' and confident that it would be his, he left the room triumphantly, and went 'over the way' to refresh himself with a glass of grog.

Another spirited competition now took place, and eventually the piano became my property at £250.

I was quite right in my conjecture that the butcher would be glad to take cattle in payment, and, before leaving the auction, we concluded a bargain. I was to deliver to him within three months from that date, seventy fat oxen, such as I had previously sold to him.

In the days of which I am writing there were no post offices in New South Wales, much less public carriers, and I had to wait several weeks before I could find a dray going to any station within forty miles of Captain Romer's abode (settlers usually accommodated each other by carrying packages to and from the interior), and it was not until after

I had myself arrived at the station, that Romer received the news of 'a large box for him at the station of Major Belrington', another retired officer who had settled in the wilds of Australia.

The dispatch of the piano I had kept a secret, and when Romer heard of this 'large box', he could not comprehend it, for he had ordered nothing, and expected nothing, from Sydney. He sent off, however, a cart drawn by a pair of bullocks, and on the third day the large box arrived. 'With great care' was painted on the lid; and with *very* great care it was removed from the cart and placed in the verandah.

The advent of a package, and the opening thereof, was always a great event at the station, even when it was expected. There would be seen Romer, with a mallet and chisel in his hands, ready to break into it, no matter whether it was a cask of sugar, a chest of tea, or a case full of slop clothing for the men, while Mrs Romer, with the youngest child in her arms, might be seen dividing her anxiety touching the condition of the stores with her fears for the children's safety—for they would all flock round their father, and frequently go much too close to the implements in his hands. But here was a *special* case—a most mysterious box. Romer said he had dreamt that some of his relations in England had sent him an assortment of saddlery, which would have been particularly acceptable; and he was hoping in his heart that 'saddlery' it would turn out. Mrs Romer had also a dream—that her father had sent a large box of clothing for herself and the children, and she was hoping for the realization of *her* dream. It would be in vain to attempt a description of the surprise and disgust of Romer and his excellent wife when they beheld the old piano.

'Such a useless thing!' said Romer.
'Who could have sent it?' said his wife.
While they were thus expressing themselves, the whole of

their children, each in a different key, were shouting out—

'Papa! Ma! What's a piano? What's a piano?'

I laughed so heartily at the scene, that both Romer and his wife were perfectly satisfied that I had something to do with 'the joke'—for as such they regarded the appearance of a piano in the Australian wilderness; and at last I confessed to them that I had bought the instrument for the amusement and instruction of their young ones.

The piano, which was locked and the key in my waistcoat pocket, had withstood all the attempts of the children to open it, in order to see what was inside; and Romer and myself carefully carried it into the room wherein the family were accustomed to dine. (It may be needless, perhaps, to inform the reader that in those remote regions where Captain Romer resided 'drawing rooms' were dispensed with.)

I was just as impatient to witness the effect of music (such as the old piano was capable of) upon the children as were the children to see 'What's inside!' I therefore hastily unlocked it, and placing my foot upon the pedal, swept the chords as vigorously as was prudent, considering the shaky state of the piano.

Alas! instead of delighting the children, I terrified them. Some ran out of the room, shrieking, 'It's alive! It's alive!' others stood aghast with their mouths wide open. One of the little boys fancied the keys were a row of huge teeth, which would bite me if I continued to touch them; whilst a little girl of four years of age begged of her mamma not to let the baby go near it. The eldest girl, observing that the instrument was perfectly harmless, was approaching my side, but was violently pulled back by two of her brothers. Presently, those who had run away returned to the door, and finding that there was no real danger, re-entered the room. By degrees the whole of them were not only reconciled to the belief that the piano was inanimate, but vastly pleased with the tunes which I played upon it. Ere long they became both bold and familiar, and, approaching the old instrument, they dealt it several blows with their clenched fists, which, had they been repeated, would have silenced it for ever.

When the children had gone to bed—and it was a rather difficult matter to prevail upon them to retire, so maddened had they become with the sound of music—I played several airs which in former days had been very familiar to the ears of Romer and his wife, but which they had not heard for upwards of sixteen years. Amongst others was 'The Girl I Left Behind Me', an air which the band of Romer's old regiment, the 73rd, used to play constantly on parade, when the regiment was marching past the colours.

When I had finished playing the air, I turned round, and said to Romer, 'You remember that, don't you?'

What was my astonishment to find my friend in tears. The large drops were rolling down his sunburnt cheeks.

'What is the matter?' I inquired of him.

'Ah, sir!' he replied. 'You have brought back to me the morning when I embarked for this country and, when, for the last time, I saw my mother and sisters. That old piano makes it seem as though it were only yesterday that I parted from them.'

And Mrs Romer was crying. *Why?* Because when she knew that Charley really loved her, and they were engaged to be married, she used to go every morning to see the old 73rd paraded, and kept her eyes upon the colours, which Charley, as junior ensign, used to carry when the regiment marched past them and played that old tune—'The Girl I Left Behind Me'. And a very happy air it was, and sweet to her ears; for shortly after it had ceased, Charley and herself had their morning meeting, and used to walk round the spot which was called 'the Government domain'. The tears that were shed by Romer and his wife were not tears of unhappiness; for, although they were not musical, their domestic life had never known a single discord.

'Play it again!' said Romer and his wife simultaneously—the latter now sitting on her husband's knees, her arm encircling his neck—'Oh! play it again. Do, please!'

I obeyed them, but was soon interrupted by the children, who rushed from their beds to the dining room, and began to dance, or rather to 'jump about' in imitation of the gestures of the Aborigines in the act of choral exercises. The boys were clothed only in their night-shirts; the girls in their bed-gowns; and to the best of their ability they followed the air I was playing with their voices. Such a scene! Had the old piano cost me double the number of the fat oxen I had contracted to give for it, I could not have grudged the price.

One of the house-dogs began to bark fiercely, and Romer went to the door, whence he saw the whole of the servants, attracted by the sound of the pianoforte, drawn up in line, and listening most attentively to the music. Romer, who was one of the most kind-hearted men that the world ever produced, entered completely into their feelings, and invited them to sit down in the verandah; and he sent them out two bottles of rum and several ounces of tobacco, wherewith to regale themselves, while the music was gladdening their souls, and carrying them back to scenes in the land which, in all probability, they would never again behold.

It was long after eleven o'clock before we retired to rest that night; and even then the children were frantic for 'more noise', as they called it.

The next morning, soon after daylight, Romer came into my apartment, and, with a smile upon his face, said: 'This old piano, it occurs to me, may be turned to very profitable account.'

'How?' I inquired.

'We may make it an instrument of terror to the blacks. Of late they have become awfully troublesome in the matter of spearing the cattle, merely for the fat wherewith to grease themselves, and only last week we lost in this way a very valuable cow. I will send for some of the tribe and frighten them, or rather *you* must, by playing on the bass keys.'

I liked the idea vastly. Besides, I was very curious to see the expression of a savage's face when, for the first time, he heard music.

The encampment of the blacks was only three or four miles distant, and a stockman was sent to bring several of them; and at noon, about eight or nine of them, in all their nudity, made their appearance. Mrs Romer had a strong objection to admit them in or near the house, and so Romer and I carried the old piano out into the open space in front of the dwelling.

The Aboriginal native of New Holland—just like the native of India—cannot help touching and examining everything that is strange to him; and no sooner did 'the blacks' whom we summoned observe the old piano, than they moved towards and examined it very attentively. One of them at last opened the instrument, and touched the keys rather heavily, and (like Fear in the 'Ode to the Passions'), terrified at the sound he had produced, recoiled backwards, his spear poised ready to be thrown, and his brilliant black eye firmly fixed on the demon, for as such he regarded the old piano. His companions also poised their long spears, and retreated cautiously step by step.

Romer now begged of them not to be alarmed, and with some little difficulty brought them back to the piano, where he represented to them that inside was a fearful demon, who would eat up the whole of their tribe if he were told to do so; but that, if they did nothing to offend or annoy him (Romer), they had nothing to fear.

I corroborated this statement by nodding my head; and, advancing to the instrument, I touched the keys and began to play as loudly as possible. Who shall describe their faces and their attitudes? Some of them grasped their boomerangs, others poised their spears ready to repel any sudden attack that the demon might make upon them. It was a scene such as I would not have missed on any account.

When I had ceased playing, Romer explained to them that I had been telling the demon what he was to do, on the next occasion of a bullock, a cow, or a calf being speared on the run; and they must have believed every word he said, for from that day forward the nuisance abated, and the tribe very rarely came near the forest where our cattle used to graze; so that the old piano, after all, was by no means dear at the price I paid for it, to say nothing of the amusement which it afforded to Romer's children.

The old piano is still extant. Not long ago I had a letter from Romer, who is now both old and rich, in which he said: 'There are thousands of pianos in the colony now, of all sorts, sizes, and prices, from £25 up to £100; but not for any one of them would we exchange our old friend here, which has a place of honour in one of our drawing-rooms, and reposes its tottering legs on a Turkey carpet.'

NANCY KEESING

Who Then Was Alice's Evil Fairy?

DURING THE 1870s the *Sydney Morning Herald* remarked that the ten lost tribes had not disappeared but were all settled in the prosperous tablelands city of Goulburn. Alice, one of their daughters, was born midway through that decade in the cool front bedroom of the stone building which, on its ground floor, housed her father's general store. The baby was immediately, and in gossip, an unusual figure since her mother, Enid Joseph, had scandalized the local Jewish ladies by engaging a trained midwife, a *goy* no less, for her confinement, and by her refusal to allow any other female to attend her.

Alice was the third child and only daughter of Ben and Enid Joseph—the last too, for Enid was forty-four at her birth. There were twelve years between the arrivals of the sleeping, wool-cocooned shape in a walnut crib beside Enid's high bed and the second son, Harry, helping with the loading of a dray in the yard below. The eldest brother, David, was so far away he might almost not have existed—in Broome, or out of Broome, with his uncle's pearling fleet.

When Mrs Morrison, the midwife, had all tidy, and the mother bathed and dressed in a fresh lawn gown whose ruffled, ribbon-threaded collar matched a ruffled, ribbon-threaded boudoir cap, she called Ben Joseph in to see his wife and child. Tall Ben, red-bearded to the chest, strode to Enid's bedside and kissed her long and warmly, then squatted by the crib to regard his sleeping daughter.

'Such a pretty babe,' clucked Mrs Morrison, 'not a wrinkle bless her.' She was about to add, 'Almost like a little Christian', but recollected herself in time and instead remarked that 'Mrs Joseph was a wonder, she really was, never a moment's trouble though not young, after all, and pretty as a picture still.'

The following day Enid Joseph received visitors and the matrons of Goulburn climbed perspiring up her polished cedar staircase to exclaim at the coolness of the room, the radiance of the mother, the beauty of the baby. They offered cakes, flowers, *'mazel tovs'*, embroidered bibs and advice. Out of joint their beaky noses may have been, but in the birth room they were cordial and determinedly kind.

They did not consider themselves exiles, these prosperous Jewish ladies of Goulburn, nor is exile what they would have admitted to feeling. But exiles they were, and not only from the Europe where many were born. (English and German most of them, French a few—Russians and Poles were seldom admitted to their circle of intimacy. A number were, and proudly, Australian by birth.) Certainly they were not exiles from their religion, for in this thriving commercial city of the plain—and what a rich, pastoral plain!—their synagogue flourished and prospered from their warm support. But unadmitted exiles from their husbands, yes! And from their sons, more! For while they cherished and fostered the warmth and closeness of traditional family life, and while their menfolk appreciated nothing so much as their 'good Jewish homes', distance of interest threatened and frightened. People who once longed for sons now valued daughters. Daughters were tractable, teachable and less given to attending town functions (certain balls excepted). Daughters did not foregather convivially with all and sundry, good business as it may be; or ride and coach off all over the countryside buying and selling stock, trading, even acquiring and managing grazing properties and eating goodness knows where, or how, or what!

Yet daughters were also a problem. More and more sons

were leaving Goulburn altogether and whom should daughters marry then?

So what, they asked themselves, for this little Alice? Whose mother was still so remarkably and obviously in girlish love with her great husband and seemed not to perceive difficulties which agitated her sisters.

Enid, propped among lace-edged pillows, her plait of undiminished black hair snaking over her left shoulder, had resolved upon forbearance, being too happy to wish to hurt feelings. At first her resolution was easily sustained. When Mrs Lazarus (Isidor Lazarus—Family Hotel) and Mrs Solomon (Solomon & Sons & Levy—Produce, Provisions) together with her sister-in-law Mrs Levy, and Miss Hannah Levy aged ten and enchanted by the baby, and Mrs Levin (Watchmaker, Jeweller, Gold Bought & Sold) had called, kindness was easy. Kindness persisted, although more edgily, during the invasion of two unmarried Misses Steiner and their mother, the Rabbi's wife. Miss Bella Steiner, despite her thirty years and a strong resemblance to a sparrow hawk, had a prospect at last—a pious young traveller from Jansoon's tannery in Sydney. Although her marriage would remove her from Goulburn, one could only rejoice.

But Enid's afternoon callers were her own younger sister Lily, May (Lily's daughter), and Lily's formidable mother-in-law Mrs Benstein.

Heat generated from Mrs Benstein as if, during her brief progress across the dusty town she had absorbed an incandescent store which, having to escape somewhere, now filled the bedroom. Heat seeped from her dark-brown corded silk bodice, her ruched skirt. A glaring sun in the form of a cameo brooch upon her great bosom seemed to illuminate the boned collar of her dress from which bulged the top of a hot, red throat supporting shining chins below a purple face steaming and melting under a stuffy, old-fashioned, hot wig. Over all glittered a beaded silk bonnet, the *tout ensemble* maintaining a steady simmer fuelled by her scarcely suppressed indignation. For the midwife had asked Mrs Benstein and party to wait in the downstairs parlour while the baby fed.

'And I should be kept from so joyous a sight!' puffed Mrs Benstein. 'I! But *mazel tov, mazel tov,* my dearest Enid.' Lily, pale of face and greying of hair although only in her early thirties, dressed drearily in grey to please her mother-in-law. Lily lived, if not to please at least to avoid offending Mrs Benstein. Lily was herself pregnant, weary and as plainly envious as Enid had feared she might be; her feelings betrayed by her quick glances at the peaceful baby, the ordered room, the freshness. Lily longed for Mrs Morrison but would, as for her previous and difficult confinements, endure ancient Mrs Isaacs and Mrs Benstein herself. As mask for envy Lily was mildly spiteful.

'You're fortunate, Enid,' she sighed, 'to escape this weather. One hundred degrees on our verandah. Our grandparents,' she added, with a malevolent glance at her mother-in-law, a more recent arrival in the country, 'might surely have chosen a more comfortable colony.' Poor Lily, married to undersized, bandy, ingratiating (and rich) Berny Benstein, found little to be proud of excepting her daughter May whose animation and beauty derived from her maternal family.

'May looks beautiful,' Enid commented with honesty. May was twelve and Byronic, having had her straight brown hair cropped during a fever last winter. It now grew at ear level—an exotic frame for her thin, eager face.

'Not decent,' Mrs Benstein uttered with a bitter glance at the grandchild. Mrs Benstein had lost only four battles in her life—none of her four daughters-in-law wore the *sheitel,* and for these four disgraces she blamed Australian Lily. Lily however, would claim one triumph only—May

Who Then Was Alice's Evil Fairy?

attended a select school conducted by a Protestant lady of impeccable credentials and had learned to speak beautifully. She murmured to the baby now. Mrs Benstein prodded its chin with a fat finger. Lily looked on and wiped her bloodless lips with a handkerchief.

Who then was Alice's evil fairy?

Alice spent her childhood like a favoured child of fortune. Her parents adored her, her brother Harry spoiled her and even the terrible Mrs Benstein, scourge of so many Goulburn childhoods, died of a heat stroke when the little girl was three to remain in her subsequent memory only as an unidentified, stale, smelling-of-perspiration kiss. Aunt Lily was a trial to be borne, a pitiful exhausted creature whose thin face was frequently agonized by pain attributed to what whispering ladies called a 'terrible time' and a dead baby that should have been nearly as old as Alice.

Yet 'poor Lil' was an influence. She had a family history to tell to any willing auditor and her goldfields childhood (Enid had had one too, of course, but seldom discussed it) fascinated Alice. *'Grandfather Benjamin was forced to hand those wicked bushrangers everything he owned, but he kept his Torah by convincing them it was magic—the Hebrew writing which they'd never seen, you know.'* '*. . . so we ran outside—all the bush was burning that day. Such flames! We jumped into the creek, all of us; our dear mother stepped into a deep hole but her hooped skirt kept her afloat and saved her.*' '*. . . we watched him ride off to join the Melbourne gold escort. He had four pistols, all loaded in his belt—he had good need of them.*' '*Every Friday, even in the calico tent, they prepared for the Sabbath. Every Saturday, prayers, and the portions of the Law for the day were read.*' '*So how could you get* matzo *for Pesach? Sometimes you couldn't, child. You ate potatoes instead, my spoiled puss!*'

Of Lily's three boys one who closely resembled his ridiculous father remained in Goulburn; two were married and settled in Melbourne. May, the pretty elegant child married at eighteen to Godfrey Jansoon, a barrister son of the Sydney tannery family. May Jansoon was mistress of a large villa at Potts Point. Once a year Lily travelled by railway to spend a month with May. Alice, in her seventh year, accompanied her aunt.

The sandstone Jansoon house overlooked the harbour and was filled with babies, nursemaids, servants, ladies paying formal calls, rich food, laughter, music and water reflections. Even Lily's female troubles abated there and she too enjoyed the Sabbath stroll down Butler Stairs, through Woolloomooloo, the Domain and Hyde Park to the new, splendid, starry-roofed synagogue. For Alice, her view partly obscured by the full bustles of aunt and cousin between whom she walked, the route was a series of glimpses of wild sailors, tall masts, cramped stone houses and Moreton Bay fig trees. There were boating parties on the harbour, carriage picnics, a children's rout (with sorbets!) in Alice's honour. But above everything was the Jansoon piano on which the little girl picked out every tune she had ever heard.

All this, Aunt Lily implied, was the result of marriage to an Australian. Cousin May would laugh. Alice, fond of her little, comical, generous Uncle Berny felt torn and uncomfortable.

'Goodness, Mother,' May said. 'Because you had a horrible old dragon for a mother-in-law! Such nonsense! Why, your own grandfathers, both of them, came from Hanover. Who is really an Australian? A hundred years ago scarcely a white man here!'

'You are wrong,' Lily cried passionately. 'I am. You are. Alice is. This is a land in the blood. After one generation, I tell you, it is a land in the soul.'

When they returned to Goulburn Aunt Lily became 'poor Lil' again, prey to exacerbated insides and misery. 'No, Enid, the Sydney doctors say it is too late for even an operation to mend the damage. Had I been allowed a modern nurse as you were. . . . '

Ben Joseph lifted Alice from the train and hoisted her high on his shoulders.

'How was Sydney, my treasure?'

'Oh Father,' she cried, 'could you buy a piano?'

In Alice's tenth year David Joseph, the brother she had never seen, brought his wife and two children from Western Australia to meet his family. They called him 'Buccaneer' because he looked like one—tanned as boot leather, as red of hair and thick of beard as his father but with unexpected deep blue eyes. David's marriage was the family miracle. How should he make a good Jewish marriage so many thousand miles from all centres of Jewish life? A few Hebrew families there were in the West—a mere handful. A remnant, truly. (David's likely apostasy had been a favourite weapon of old Mrs Benstein's.) David, however, claimed American Miriam from her father's clipper which, being damaged by an Indian Ocean cyclone, put in at the pearling port for repairs. Now, in a whirl of late summer dust here was Miriam in Goulburn, a woman as bleached as the paddocks surrounding the city, her twin boys as fair as their mother and their Bar Mitzvah to be held in the Goulburn synagogue.

Lazarus' Family Hotel and half the Jewish households of the town nearly burst at the seams as visitors arrived for this Bar Mitzvah. The Jansoons and their family would stay at Lily's house, but cousins and cousins' cousins and retinues of nursemaids were all to be accommodated. Harry Joseph, a bachelor yet, and Alice had temporary quarters in rooms smelling warmly of treacle, onions, mice and recent scrubbing, which had been cleared out behind the store front.

Ben Joseph invited half Goulburn and the surrounding district to the afternoon reception held in a marquee on Israel Levin's large lawn. It was the most joyous occasion of his life and no premonition that this was not only the fullest flowering, but one of the last, of Goulburn's Jewry, disturbed his pleasure in watching his family, friends, his Protestant and Catholic acquaintances, all for this day happy, feasting, benevolent. Even poor Lil, that afternoon, forbore to correct little Uncle Berny's thick accent and clumsy manners. Enid was serene and splendid in David and Miriam's gift of matched black pearl earrings.

Enid hoped Harry might stay at home, or establish a branch of the family business in some nearby centre at least. He was a tall young man, clean shaven and somewhat of a dandy. Harry kept the music box beside the piano filled with the latest music hall tunes which Alice loved to play and he to sing. For his twenty-third birthday she composed a song for him—the 'Nanarrama Waltz', Nanarrama being the name of May Jansoon's Potts Point house. For her next birthday Harry's surprise was a gift of the song in print—during a Sydney visit he paid a musician friend to arrange and improve Alice's composition. To everyone's surprise it sold a few hundred copies in the Sydney shops.

But Harry went. He travelled first to the West at David's invitation, but pearling was not to his fancy. For a restless year or two he wandered, working as a station book-keeper sometimes, sometimes speculating in stores. Eventually he reached Queensland, nearly died of typhoid at a goldfield near Townsville, opened a store and, like his grandfathers before him, made his first fortune indirectly from gold. Unlike his grandfathers he abandoned piety, invested in land and cattle, grew very rich, very remote and married a local (Presbyterian) heiress.

When this news reached Goulburn Ben raged, Enid cried

for a week indoors but powdered eyes and nose defied all attempts at discussion, commiseration, conjecture and plain spitefulness in street, synagogue and parlour. Lil sniffed, indignant but inscrutable. Alice, who had dreamed sentimentally that the prodigal would return, ill and poor, to be nursed back to health and prosperity by a devoted sister, was disconsolate and, unaccountably, angry to the depths of her fifteen-year-old soul.

The ten lost tribes were dispersing. Enid was frightened and Lily no comfort. 'Australians do not stay in one place,' she insisted.

'Then how shall we keep our children?'

It was Lily's turn. Death claimed her at May Jansoon's house, an early victim of emergency surgery.

Enid, Ben and Alice travelled to Sydney for the funeral. Alice, at May's insistent invitation, remained at Nanarrama when her parents returned to the plains—a comfort for dear May, it was agreed. As it happened, Alice never saw Goulburn again.

She was seventeen. Her dark hair curled, her brown eyes shone, she had a 'neat figure' and was pretty enough although not remarkable in May's handsome family. However her facility as a pianist kept her in demand for the musical evenings so much a feature of Potts Point society. At one such evening in Mrs Moses Abrahams' lacy, pillared house, she met a young artist, Jack Sommers, who had returned a year before from France and was already making a popular reputation by translating new theories of light into a series of paintings of Sydney Harbour. The month succeeding this meeting was the happiest of Alice's life. Its end saw the end of all her real happiness.

Without doubt Alice was deceitful. Equally deceitful was young Mrs Ernest Abrahams, her chaperone. She, with all the tact of a High Romantic, happily married seventeen, enthusiastically embraced metaphorical blindness and contrived actual disappearance day after day during which, in a dazzle of calm autumn, Jack rowed Alice to white harbour beaches. Whatever their setting every painting of his from this period has, somewhere, either centrally or in the background, a girl whose face is invariably hidden, either veiled or half turned away. She wears bustled, pastel-coloured dresses, overburdened hats, long gloves and carries a parasol. From none of these props to virtue, indeed, was Alice ever parted until the calamitous day in late April when a sudden squall overturned the boat, fortunately near its Balmain mooring. Alice slunk home by cab wearing Jack Sommers' landlady's clothing. Luckily she gained her bedroom unobserved and no one, not even Hetty Abrahams, ever knew.

Her ducking and rescue, during which she had, perforce, been enclosed in Jack's arms, convinced Alice of what she had chosen to disregard before. She loved the scallywag painter to distraction, but would and could never marry him. Australian she might be, religious she was not, but Jewish enough and sufficiently of her family to make 'marrying out' unthinkable. She never saw Sommers again either.

Within three months she stood beneath the *chuppah* in the Great Synagogue, supported by the comfortable rustle of Enid's silk behind her, and the sound of Ben's beard rasping against his starched collar, to marry Sigmund Jansoon, Godfrey's recently widowed uncle whose two married daughters, together with May, attended the bride.

Sigmund was a kind, amusing, rich old man. For the twenty years that remained to him he and Alice travelled widely in the East and in Europe. They had no child and never owned a house. Sigmund died in a London hotel.

Alice returned to Sydney—no ties with Goulburn now. Enid and Ben were dead. She had barely kept in touch with David. Occasional letters had reached her from Harry over the years—these she refused to answer. Only a tenuous

Who Then Was Alice's Evil Fairy?

friendship with widowed May Jansoon remained.

In the opulent, dark, polished Hotel Australia she rented a suite of rooms and when occasional great-nieces and nephews from Western Australia turned up in Sydney they endured, usually more from obligation than pleasure, her heavy, rather stuffy hospitality. She refused to meet Harry's progeny. Harry had 'gone over'. One of his sons tried to visit his aunt before embarking for France in 1915 but was told by the desk clerk: 'Madam acknowledges no relative of your name.'

In the late 1920s her refusal to adopt present-day fashions became noticeable and queer. Alice was, unknown to herself, a curious, conjectural character in Sydney's streets, theatres and concert halls. Always alone, always unapproachable, she snubbed any acquaintance from past times who recognized or greeted her. Once a week she took tea with May Jansoon but wished to meet none of May's family or any of her girlhood friends. Once a week too, she walked very stately through Angus & Robertson's cavernous bookshop to the lending library in the nether regions, consulted a certain Miss Skein (the only assistant she would deal with) and exchanged one leather-strapped collection of sentimental novels for another. She then crossed Castlereagh Street to David Jones where Miss Crew (stockings), Mr Porter (shoes) or Miss Standish (dress materials) supplied her needs. Twice a year Mrs Katinsky, a dressmaker, was summoned to the Australia to replenish Alice's wardrobe—coats, dresses and underwear as well, all in the outdated styles she favoured. Alice was always polite, generous with tips, unsmiling.

In 1932 she lost in a week nearly every penny she possessed and moved from the Australia to a newly opened and fairly cheap boarding house at Potts Point—Nanarrama in fact, which May had sold two years ago when she removed to a flat in Macleay Street.

Alice's income was now a small salvage from Ben's estate supplemented with difficulty—for the times pressed on the Jansoon interests too—by May. In 1935 Alice consented, graciously and coldly, to receive her brother Harry, grown so old and deaf he could not converse much. They got on together rather well but neither desired another meeting before he returned to Queensland. If Alice subsequently guessed that a small, mysterious six-monthly addition to her meagre bank account came from that quarter she gave no sign. In this year David died. Miriam's letter to Alice remained unanswered.

Nanarrama Private Hotel was a well-conducted establishment housing some twenty 'guests'. The proprietor, Mrs Mullen, liked to foster a 'friendly atmosphere'. Most of her guests were people in their sixties who had expected to die in their own houses with a servant or two, but the Depression had altered all their careful plans and arrangements. May's large drawing room, its high windows still draped with their original, indestructible Indian brocade curtains, was now The Lounge, furnished with big, comfortable leather chairs and sofas, several bridge tables stacked in one corner ready for anyone who wished to play. On a central table stood a vast bronze jar filled with leaves and a few poppies, gladioli or strelitzia—whatever was cheap at the florist. Little was left of the harbour view for the garden was given over to textured-brick flat buildings.

Mrs Mullen, a stout, breathless, capable widow, had only one vice, shared by all of her staff and many of her guests— the 'gee-gees'. On race days a cadaverous radio console near the gas fire stuttered out its messages of fortune and disaster. When 'they were on' at Randwick Mrs Mullen, together with two of her boarders, Mr and Mrs Gladstone, jolly retired (and nearly ruined) hotel-keepers, often went by tram to the races. If the fates were kind they returned by taxi, the more cheerful for a 'spot or two' along the way. On days when they broke even, a spot or two helped them to endure the overcrowded discomfort of the return tram ride. Then Mrs Mullen, the red rouged discs on her cheeks as symmetrical, her yellow marcelled hair as tightly corrugated as when she left home, and despite the fact that her fat feet in brown patent shoes were 'killing her', would be optimistic and hopeful of better luck next time. Sometimes luck was out. Spots were consumed but did not avail. Gracious good humour deserted. Mrs Mullen's rare bouts of bad temper were terrible; the more so because no one could predict where the lightning wrath would go to earth. Whether Cook would be struck, or Parsons the porter, or the Gladstones, her companions in disappointment. One Saturday the bolt fell on Alice.

'Keeping yourself to yourself. Stuck up. Won't have your potty old ornaments dusted. Dirty. Have all tried to be friendly. Never a friendly word. Dirty. Smelly—yes, smelly. Yes you are. Out!'

At the doorway of her room, surrounded by the grime-encrusted objects which represented her life, bent nearly in a bow by rheumatism that day, Alice seemed to submit to the storm.

Her dulled eyes blinked, for behind Mrs Mullen the hall was well lit and Alice had kept to her curtained room for some weeks, eating a little from trays sent in to her. Indeed Mrs Mullen had not, before this, been unkind. Forbearing rather, and worried also about her eccentric lodger. Mrs Mullen had cogitated the problem. She had not wished or intended her present outburst. The old woman's seeming inattention provoked her.

Yet Alice only seemed inattentive. Behind the blatant assault of words she groped strenuously into her memory to discover when, where, she had heard, or heard of, something similar. She could not place it although Mrs Mullen's dusty, stale-scent smell seemed to apply to her search. What she could recall were some words of her mother's which suddenly came into her head and seemed to apply—so she repeated them:

'She was an ignorant, common, trouble-making old woman!' Alice said suddenly. 'That is, you are! And cruel. You pretend to be nice only. I will leave as soon as possible,' she added. It was a long time since she had spoken so many words together.

May, now incapacitated by heart trouble and soon to die, discovered a room for Alice in the small Rushcutters Bay house of a Jansoon ex-manservant called Simpson. All was arranged by telephone. Mr and Mrs Simpson came by cab to Nanarrama to help with the removal. They had met Alice a few times only when, during her Hotel Australia years, she had been May's afternoon guest. Ageing they were prepared for; premature senility was unexpected and disturbing. However they were a kindly loyal couple and suspicious too, for behind Mrs Mullen's cordial joviality they sensed something wrong. Mrs Simpson guessed, mistakenly, prolonged cruel treatment. Simpson was convinced the old lady was mad, though plainly docile. The couple consulted in whispers as they packed for their new lodger and decided to keep her with them on trial—'There's Homes and so on if it doesn't work out,' said Simpson.

In a small room off the central hallway of the Rushcutters Bay cottage Alice, on shelves and tables, set up her life again. One brass gold buyer's balance with weights; a cameo-carved emu egg mounted on ebony—once Ben's paperweight; a glass case full of pearl shells of various types, one with a blister pearl on the surface; six ebony elephants (purchased by Sigmund in Ceylon); a silver *kiddush* cup brought from Europe by some forgotten grandparent; a photograph of May Jansoon aged twenty-five (the only photograph on display); a sampler worked by Lily and Enid together when they were children, its legend: 'Be good, sweet maid, and let who will be clever'; a largish flat box inlaid with pearl shell and having sturdy brass hinges and lock; and (how did she come by these?) a glass jar of beads from one of Mrs Benstein's bonnets.

Alice refused to allow Mrs Simpson to unpack more than one suitcase of clothes but was grateful for the garish shawls her landlady crocheted for her to wear across her shoulders and round her swollen knees. Every fortnight Mrs Simpson washed Alice's hair, trimmed it as best she could and commented that it 'would be real pretty if you'd have it properly cut'. Alice seldom left her room and only crossed the threshold of the house on election days when Simpson escorted her to the polling booth—he once tried to explain to her that she could apply for a postal vote and earned a warm lecture on citizens' rights. One election morning Mrs Simpson, 'being no more than human', opened several trunks, tut-tutted at the slowly ruining clothes they contained and wept a genuine tear for a smiling photograph signed 'Loving Alice to dear Aunt Lily'.

1943 found the Simpsons' son fighting in the Middle East and the couple rented his unoccupied front room to an American captain stationed indefinitely in Sydney. He was a brash, pleasant, clever young man of, they were thankful to find, impeccable morals despite his hobby of painting.

Captain Silver, passing Alice's room one stifling day when the door was ajar, noticed the *kiddush* cup and unceremoniously barged in to enquire its origin, for his mom owned its twin back in Chicago. Whether she wished or not Alice, huddled despite the heat into a purple and yellow shawl, had no choice but to hear the story of Captain Silver's heirloom. Uninvited he pulled up a chair. Glumly, picking at hairs sprouting from a grey mole on her left cheek, she listened. Captain Silver told his family history, expressed his pleasure at finding a fellow Jew in the house, gossiped for an hour and returned the next day with flowers.

The day after he intruded bearing a cake and some 'real, but *real* American coffee—I brewed it myself'. Then he proffered an ink and wash sketch of Alice which he had drawn from memory.

Alice held the sketch in her shaky, grey, rheumatic fingers and looked at it closely for so long that Captain Silver began to feel awkward. At last, impatiently refusing his help, she pulled herself painfully from her chair, shuffled to a shelf, took down and unscrewed the jar of beads and rummaged until she found a tiny key. With the key she unlocked the inlaid box—it had been fitted to hold a small, framed oil painting.

'Mr Silver,' she said, 'difficult as you may find it to recognize, I have sat for my portrait before. This was how I looked then. A girl, a country girl—yes, yes, from the country.' He took the painting from her hands and carried it over to a window seeking light. There he scrutinized it for some time. Then, 'Man! That fellow could paint,' he said, 'and do you know, it reminds me so very much of my wife. And that's curious—Betty isn't Jewish.'

Alice glanced up sharply. She drew in her lips. She picked at balls of matted wool on her shawl.

She said, at last: 'Indeed. A pity, I think. But I am sure she is a sweet girl.' After a pause she added: 'We used to consider such matters of great importance once. Times change.'

And while Captain Silver continued to study the only token Jack Sommers had ever presumed to offer, Alice recounted the story of her ill-fated boating expedition. She began, apparently, to enjoy this first telling of her tale for he heard overtones of lightness to her usually monotonous, slow speech. She explained how she'd sneaked into May's house and had nearly been discovered by a maid. She remembered Mrs Ernest Abrahams' agitation too, when that distracted young matron arrived at Nanarrama agog to discover what had prevented their conspirators' rendezvous inside a city shop whence, on other days, they had walked, or travelled by horse bus, sedately home. 'For you must realize, Mr Silver, that a chaperone was at least expected to deliver her charge safely. Poor Hetty Abrahams, her face!' But his eyes were fixed on her own where, although she seemed unaware, a smile spread from the corners of her downward sloping lips, creasing her smooth, puffy cheeks until before she knew what she was up to, she laughed. Her dulled eyes sparkled until she groped down the side of her chair for a handkerchief to wipe away the moisture. 'Fancy,' she said, inconsequentially as it seemed to him, 'I doubt I'd know Goulburn now.' Mrs Simpson, hearing this extraordinary laughter, crept to the door to make certain all was well.

From this time Captain Silver began bringing his friends to meet 'my honorary grandmother'. Their girls drifted in and out of Alice's room. One visitor gave her a radio which, to everyone's surprise she as often tuned to modern dance music as to classical programmes. News broadcasts she switched off. She was guest at several wartime weddings and a number of impromptu parties—to these she wore resurrections from her antique wardrobe and, although bent and frail, looked oddly splendid. For an enthusiastic song collector she would sing by the hour in a sweet, if damaged voice and, leaning on a silver mounted walking-stick she embarked on shuffling progresses through Rushcutters Bay Park where she made several friendships among the young mothers who knitted by the playground, watching their children. On the very day of her seventy-third birthday, returning from one of these excursions, she was run over by a delivery van and killed instantly.

NATHAN SPIELVOGEL

Mr Bronstein Learns His Lesson

LET ME SEE!

Yes! It was at the beginning of the year 1914 that I took charge of the school in a large country town in Victoria, the name of which is no business of yours.

A few days after I had settled down in my new home I was visited by one of the clergymen who inquired if I belonged to his flock. When I told him I was a Jew he apologized for intruding and would have withdrawn. But I liked the look of him and detained him for a chat.

I soon found he was not only a cultured gentleman but also a member of the Craft, so you will understand that we spent quite a pleasant hour together.

During this conversation I asked him if there were any of my co-religionists living in the town.

'I am not sure,' he replied with a smile. 'There's Mr Bronstein who owns the Big Store. When he came to our town three years ago, we all thought he was a Hebrew. But he boasted much about being a German and praised German ideals and German business methods. But when Hebrews were mentioned he had nothing to say. Some of the naughty lads at the Club conspired to draw Mr Bronstein out. So one night they told a lot of nasty stories about Jews. You know the sort of thing!

'But Mr Bronstein made no protest and laughed as loudly as the others. So you see I do not know yet whether Mr Bronstein is one of your faith or not!'

In course of time I met Mr Bronstein. He was a typically successful business man, bubbling with enthusiasm about his establishment and with the foreigner's difficulty of using the sounds of 'ch' and 'w'.

He proudly showed me through his store. There was no question about it being organized on most efficient and up-to-date lines. Everything showed that the owner was a man with big ideas and keen business acumen. He led the way into his office and produced a bottle of fine old brandy.

When I raised my glass I murmured the old greeting, *'Chayim!'*

He looked at me blankly and went on with his story of how he had with hard work and much thinking built up the best business by far in the town.

'Yes, Sir! Ven a shanse gomes to me I take it! Shermany is a great country because she always takes her shanses.'

He lifted his glass and said *'Prosit!'*

When *Pesach* came, I celebrated it with my family as well as we could. After the festival was over, I took a few tea *matzos* to the Club and placed them on the biscuit tray on the bar counter.

Some of the men were curious about these strange things and when I explained what they were, no one was more interested and intrigued than Mr Bronstein.

'Very gut!' he said. 'Dey go vell mit good beer!'

After that I met him frequently at the bridge table, and though he was noisy and rather boastful, I got to like him because of his very kindly nature and his unbounded generosity.

Then came the war!

One of the first results that followed the outbreak of hostilities was a widespread suspicion of everything and everyone that smacked in the least way of Germanism. Sometimes I wondered how my German-sounding name was being discussed in barber shops and bar parlours. Sometimes I fancied I saw hostile glances as I passed down Main Street.

One afternoon while I was smoking a pipe on the Club balcony I overheard some voices in the committee room. I took no notice till I heard my own name mentioned.

'He's a German and we must expel him from the Club!'
'He's no German! He's a Jew!'
'But there are German Jews, too?'
'Oh! Rats! He was born in Ballarat! Many a time I was in his old man's shop when I was a kid! I tell you he's a Jew and I vouch that he hates the Hun as much as we do!'

I waited to hear no more but quietly went home.

A few days later one of the big plate-glass windows at the Big Store was smashed and the word 'HUN!' was painted in big letters across the front tiled pavement. The next week the town was plastered with printed posters:

'Don't shop with Huns!'

Mr Bronstein donated a large sum to the local branch of the Patriotic Fund; he took a whole page of the local newspaper to advertise that his sympathies were all with the Allies; that the full salaries would still be paid to all his employees who enlisted; that wives and mothers of soldiers at the front would receive a discount of twenty per cent on all their purchases at the Big Store.

The response to these generous gestures was that late the same night, every window in the Big Store was smashed. The window spaces were boarded up and Mr Bronstein bravely attempted to carry on by means of a tremendous cut-price sale.

But it was all in vain!

His shop employees refused to continue in his service and he could get no others. The townspeople refused to buy anything from his establishment. Yes! And many of his customers refused to pay their book debts.

In a few weeks the sumptuously appointed Big Store was a desolate wilderness, while the other storekeepers chuckled to themselves and congratulated each other on having got rid of a powerful business rival.

One evening I was smoking my pipe and reading in my study when a visitor was shown in. It took me a minute to recognize in the haggard and nerve-shaken man before me the jovial and self-satisfied Mr Bronstein of only a few weeks ago.

Timidly he held out his hand.

'Mister,' he whined. 'You von't turn me down like all my fine friends! Gott! Dey none of dem don't know me anymore!'

'I'm sorry for you but what can I do for you?'

'But you're not a *goy* anyway,' he interrupted.

Harsh, sarcastic words came to my lips, but so abject, so miserable, so pitiable was the broken man before me that I could not utter them.

'And now dey tell me dey get me interned! I do notings bad! I give! I give! I give! And now dey say I be interned! *Oi! Voi!*'

Suddenly he gave me a crafty look.

'Vy do dey do noting to you? Your name, Spielvogel, is as *Deutsch* as Bronstein! Hey!'

I could not resist the thrust!

'Because they all know that I am a Jew and they all know that you are a German!'

He shrugged his shoulders in true ghetto style.

'Me a German? Yah! A German from Vilna!'

'But you always said—'

'Ai! Ai! I know! I know! I know!'

And the poor wretch put his head down on the table and groaned aloud. I felt very sorry for the poor fellow.

'If a few pounds are any good,' I began, but he shook his head.

The next thing I heard was that Mr Bronstein had disappeared from the town!

Then the whole '*truth*' came out!

Bronstein was a German spy! Did he not have a secret wireless hidden up on the roof of his store? Had he not received many registered letters from Berlin? Had not black-bearded foreigners come in big motor cars to his place late at night and left early in the morning? Had he not collected plans of the bridges and roads of the whole district?

All these things were whispered round the town and believed by the credulous folk.

A week later I had a visit from a Commonwealth Inquiry Officer who, because of 'information received' had been sent to investigate about a man, Bronstein, who was reputed to be a German spy.

When I explained to him that Bronstein was a rather stupid Polish Jew who considered it better for his business prospects to be accepted as a German rather than as either a Pole or a Jew, the officer laughed sardonically.

'The same old story! I've had a dozen similar cases to investigate! Poor devil! But he is paying a big price for his stupidity!'

I made no inquiries about what had become of Mr Bronstein, but everybody in the town *knew* that he had been interned. One or two of the very best informed of the inhabitants had it from very reliable sources that he had been shot in Melbourne Gaol as a spy.

And that was the end of poor Mr Bronstein!

No! Not quite the end!

Some years later I was having a vacation motor tour through southern New South Wales. One day I came into a large country town. In the main street I saw a fine store with well-filled show windows and every sign of affluent prosperity. But what attracted my attention was a huge Neon sign above the building:

ISAAC MOSES BRONSTEIN!

I stopped the car and got out.

I looked at the crowd of people admiring the attractively displayed goods and passing in and out of the elegant portals. The place seemed as busy as a beehive!

Out came Mr Bronstein as prosperous and self-satisfied as ever. His eyes lighted up when he saw me. He seized me by the arm and dragged me through his busy store till we arrived at his palatial private office.

'*Shalom Aleichem!*' he cried. 'Vot do you think of my new place? You see dey can't keep a *Yidella* down. No! No! Dey can't keep a *Yidella* down! Vait a minit! I want to open a bottle of wine!'

He filled my glass with some superb sparkling burgundy and then filled his own glass. He held it up and with a sly grin he merrily said, '*Chayim!*'

Not a word was said about past happenings in that far-off Victorian country town, but I perceived that Mr Bronstein had learnt his lesson. Yes! And learnt it well!

While we finished that bottle of delicious wine, he told me that he had three or four friends coming to hear him read the *Haggadah* at his *Seder* next week.

Wouldn't I stay for it, too!

Yes! I saw that Mr Bronstein had learnt his lesson!

LYSBETH ROSE COHEN

Original Anzac

THE PIPES of the Black Watch Band increased in volume as the column swung around the corner, the campaign medals at the end of their bright ribbons jangling gently in time with the marching feet of their owners.

The people were cheering in this part of the city just as loudly and enthusiastically as at other points along the route, and every now and then he would hear an excited cry above the general hubbub: 'Look! There's —!' He kept facing straight ahead, as in the old days as sergeant he had urged his platoon to do. It would be pointless for him to gaze around, anyhow; who could possibly be there watching for old Bert Langton?

Not his son Harold, who had forsworn marching or watching marches or even attending reunions after his repatriation from the enforced marches of the Burma-Thailand railway: so Harold's wife and children would not be there either.

Not his daughter Elva, with the black hair and blacker moods, who condescended to acknowledge her family once or twice a year in between her oh-so-important social and business commitments.

Not, no certainly not, his wonderful, worthy wife Ilma.

'Haven't you got over all this playing soldiers at your age?' she had demanded that morning, wiping her plump hands on the comfortable expanse of checked apron, exactly as she had reiterated every year for the last five. 'If you're too old to work, surely you're too old for all that marching.'

'I like it. I like seeing the boys again.'

'Huh. Those of them that are still around.' She turned back to the cake she was mixing. There was a Red Cross fête on Saturday.

How cruelly that was true. Every year there were fewer of the original Anzacs, every year some well-remembered face was missing. Today the ranks were smaller again. Last year old Harry Thompson had collapsed on the way and died in hospital the next day. It had been in all the papers with the appropriate blurb about the March and the Landing and so on. Well, we all have to die some day, don't we? he thought, angry at the memory, and wished he'd had the courage to say this to Ilma.

Himself, he had never felt better. The sun warmed his still straight back and highlighted the good tan that constant attention to his garden gave to his barely lined face. The slight nip in the air lifted his spirits. I'm good for years yet, he told himself, even though Ilma's so sure my liver is covered with knobs. Somewhere she had read that that was what happened to hardened drinkers. And she had always considered his drinking far worse than it actually was. Of course he could refuse a drink if he wished. How like a woman to blame the succession of bad luck he had had in business on a few drinks.

There was that time during the Depression. Ilma had saved them all from the dole by making cheap and tasty cut lunches which he had delivered to the factory in the next street. The children had been able to complete their schooling. Later something always seemed to go wrong and when, helpless and bewildered, he had a few extra drinks to help himself cope—well, somehow she always managed to rescue them, but did she ever let him forget it?

The ultimatum five years ago, threatening to leave him for good if he ever drank again—that was not really necessary. The way she spoke, a person would think he drank all the time, instead of just now and again when he was depressed and things went wrong. For a while things seemed to go wrong so often. A few drinks would make him feel successful and important and respected all at once—until the awful hangover, of course. So for five years he had kept his promise—most of the time—with only an occasional lapse, limiting himself with difficulty to one small drink each time—and Ilma never knew.

A childish voice beside the police barricade piped: 'Look at the old ones!' causing a clear adult reply: 'They're from the first world war. They're the men who fought at Gallipoli. Remember—the Anzacs?'

Subconsciously the veterans in his row straightened their backs and marched a little more smartly.

How proud his children had always been at school when the lesson of Anzac was taught! In those days Ilma, her brown hair still unflecked with grey, had packed up a picnic lunch of all his favourite things—salmon patties and hard-boiled eggs, freshly baked cup cakes, he could smell their inviting aroma now—and with a child on either side had travelled to the city at the crack of dawn to watch from a position of vantage. In those days he would look across and grin and half-raise his hand in salute to his family, and the children would jump up and down in excitement and recognition. In those days they were hard up, but not desperately so. That was before the drinking became a problem, before the years of bitter rows.

And Elva, critical of him even at that tender age, had become quite affectionate for a few days, only to return to her usual sullenness when the excitement of the March was over.

'When I grow up,' she would say bitterly, 'I'm going to marry a man with plenty of money and a car and have lots of new clothes whenever I want them.'

She had done just that, but he doubted whether she was any happier as, childless, she travelled round the country with her estate agent husband, buying well and waxing wealthy.

Bill Jones, marching beside him as they had marched each Anzac Day for a lifetime—as they had marched to the transport ships in 1915, their slouch hats at the smartest angle, band playing, crowds waving—Bill Jones spoke beneath his moustache without turning his head.

'Goin' to join us for a drink, after, Bert?'

For the past five years he had managed to avoid this temptation, managed to talk about other things and escape before the invitation had been proffered.

'Promised the Old Woman I wouldn't.' He tried to sound cheerful and nonchalant.

'Aw, come on. It's Anzac Day, after all.'

'I'd love to,' wistfully, genuinely meaning it, adding 'See about it later,' while conscience (or was it fear of Ilma?) smote him as he spoke.

What harm could there be in a drink with the boys anyway? Just one. Just one little one for old times' sake. But in his heart of hearts he knew that in this company he would not stop at one, could not stop at one, would probably go on drinking for a week the way it used to be. No, it was not worth the risk of Ilma's leaving him. It was not worth those terrible feelings of sickness and remorse that would follow.

The pipers ceased and the Junior Air League Band behind them struck up a different tune, a cheerful brassy march. Fresh crowds began cheering and the tangy odour of oranges tantalized his nostrils as they passed a group of youngsters sitting on the kerb, bright play-shirts, bright eyes, quite oblivious of the fact that their picnic was being televised by the cameras opposite.

He became aware of a break in the rhythm of marching feet beside him. Looking to his left, he saw Perce Hopkins faltering.

That dawn of the Landing, Perce had faltered as they climbed and groped through the scrub, Perce beside him hit by a Turkish bullet—and others in front and behind, too.

'You all right, Perce?' The years seemed to melt away. He looked around for stretcher-bearers, expecting to hear the reply: 'They got me leg, Sarge,' when the present returned with a jolt as Perce quavered: 'No. I feel crook. I'll have to step out of line.'

'Look, go across to that cop, there. He'll take care of you.'

Perce was an awful grey colour. He staggered to the barricade. Thank goodness he made it. Hope he'll be all right. With relief he saw an ambulance man materialize as the policeman raised his hand.

'Perce's out,' Bert muttered to Bill Jones, marching more briskly himself to regain confidence.

Bill missed his step and skipped to regain the rhythm of the others.

'Gawd! Not another one this year. We'll certainly need that drink, Bert, when the March is over.'

Bert passed his tongue over his dry lips and suddenly felt much older. He would need that drink when the March was finished. He was tired and thirsty and horribly depressed, and there was still quite a way to go. And why shouldn't he? Resentment swelled up inside his breast. If that had been himself instead of Perce, he would be in the Casualty Room now, his spare form taking up about half of the examination couch, being stimulated by good hospital brandy. The very thought of it made his stomach contract.

Left, right, left; left, right, left; left ... left. ... I had a good wife and I left. ...

He wished Ilma had come to watch today. Each year, as he became more dependent on her, she seemed to need him less and less. Her tremendous vitality, used for so long to keep the family off the rocks, had now been channelled into Red Cross work and she seemed to be perpetually attending meetings or organizing card parties and fêtes for charity. She had never looked so well and happy. Sometimes he would suggest that she stayed at home while he worked in the garden—just for company.

'Oh, you'll be all right there,' she always replied. 'I shan't be away long and you can get that vegetable patch (or that rose garden or something) turned over by the time I get back.' But he could tell she was pleased by the warm tones that replaced her usual staccato.

If she were to die before him, what would become of him? Who would look after him? Who would care? He supposed Harold and Jean would, and their two little boys—but an old man does not always fit in so well with a young family. Ideas of bringing up youngsters vary so much from generation to generation. And there was always beer on ice for their frequent callers. If he disgraced himself there they would probably never want to see him again. Jean had been strictly raised by very religious parents; he knew Harold's views about excesses of any kind. He thought with affection of Terry and Ricky; it wouldn't do for them to see him the worse for drink. No, it was not worth it. He'd buy himself a milk-shake after they dismissed.

Some Anzac Day celebration! A milk-shake by himself because his own family did not care sufficiently to come and watch the March and his pals were all drinking the beer he dared not touch, he thought bitterly. Some Anzac Day! Come to think of it—some life!—frustrated, failing, drinking, and now fearful of the future, cared for in his old age by nobody. Ashamed of himself, he could not fight off the unaccustomed self-pity that welled up inside him until he felt he would burst. Bill Jones would have some drinks with their mates and then wander happily home to a traditional roast beef dinner that somehow his wife would have managed to keep hot for him. And he, himself? Why even the cake Ilma was making that morning was for some fête, not for him. There was a sour taste at the back of his throat as they reached the last section.

'Now, what about it?' asked Bill, as they began to disband.

Desperately, miserably, the memory of that cake still rankling he still could not bring himself to agree. He pretended he had not heard, waving to an imaginary friend as they sauntered towards a group of former comrades. The spectators were mingling with the marchers now, happy laughter, hugs and kisses all around him, families of returned men of two great world wars and several smaller ones. And his? He tried to grin, tried to keep the grim thoughts from showing in his face. In a minute he would have to make his decision: either leave the group or go with them into the nearest pub.

He stepped aside to avoid two small boys hurtling towards him, apparently intent on knocking him off his feet. The next moment, to his delighted surprise, he found himself hugged on both sides, while one squealed: 'We saw you, Grampa!' and the other jumped up, crying: 'Can I touch your medals, Grampa?'

He stopped in his tracks, hardly daring to look in case he was having hallucinations. Then, when he could control the lump in his throat, he asked them gruffly: 'Well, now, and how did you get here, eh?'

'By bus,' said Terry, stepping back proudly. 'All by ourselves. And Mummy says we have to bring you home for lunch.'

'And Nana's coming and bringing a special cake!' added Ricky, between bounces.

'Sssh! That's supposed to be a secret!'

He waved to Bill Jones. 'You go on without me,' he said, nearly bursting with joy. 'I'd better see my grandsons get home safely. Have a long one for me, won't you?'

And, with a small boy clinging to each hand, he marched across to the bus stop, his footsteps ringing on the pavement.

JUDAH WATEN

'Well, What Do You Say To My Boy?'

WHEN I WAS A BOY most of the women in our migrant community did not want their sons to follow their husbands' occupations. This was the case even when a good living was being made and money was not short. The women wanted their sons to become educated men—doctors, lawyers, professors and the like. For why did they come to Australia if not to educate their children, to avail themselves of the schooling which was to be had here and not in their old homes?

The men did not oppose their wives. Clearly the professions were better, more dignified, more secure than, say, bottle-buying, hawking with drapery, labouring or even carpentering, which was said to be one of the best trades. Besides, the men, too, wanted their sons to be somebodies in the new land. Of course businessmen were the only ones with any chance of attaining to fortunes, but learning came before money. Or so everybody said.

From this it mustn't be concluded that all the boys in our community became educated men. Many did, but in quite a few families the sons, when they turned fourteen, left school and joined their fathers at whatever they happened to be doing.

In our community no women desired more ardently to educate her five sons than did Mrs Minnie Green. And no woman extolled more rhapsodically the virtues of learning than she did. And her husband seemed to be one with her in her aspirations, always keeping a serious mien, always nodding his head whenever she spoke on the matter of education, which was very frequently.

Mrs Green, however, had no fortune with her two eldest boys, Les and Izz. Neither of them had liked school and as soon as each reached fourteen he had joined his father on his clattering, honking truck, buying bottles for three days a week in suburban streets and on the other three working days buying hides, skins, tallow and animal bones from farmers in country districts.

Mrs Green had not tried to stop Les and Izz from becoming businessmen. She had accepted the position realistically, without fuss. Concluding that her influence had not been strong enough to offset the pulls against learning to which they had been subjected, she set about making the home the all-conquering influence, a bastion of culture and learning, so that her other sons would not be lost.

Her third son Benny, who was then approaching fourteen and was a promising scholar, benefited from her policy. She surrounded him with objects which she believed would inspire him to higher things and cement his ties with learning and culture. She could not do anything else for him; she could not discuss his school work with him nor could she help him with his homework. The truth was that Mrs Minnie Green could not read or write in any language and she could not speak any language correctly, least of all English.

Thus it came about that she bought a piano on time payment. It might be asked, 'Why a piano?' when nobody in the house knew how to play the instrument and when not one of her five boys was receiving piano lessons? Partly it was because Mrs Green looked upon the piano as something inspiring and refining. And besides she was convinced that only the piano could counter the baneful influence of the

'Well, What Do You Say to My Boy?' 139

guitar which her eldest, Les, was for ever strumming inside the house. She sniffed at that stringed box as at an unclean thing that mocked at the higher things.

Mrs Green spent much time with the piano, dusting it every day and lovingly polishing it at least twice a week. It stood out among the rest of the furniture in the dining room, a formidable if silent ally of the mistress of the house. Silent it was for most of the time, but now and then the only musical member of the family, Les the guitar player, would run his grimy, thick fingers over the keyboard and produce a frivolous tone reminiscent of the guitar. It would grate on his mother's ears and make her wince as if with pain.

'Why must you do that to the piano, Les?' she demanded. 'It is desecration, nothing but desecration,' she added almost breaking her teeth over that stern word.

Les looked at her with feigned earnestess.

'The piano'll pine away, Mum, if it isn't touched sometimes—caressed,' Les said. 'You know what I mean. It's like a human being,' he concluded, inclining his head respectfully, his lips set firm to prevent his face breaking into a smile.

She did not answer him. She gazed at him with a puzzled frown as if trying to divine exactly what he meant. His earnest features set her at ease but she could not rid herself of her suspicions. Les had a most peculiar sense of humour. Vulgar, it could almost be called. God knows where he got it from. He certainly did not get it from her and she was convinced he did not get it from her husband who, she was sure, was very refined despite his uncouth occupation. Ah well! she sighed. The outside world, that rude world of money-grubbing and vulgarity, had a habit of twisting people to its own image.

But for all this she was happy with her sons, particularly Benny the promising scholar, and happy with the piano which on the whole was performing its requisite cultural role.

The piano was not the only object she brought to bear on the boy. There were the books, in great numbers, cluttering up the sideboards, tables and dressers, for there were no bookshelves as yet. To her great joy Benny devoured the books as if they were slabs of fresh honey-cake. She watched him read with that look of pleasure and pride which young mothers ordinarily wear when their first-born utters its first halting words. Benny was more than making up for her failure with Les and Izz.

Mrs Green bought most of the books from second-hand dealers, acquaintances of her husband. They sold them to her for next to a song. There were complete editions of Scott, Dickens, Thackeray, Kingsley, Marryat, Reade, Lever, Collins and other eminent nineteenth-century writers including some leatherbound volumes of poetry. Now and again a dealer, taking advantage of her inability to read, would palm off a cookery book or an abstruse, learned work like Locke's *An Essay Concerning Human Understanding* or Hobbes's *Leviathan*. It did not make any difference to Mrs Minnie Green. She did not know one book from another, but she blindly revered the printed word from which stemmed learning and thus happiness.

On almost all her shopping trips she dropped into the second-hand dealers first. Invariably she bought some books, which she placed at the bottom of her large shopping basket. But she could never resist carrying one or two under her arm like a student and she would succumb to the temptation of showing off, even boasting in the butcher's shop where there was always a goodly congregation of ladies, gossiping, treating the place as if it was a street or a back yard.

'My Benny only reads the best,' Mrs Green often boasted to the ladies. 'Penny dreadfuls never show their noses in my house,' she added with a faint blush for her words were not strictly accurate. Still, they were nearly true.

Once after she had made her familiar remark a lady who could read English looked at the book under Mrs Green's arm and asked mischievously, 'Does your Benny enjoy Christian sermons too?'

For a moment Mrs Green did not know what had been said to her and she stared blankly at the lady who added ironically:

'Of course if you have to give him sermons it's as well that they should be by a bishop of the English church. After all what greater authority on Christianity can there be in an English country?'

It suddenly occurred to Mrs Green that she was carrying some kind of religious book and that she had been had by that grubby, oily-mouthed second-hand dealer who often talked about Benny's reading, pretending to be interested. But suppressing her annoyance, with unexpected presence of mind and at the same time rising above her own beliefs and prejudices, she answered calmly:

'My Benny said, "Mum, please get me a book by an English bishop," and I hunted everywhere for it until I got it. My boy is very interested in religion and history and everything,' she added with a satisfied smile.

And before the other lady could open her mouth to cast doubts Mrs Green, speaking rapidly, said that her Benny in the pursuit of knowledge would read everything, even the writings of Christians and heretics. He was like her late uncle, possessed of courage and curiosity. Her late uncle of blessed memory was not even afraid to dip into the pages of socialists and writers who said we stemmed from monkeys and once walked around the world with tails in the air.

For all her words and her calm manner the ladies in the butcher's shop did not believe Minnie Green. A sly second-hand dealer had palmed the book of sermons on to her; how would she tell which was a book of sermons or which a joke book if they were both placed in front of her? This was said after Mrs Green had left the shop with the parcel of meat on top of her basket, the sermons still under her arm.

Yet the community could not help admiring her. Granted, it was said, that she was a little green—'a plain greener' as they termed starry-eyed, excessively optimistic newcomers. But there was no doubt that Minnie Green was naturally a refined, cultured woman, a kind of nature's lady with genuinely lofty ambitions for her sons. But how she had ever come to marry Sam Green, that coarse animal, that Samson of a man, was almost beyond their understanding. It was a great source of discussion in our community.

One of our most respected and best informed gossips, Mrs Fanny Snider, told a group of ladies at an engagement party that it was a fact that refined girls were often drawn to unrefined men. How could she say such a thing? everyone protested. Mrs Fanny Snider then repeated her statement, saying that it was as much a fact as that the sun rises in the morning. She gave instances. Minnie Green was one.

Whatever it was that had caused Minnie to wed Sam, it was undeniable that they were still fond of each other nearly twenty-two years after their marriage. And she looked up to her husband to such an extent that she could not understand why sometimes she heard him referred to as that 'happy bandit'. Maybe it was only a joke. But Minnie Green said: Ask yourself what sort of a joke it is? She did not like it although she let it pass.

But when she overheard Sam described as a bushranger she spun round aggressively ready to do battle for her husband's honour and put an end once and for all to these unpleasant jokes which were not jokes at all. What was the meaning of it? she demanded.

'Now, now, Mrs Green, what is there to get excited about?' came the answer. 'Bushranger! Pah! Shame on you

'*Well, What Do You Say to My Boy?*' 143

Mrs Green for raising your voice. In this country bushrangers are the aristocrats, the leaders of society, honoured by everyone. You have something to boast about with a husband a bushranger.'

These exaggerated, swollen words placated her. Her husband was certainly not a bushranger, a leader of society; but maybe he was a tiny bushranger. In a kind of way she was proud of her husband for his achievement. He was only a newcomer but he was a somebody already. Thus she accepted the explanation, relieved, too, that she did not have to quarrel, for she was a peaceful woman and she cared for her dignity. But all the same she had many misgivings, deep inside. Who ever heard of bushrangers honoured! Honour was for learned men, she had always believed. Evidently she did not know as much about her new land as she imagined. And that came from looking at the world with the eyes of a 'greener', the wise ones in the community said. But she could not help it. Everything about her told of a guileless nature, even her face which was broad and pink and unwrinkled, with an expression which reminded one of a question mark, and her fair hair was done in a girlish Gretchen manner.

So it was not surprising that her husband, Sam, was not altogether as she saw him. He was regarded in the community as coarse and crafty and there was no doubt that he was worldly. It had not taken him long to know the new land, to become a real expert, a native in fact. And he had prospered as a bottle-oh and a buyer of junk and animal bones which he sold to the fertilizer works. So well had he prospered that he had long ago discarded a horse and cart in favour of a motor truck; a poor spluttering thing it was, but it suited Sam better than a healthy good-looking truck which only flaunted one's prosperity. In no time he had needed assistance, partners in fact. And what better partners than his own sons when they were like Les and Izz?

Sam had taken the two boys from Minnie without her knowing it. Behind her back he always encouraged them to play truant and to come with him on his rounds, where he scoffed at the school, extolling the self-made man as the best of men. What did they want education for? To make money all they had to know was how to read and add up and subtract in their own favour. They knew that already.

The boys had quickly fallen in with their father. They were very like him in many ways. The same humour, the same craftiness. And, in appearance, the same heavy, powerful bodies, the same jet black hair. They made a fine team.

Thus on their round they were rarely out of one another's sight; Sam generally doing the buying and then helping the boys carry the bottles or the junk to the truck. They must pay for what they took; no thieving like other bottle-ohs. Sam had laid down that rule at the very inception of the partnership.

'You make more by honest commerce than by thieving,' he explained to his sons. 'Ever hear of a thief becoming a Sir or a Lord or even a mayor? I bet you haven't. But plenty of businessmen have. There's that grocer, for instance, who is not only the mayor but was knighted too. See what I mean boys? You've got to be legal to get on.'

They understood him quite well. You had to pay. That was the rule. There were no other rules.

When the boys had acquired plenty of experience and could take good care of themselves Sam allowed them to open up new territory, to go into back yards without him. When they returned to the truck they would relate all their experiences, tell their father everything. Sam had an easy way with them so that they always treated him like a companion, a friend of their own age and not a parent.

One day Les said to his father, pointing to an apartment house which had issued up a regular gold mine of bottles, 'The old girl in there fell for Izz as soon as she laid eyes on him. She told him he looked like a movie actor. "Come round as often as you like," she said to him. "On your own."' he added, mimicking a woman's voice.

Sam looked admiringly at Izz who was the darkest, the best looking and biggest of the three.

'She thought you were an amorous drake,' Sam observed, 'and I don't suppose she was too far out.'

'What would I want with an old piece like that?' Izz asked. Sam shrugged his shoulders and smiled.

'Come to think of it she was an ancient piece', Les said. 'Forty if she wasn't a day.'

'So forty's old, eh?' Sam turned on his son. 'I ought to be shuffled off the stage, eh? Is that what you think?'

Les spoke placatingly. 'A man's not old in his forties; a woman is, though.'

'Too right,' Izz said. 'For mine, they're old when they've turned twenty-one.'

Sam looked his sons up and down with contempt.

'A fat lot both of you know,' he said sneeringly. 'When you grow up you'll find out that old bones make very good soup.'

The boys winked, digging each other in the ribs with their elbows.

'You break your teeth on old bones,' Izz cried.

'You sharpen them, you fool,' Sam retorted. 'You don't on jelly.'

The argument ended in laughter. Most of their arguments did. The other bottle-ohs and the men who worked the streets envied them their capacity for enjoyment. Father and sons found each other amusing and they were happy with each other. Their business kept growing.

When Benny was sixteen and in the leaving class at school his father was seeking an assistant for the dealers' yard he had just opened, one who could write letters, keep books and 'talk nice' to important buyers, as he put it. And Sam

Green thought of Benny—an educated boy if ever there was one. What a triumph it would be to snatch him from Minnie now that he was on the threshold of the university! The more Sam thought about it the more attractive the idea seemed and he was determined to capture his son.

But he could not inveigle Benny as he had Les and Izz. His third son was aloof and cool and rarely talked at the meal table, rationing his words as if they were really valuable. In a way he was a stranger to his father. How to get intimate with one like him was indeed a problem.

So it came about that Sam began to affect an interest in books and when it occurred to him that his son spent more time than was normal at his desk absorbed in writing, he asked Benny what he was doing, pretending that he was much concerned, although the boy's scribblings were as much on his mind as yesterday's breakfast. Benny looked at his father shrewdly and answered non-committally, giving him no information at all. Sam was rebuffed again and again.

'He won't talk, devil take it!' Sam muttered to himself. 'He looks like Minnie, the same fair hair, the same pink face, but he hasn't got her innocent tongue or her simple heart,' he thought with self-righteous indignation. 'That boy of mine is really tough, tougher than he looks.'

Presently Sam lost patience and cast away all pretences. He approached his son directly and without any apparent guile.

'I want you to come in with me, Benny,' he said. 'In a couple of years we'll have a great business. Green and Sons. Metals, scrap, import, export. We'll be rich.'

From the expression on Benny's face Sam could see that he had sounded the wrong notes and he hastily began to sing a new tune.

'You'll have an easy life, son,' he said. 'I'll get you a motor-car. You can do a lot with a motor-car. You can take your girl friend for rides all over the place,' he added, honestly believing that if the promise of money and an easy life couldn't do the trick a girl friend in a motor-car with its saucy implication most certainly would.

To his astonishment, however, Benny screwed up his face in an expression of utter repugnance.

'What makes you think that I would put a motor-car and a partnership in Green and Sons as the height of my ambitions?' the boy asked haughtily. 'I know of a higher aim,' he added to his speechless father.

Sam was still furious when he spoke to Les and Izz a few hours later.

'What sort of a fellow's your brother?' he demanded.

'What do you mean?' Les asked.

'You ought to know,' Izz said, glancing slyly at his father. 'You made him, Dad.'

'I don't know him,' Sam snapped. 'He's a cold devil, that's what he is. Ever notice that?'

'He's all right,' Les said. 'He's got a lot of brains, Benny has.'

'Deep as the sea if you ask me,' Izz said.

'Deep as my old boots,' Sam snorted. 'Got plenty of airs though.'

For all his anger he was now more determined than ever to ensnare Benny into the dealer's yard. And Minnie, who did not know anything about her husband's intention, had no doubt whatever that Benny would go to the university the following year. In the butcher's shop she boasted without pause. Although she did not know whether Benny wanted to do medicine she could not imagine that he did not want to become a doctor. So she announced that her son was going to study medicine. It was a fine, noble profession. Doctors were respected and honoured everywhere and if they were not respected and honoured they were feared. And they always looked clean and very dignified, which was more than could be said for most of the husbands of the ladies in the shop. And as if making a concession to vulgar opinion she said that doctors were never short of customers, which could not be said of other professions from what she had heard.

Minnie Green should really have gone into conference with Benny before speaking so emphatically in public. She would have discovered her boy had his own ideas. She did not learn what they were until early the following year. It was at the dinner-table the day Benny obtained his leaving certificate with many distinctions.

In honour of this signal occasion Mrs Green roasted a turkey stuffed with rice and garlic and hid the table with her best damask cloth and heavy silver cutlery, both wedding presents. And Benny was seated next to his secretly proud father, where he was fed the best pieces, fussed over by his admiring brothers and beamed upon by his mother who kept calling him 'Dr Green'. The boy looked at her with a puzzled expression, repeating to himself the words, 'Dr Green'. And all at once it dawned on him why his mother had bestowed that honourable title on him. He must put a stop to it. He would never be guilty of false pretences, he would never fly under false colours; he had long ago sworn an oath to himself to serve truth in all things.

'Mother,' he began in a solemn voice, 'if you think I am going in for medicine you are mistaken. In fact I am not even going to the university.'

Father and brothers suddenly stopped eating as if felled, while Minnie Green kept repeating, 'No university?' and going into a kind of daze, staring wide-eyed and blank across the table.

'That's right, Mum,' Benny said, relentlessly faithful to the truth.

Sam glanced at Benny appraisingly and smiled cautiously, pleased with the latest turn, his hopes rising, yet held in check—for God alone knew what his son had boiling in that head of his.

'What do you intend to do then?' he asked quietly in a matter-of-fact voice.

The boy glanced at his father with a determined, almost truculent expression on his face.

'I'm going to be a writer,' Benny said aggressively.

'A writer!' Sam exclaimed.

'Yes, a writer,' Benny repeated pugnaciously. 'A writer.'

That brought Minnie to. She roused herself from her daze, fixed her eyes on her son and asked, 'What are you going to write, Benny?'

'Stories of life, Mum,' he answered.

She did not understand him.

'Stories,' she repeated to herself. 'Do you mean books, Benny?' she asked hopefully.

'Yes, books, Mum.'

'Books,' she cried. 'Books! That's wonderful. Did you hear, Sam? Benny's going to write books.'

She was filled with an elation which drove away every vestige of her former disappointment. What greater happiness could there be than to have a son a writer, the supreme kind of learned, educated man who wrote the books which others read and studied—even doctors?

But Sam was alarmed. Now he knew for certain that he was in danger of irrevocably losing his son who could have become an ornament to the firm, a letter-writer and a talker of good English, necessary sometimes in business. But Sam did not bow to fate:

'Benny, how are you going to earn a living?' he asked.

Confidently the boy answered, 'By writing, of course.'

Sam looked at him pityingly.

'You don't know anything yet, Benny,' he said. 'I'll tell you something you ought to know. On my rounds I've collected bottles off a poet, a big poet, they say. You'd know him if I could remember his name. Do you know his name?' he turned to Izz and Les.

They didn't know his name either.

'Well,' Sam continued, 'that poet makes less out of poetry in three years than a shopkeeper makes in a week.'

The boy exclaimed angrily, 'You're always bringing money into everything!'

Sam ignored his son's outburst.

'Look here, Benny, if that poet I'm telling you about didn't work at something else besides his scribbling he'd starve like a homeless dog. In this country writers are on the lowest rung,' he added in a superior tone.

'We've got different ideas about the lowest rung,' the boy retorted hotly.

'Each one to his own opinion,' Sam said, winking at Les and Izz. 'But to get away from that, Benny—seriously, you ought to get into something that'll bring you in money and leave you time to write. Writing's only a hobby after all.'

The boy was speechless with indignation, but his mother suddenly found tongue.

'Sam, what are you saying to Benny? I'm amazed at you, I thought you would show more understanding.'

'You misunderstand me, Minnie,' he said and proceeded to tell her that he was thinking of nothing else but how he could help Benny with his writing career.

She was only too ready to believe him. And in a kind of way he was relieved that once again she believed him. He did not want her to know the truth; he did not want her to suspect how he schemed against her. Till his dying day he wanted to keep up his pretence.

But more than anything else he wanted to get Benny into the business. He made another sortie just before the end of the meal.

'I've been thinking, Benny,' he said, 'That a writer needs to see everything. If you'd come down to the yard sometimes or go on the truck with the boys you'd see things that'd make you old in the head before your whiskers come up.'

Benny was not misled by his father. With pleasurable malice he said, 'Dad, before I forget—my head, Mr Fitzsimmons, wants to see you.'

'See me!' Sam exclaimed. 'What's he want to see me for? He doesn't drink, does he? Or maybe he's been collecting brass door handles he wants to get rid of.'

'Sam!' Minnie cried disapprovingly. 'What's come over you tonight?'

He instantly changed his tone.

'I can't see him tomorrow, Benny,' he said earnestly.

'Any day will do, Dad. He's spending his holidays at his home.'

Several days later Sam Green was shown into the headmaster's study. Mr Raynor Fitzsimmons, a tall imposing pedagogue with a silvery mane, extended his hand and declared in a deep, carefully measured voice, 'I've wanted to see you for weeks, Mr Green. I have most important news for you.'

Under the magisterial gaze of the pedagogue Sam Green was suddenly oppressed by a premonition of defeat and he went as meek as a lamb, thus confirming his saying that often a lion among lambs became a lamb among lions.

'You've got a son a genius, Mr Green,' Mr Raynor Fitzsimmons went on in a voice that brooked of no contradiction. 'A genius!'

Bending over his desk he extracted a bulky handwritten manuscript from a drawer and thrust it under Sam's nose.

'Did my Benny write all that?' Sam asked weakly.

'Unaided, Mr Green,' came the reply.

'Unaided,' Sam repeated seemingly overwhelmed by the information.

'Only a genius could have written this work,' Mr Fitzsimmons declared. Putting the manuscript back in the drawer he fixed his steady gaze on the parent and spoke in his best manner.

'We must face the facts, Mr Green. Geniuses are never successes in the ordinary sense of the word. To put it another way, they never make money. In fact they rarely make enough to live.'

Sam paled. He could not help it. It was that premonition come true. Mr Raynor Fitzsimmons was making his defeat complete and almost ignominious. For a moment he wondered if Benny hadn't put Fitzsimmons up to it; you could expect that kind of thing from a son of Sam Green. He could not suggest that. Instead he struggled with his voice which had gone feeble.

'I had a plan for putting Benny in my dealer's yard and giving him....' He was interrupted.

'Are you joking, Mr Green?' the headmaster almost hissed out the question.

'I was joking. Believe me. But I thought....'

Sam was interrupted again.

'Benny will bring your home honour,' Mr Fitzsimmons continued victoriously. 'But he needs freedom from all worries and petty concerns. I'm sure you'll be proud to see to that.'

And with that the headmaster escorted a bewildered Sam to the front door where he dismissed him with these words:

'Mr Green, your son is the pride of the school. The school looks to you to give him every opportunity.'

With a heavy heart Sam drove through the street. Curse the pedagogue! Why was he so foolish as to call on him? Yet it was not that he would have to keep Benny for the rest of his days; it was that he hated to lose. And Sam showed his chagrin, his unhappiness when he returned to the yard.

'You don't look too well, Dad,' Les said glancing at Izz.

'Some rotten cow take you down?' Izz asked.

'We've got a genius in the family,' Sam said mournfully. 'A genius, that's what Fitzsimmons said. And I suppose he knows, the old coot.'

'Cheer up, Dad,' Les said. 'It could have been worse. Benny might have turned out a tea leaf and not a genius.'

'I don't know whether it's any better,' Sam replied. 'A thief's got a chance, but what chance has a writer, I ask you? You've seen that poet bloke. You know.'

'Benny won't take much keeping,' Izz said.

The boys were getting on their father's nerves without knowing it.

'Maybe it won't take much to keep him,' Sam replied angrily, 'but enough to cut you two out of a car. We'll have to economize.'

'Now, Dad,' Les admonished.

'You're going too far,' Izz said.

'Perhaps I am,' Sam said wearily. 'I just can't get over it. Benny's got brains. And they could have been put to something. We need letters written.'

'I'll write 'em,' Les said.

'You, God help us!' Sam said.

Suddenly his mood lifted as he recollected something.

'You know, boys, that headmaster showed me what Benny did. A whole book of writing. I'll swear it was sixteen by eight by three and a half. Remarkable,' Sam added proudly and returned to his work whistling.

But his lightheartedness was only temporary. Soon he thought of his great loss and he was disconsolate again.

Not so Mrs Minnie Green. She walked as if on air. Her Benny was a writer, a genius. In the butcher's shop she faced the ladies with great confidence.

'Well, what do you say to my boy? A writer he's going to be. A writer of books. Truly our house has been blessed.'

JUDAH WATEN

A Peaceful Life?

ONE SUMMER MORNING the migrant ship *Liberté* entered Port Phillip Bay and moved over the quiet water towards Melbourne. The decks were crowded. Far away to the left there was a range of pale hills; to the right, behind the twisted, low, scrub-covered sandhills, were the houses of the bayside townships. The sun rose and a broad streak of light stole over the ship.

Soon the wharves came into sight and the city in the distance, a facade of lofty sombre buildings without depth, like a stage set, yet forbidding and mysterious. The ship drifted nearer and began edging into its berth. A thousand people were standing on the decks peering at the treeless sea-front with silent factory buildings, a gasometer and a few wooden shops. This was the gateway to the new land! It had a deserted look as if everybody had gone away. Impossible to set foot there and eat and work there.

The ship tied up. The wharf was crowded with people waving and shouting. The migrants on the decks became individual entities, waving back, shouting down to the wharf, their hoarse, tear-filled words lost in the din.

On the upper deck Joe Becker, a small, slight fourteen, stood between two men and watched his fellow migrants with cases and satchels walking gingerly down the gangway. On the wharf people from all sides moved towards the pale, bewildered newcomers. There were cries and tearful embraces.

The boy shifted his gaze to a group of men and women evidently waiting to come on board. There was one among

A Peaceful Life?

them who would come to claim him. His new guardian, a cousin of his dead mother, would from now direct his life. Joe Becker felt a hostility towards this man whom he had never seen and hardly knew anything about. This man would take him away to some distant place, take him further away. His only other relative, an uncle, had taken him away too. The boy had a deep mistrust of kinsmen.

As though to hide, he hurried away from the deck to the end of the ship above the seamen's quarters. Here he was alone. He leant over the taffrail and looked around. There were other ships in port and an oil tanker was creeping towards a storage wharf some distance away. Close by on a narrow strip of sandy beach, boys of his own age were playing with a dog. Joe Becker wondered if he would ever be as carefree as those boys seemed to be.

He went to the other side of the ship. From there he caught a glimpse of the railway station with an electric train sitting comfortably alongside and a loose engine trundling back and forth on another line. He remembered train journeys. They had always taken him away from all that he had known and loved.

Restlessly he walked back to where he could see the boys playing on the beach. Suddenly he pressed his face against the rail and cried. A passing sailor stopped and spoke to him in French.

'What are you crying for?'

Joe tearfully muttered something.

'Never mind, never mind,' the sailor said. 'You've got nothing to cry about. You've got your life before you.'

Joe stopped crying, dried his eyes and blew his nose.

'That's better,' the sailor said. 'You're being met, aren't you?'

'My new guardian,' Joe said in a nervous voice.

'You're a lucky boy,' the sailor said.

That, Joe didn't believe. He remained silent although he

could have told the sailor much. His uncle had left him in an orphanage outside Paris where he had lived before coming to Australia. Before he had been brought to France, for as long as he could remember, he had lived with a peasant family outside Warsaw and he had regarded himself as one of them. It was just after the war ended that a young/old-looking man came to the village, announced that he was Joe's uncle and after a talk with his peasant parents told the boy to collect his belongings and come away with him. The peasants were not his parents; they had taken him in when he was still a baby, a few days before his real Jewish parents had been sent to Auschwitz where they had perished.

Joe cried and pleaded with his strange uncle not to take him away: he belonged to the peasant family, he was theirs. Uncle Aaron would not listen to him. He had promised Joe's parents to bring up their boy as a Jew if he survived the war and found the village where Joe had been left. Aaron was one of the few survivors of Auschwitz and he was determined to take Joe to another country where they would begin their lives again. His memories were too painful for him to remain in Poland; of all their family only he and Joe remained, and there was a cousin in Australia.

There was a warmth of fury and sorrow in Uncle Aaron's words, but it did not touch Joe. He did not know his parents who had been gassed in Auschwitz; his only parents were the peasant couple in front of him. They had loved and protected him. He flung himself into his peasant father's arms. But the peasant with a heavy heart returned the boy to the uncle; he recognized Uncle Aaron's right, more so as he was one of the few to come back from concentration camp.

Uncle Aaron was stooped, thin, with a tight skin that stuck to his bones like yellowed elastic, but once he was a fleshy man. He had a sharp, foxy face with unblinking eyes that seemed to lack eyelashes. His nature was by turns unexpectedly warm and unexpectedly callous, and he was shrewd. That had stood him in good stead in Auschwitz. He had hidden under a heap of corpses when the guns of the liberating army could be heard and the guards, before fleeing, had shot nearly all the inmates.

Joe went with his uncle tearfully and sullenly and longed for his village parents and the village. Uncle Aaron understood what was going on in the boy's heart and set out to win his affection. He became absorbed in his task and in one burst all his belated love and accumulated pity were poured out on Joe.

As they travelled over Europe he rarely left Joe for a moment, dressing him in the most expensive clothes and feeding him extravagantly. He stuffed food into the boy's mouth as though he were fattening a goose. His own appetite was enormous and he could never eat enough.

By the time they had reached Paris Joe quite liked his uncle although he remained reserved and had the passive watchfulness of a captured animal. For the first month in the great city they were rarely out of each other's company. There was nothing Uncle Aaron enjoyed more than a film, particularly a love story that ended happily. Every day they sat in a picture theatre feasting on the idle, untroubled lives of good-looking men and women. Afterwards they sat in cafés where Uncle Aaron talked with new acquaintances of the life he intended to make for himself and his young nephew. But he was constantly changing his plans.

Months passed and still Uncle Aaron made no move to leave Paris. Instead he had gone into business with another ex-inmate of a concentration camp and they were making money. He ate gluttonously and grew fat and sluggish, only his unblinking eyes retained their sharpness.

As he found it impossible to take Joe with him to his business, for days on end he left the boy alone in their flat, only seeing him at breakfast or for a while during the day when he brought an armful of foodstuffs and left it on the table. And he was so absorbed in business that he hardly ever talked with Joe. Sometimes he behaved irritably as if the months alone with a small boy had given him enough of youthful society for the time being.

A feeling of wretchedness was always with Joe. He sat in front of the window of the flat and stared at the passing buses and the people walking in the street. Now and then he breathed on the glass and smudged it with drawings of his village. He was afraid to leave the flat; he could not speak the language and he was sure he would not be able to find his way about the city.

Late one night when Joe had fallen asleep Uncle Aaron came into the room and sat down on the edge of the boy's bed. A feeling of pity for his nephew came over him.

'Joe, Joe,' he whispered. 'Wake up, Joe.'

The boy stirred, opened his eyes, looked reproachfully at his uncle and then closed his eyes again.

'Wake up, Joe,' Uncle Aaron said, shaking him. 'I must talk to you.'

Joe opened his eyes again and sat up slowly. His uncle's face was pale and drawn and contrasted oddly with his heavy body.

'Would you like to go on a long journey in a big ship?' he suddenly asked the boy.

'I wouldn't,' Joe said agitatedly. 'I want to go home. Send me back, Uncle Aaron.'

'I can't do that,' he said. 'I don't even know that they'd want you now.'

'They want me, I know they want me,' the boy said passionately.

'What are you to them?' Uncle Aaron asked and answered himself. 'Nothing. They aren't even Jews.'

Joe looked at him with a pained, bewildered expression. Uncle Aaron averted his eyes and bent his head.

A Peaceful Life?

Suddenly he caught hold of the boy's hand: 'Forgive me Joe. I've let you down. I didn't mean to. I thought I could look after you as well as myself. But I see I can't. When I took you away I was still living with dreams. They've all gone. A thousand curses on Hitler, that madman. He made me into a wolf just as surely as he took your parents away from you.'

He stood up from the bed and paced up and down the room. He stopped near the stove at the far end and, to distract his thoughts, he lit the gas jet and placed a pot of cooked spaghetti over the flame.

'Have something to eat with me, Joe,' he said.

'I don't want anything,' the boy answered sulkily.

'Have a piece of chocolate then.'

Uncle Aaron walked over to the bed, pressed the chocolate into the boy's hand and returned to the stove. He emptied the spaghetti into a large dish, poured a tin of meat balls over the top of it and sat down at the table in the middle of the room to eat the mixture.

'I've asked the Bureau to find your mother's cousin for us,' he said between mouthfuls. 'They'll get his address if it takes them months. It's somewhere in Australia. From what your mother used to say he has a golden heart. When he learns you're in the land of the living he'll jump with joy. He'll want you to come with him straight away.'

In a resigned tone the boy said:

'I must go where you go.'

'I'm not going,' Uncle Aaron said, staring down at the table. 'I leave for America next week.'

A week later Uncle Aaron took Joe by train to a village where there was an orphanage for the boys of Jewish parents killed by the Nazis. He would be taught to speak Yiddish as well as French. It might be years before he went to Australia. In the director's office Uncle Aaron embraced the boy and kissed him passionately on the face and, as if overcome by a rush of sad memories, tears filled his unblinking sharp eyes.

'Don't think badly of me, Joe,' he pleaded. As though to snatch a last sympathetic glance or word from his nephew he said in a broken voice:

'I swear on whatever is holy in this world I'll always keep an eye on you, wherever you are. When I've made my fortune in America you will share it, I swear.'

Uncle Aaron was determined to wipe out the memory of his years in Auschwitz, to avenge himself for his sufferings by making a fortune. He thought he could in America. He told Joe his plan. But the boy looked at him bitterly and even when Uncle Aaron had left the office the bitter expression remained imprinted on his face.

As Joe waited on the deck for his new guardian, he recalled his uncle, the orphanage, and his Polish parents he still longed for. It was getting hotter and the sun shone straight down on the ship. A curious thought crept into his mind. His guardian might not come for him. What would he do then? He would look out for that sailor who had spoken so optimistically and pour out all his troubles to him. The sailor would take him back to Marseilles. Then he would find his way to the village in Poland.

Joe walked a few paces and looked down the main deck. Most of the migrants had gone ashore.

All round him the wharf labourers were taking possession of the ship. When they passed they spoke to him in their strange language and he stared back with a strained, startled expression.

A few more minutes passed and he saw two men coming towards him. One was the welfare officer who had kept an eye on him during the journey, the other was a stranger.

'We've been looking for you everywhere, Joe,' the welfare officer said in French.

'Hullo, my boy,' said the stranger and put out his hand.

A Peaceful Life?

'This is your guardian, Mr Zeitlin,' the welfare officer said.

Mr Zeitlin was a short, heavy man in his early sixties. From his large, shiny unwrinkled face genially peeped two tiny blue-grey eyes. Although it was oppressively hot he wore a blue serge suit and his stiff white collar drew a fiery red circle around his shaven sunburnt neck. He was dressed as for an important occasion.

'So you're Gittel's boy,' he said in a tone of wonderment. 'Let's have a good look at you,' he said in a mixture of Yiddish and English, eyeing Joe up and down.

He noted the boy's troubled eyes, his small and delicate features, his slender figure, his expensive, unusual clothes.

'My word,' Mr Zeitlin continued, 'you're the living image of your mother, may she rest in peace. I can see her clearly before my eyes as I speak, though when I left the old country, why that's over forty years ago, she was only a little girl. Wonderful how well I can remember her though. They say I've got a good memory. Out my way they often ask me about things that happened a long time ago.'

As the welfare officer left, Joe looked at Mr Zeitlin and he saw a smile on his face. That smile seemed to say, 'You've landed in a safe haven, you're in my hands.' Mr Zeitlin seemed to be full of happy spirits; on account of the strange mixture of languages he spoke, his voice ran easily into comic oddity.

'Well, we better get down to the car,' Mr Zeitlin said.

They left the ship and walked along the wharf to a parking allotment. Then with the boy next to him Mr Zeitlin drove slowly towards the city.

'You wouldn't believe it,' he said, 'that I who was brought up in a city should prefer the country. Of course I've lived in the bush for the last thirty-five years. A day in the city does me now. Of course, there's a lot to see and talk about but I'm always glad to get back home.'

'You a farmer?' Joe asked with a sudden interest.

'Do I look like a general?' Mr Zeitlin asked.

Joe smiled.

'I grow fruit,' his guardian said.

Mr Zeitlin continued to tell the boy the story of his life while they drove through the city. Only two of his children were on the orchard now; the others were grown up and in the city.

On the farm back home in Poland his peasant father had grown fruit trees as well, apples and plums, Joe said.

'I had a letter from your uncle Aaron the other day,' Mr Zeitlin said. 'From America. He writes me quite often since he's had my address. And he always sends me money for you. When you're twenty-one you'll have a nice nest egg. He must be a good man, your uncle.'

Joe did not say anything. Mr Zeitlin glanced at him quickly. Then looking straight ahead, his hands steering the car through heavy traffic, he said:

'He suffered a lot, your uncle. He's a stranger to me of course. So was his brother, your father, although I knew about their family. They belonged to the same town as us. There were so many in both our families, your mother's and your father's. Now there's only us and your uncle Aaron left.'

After which he fell silent for a moment. Then he said:

'We'll never know those terrible years again. Things are going to be different from now on. You take my word for it; the world is different. It has learnt something.'

Mr Zeitlin had spoken these words to lift the boy's spirits, but why shouldn't it be true? he asked himself.

On Joe's face there was a look of disbelief. He was suspicious of the future; only the past had any reality. He could tell his new guardian a thing or two. He recalled a winter's day when he had been hidden under the sacks on the floor of a cellar because the German soldiers and the S.S. men

A Peaceful Life?

were searching every house in the district. His two peasant brothers, both older than himself, had been herded into a lorry a few weeks later and sent to some distant place never to be heard of again. He remembered a neighbour hanging from a gallows in the village square, his livid face resting on his chest like Christ on the cross. He could not accept his new guardian's assurance, but he did not speak, his mind agitated, confused.

Mr Zeitlin went on speaking:

'You will have a peaceful, a secure life.'

Joe gazed out of the window at the unfamiliar places while the car flew by. There was a large swamp littered with rusty tins and broken boxes and seagulls flew overhead. He caught glimpses of ships' masts behind the swamp and clouds of smoke rising from factories. Soon they were out of Melbourne and driving in the country, the sun blazing down so that quivering heat waves rose before the moving car, making the whole earth tremble. How terrible to be abandoned here in this hot, strange land, Joe suddenly thought. That could happen to him. Yet he could not help liking his new guardian who seemed so ready and pleasant with him, telling him about the trees and places they were passing. Perhaps he would not be like Uncle Aaron who had deserted him. Joe lowered his head and tried to envisage the new, unknown life that had begun for him. Would that life be like Mr Zeitlin had said? Maybe Mr Zeitlin was speaking the truth.

JUNE FACTOR

Made in Czechoslovakia

THE WEATHER was exactly as he had expected. Hot. Bright sharp light. A sky very high, pale blue, with only a fleck of white in the distance. It had been snowing when he left Warsaw. Melbourne, at the other end of the world, must, therefore, be sunny. His smile expressed relief as well as vindication.

Yossel Freeman was twenty years old. He knew no one in Australia, but he had the address of a rooming house where he could stay until he had established himself. The address was carefully folded in the breast pocket of his cream jacket. He fingered it now, as he walked down Drummond Street, examining the houses. He knew the address by heart.

First I'll meet the landlady. Then I'll leave my cases in my room, and look around a bit. See the town. And maybe I can find out about a job.

It was amazing. He had walked all the way from Port Melbourne to Carlton, and he wasn't at all tired.

'Just got off the boat, have y'? Why didn't y' get a taxi? Luggin' those two 'eavy cases. . . . Don't tell me y' haven't got any money. I'll want a week's rent in advance.'

Yossel understood the words 'boat' and 'money'. He took out his wallet and offered it, open, to the woman. She extracted two notes, inspected them suspiciously, then returned the wallet.

'Glad t' see y' got the right currency. Change it on the boat, did y'? Where do y' come from, anyway?'

Yossel smiled. 'Yes. Good boat.'

'Jesus wept. . . . Come on, I'll show y' your room.' She glanced scornfully at his brown linen trousers and cream jacket. 'Don't expect no palace.'

The room was at the back of the house. There was an iron bed, a varnished wardrobe with a mirror on the front, a small chest of drawers and a chair. The linoleum was a faded green. The fringe on the blind was torn.

'You can have breakfast, but the rest of y' meals y' eat out. Understand?' She mimed eating, and Yossel nodded enthusiastically. He was hungry.

'No, not now, in the mornin'. God, why the dickens do they let you fellas in without a word of English! In the mornin'! Sleep. Up. Eat. Got it? And this here's the bathroom. And out here's the dunny. Toilet.'

Yossel's fair skin coloured. 'Thank you.' He was uncomfortable now. The sweat made his shirt stick, and his legs chafed from the heat. His lack of comprehension puzzled him. He'd taken English lessons conscientiously on the boat coming out. One hour every day of vocabulary, declensions, tenses. The Scotsman who'd instructed him had been very encouraging.

'I go out.' His awkwardness made him fumble with the key she gave him, so that he was forced to kneel to retrieve it from among the dustbins at the back door. He noticed her down-at-heel slippers. One lisle stocking had a hole in it.

Out in the street, he was ashamed of his revulsion. There was plenty of shoddiness and dirt back home, after all. I must be careful not to judge people too quickly. There are good and bad everywhere. First, something to eat, then a look around the town. A map would be useful. And tomorrow I'll start looking for a job. The men seem to wear their hair very short here—there should be room for a good barber.

Yossel walked down Lygon Street, following the tram

line into the city. He was familiar with trams, but the wide, right-angled streets seemed severe to him, sharp and angular. Once he was stopped by a decrepit-looking man, whose mournful face peered at him from under a greasy grey hat brim.

'Got a bob, mate? Be a sport, give us a bob.'

Yossel recognized the urgency beneath the whine. He had seen men like this before. He pressed a coin into the man's hand, and walked on.

The café he found was small and dark. A relief from the sun. A young girl came up with pad and pencil.

'What'll y' have?'

Yossel smiled but she didn't respond. There was no menu. What do they eat in Australia?

'Coffee, please, and eggs.' His stomach was rumbling.

'How do y' want y' eggs?'

Was she saying there were no eggs?

'Fried? Poached? With bacon?'

He nodded energetically, hopefully. Surely she'd bring him something to eat.

She slapped down a thick white cup and saucer. He tried not to notice the crack near the handle. A small pot of dark liquid, a small jug of milk. Some slices of white bread. A tiny dish with a slab of butter on it. Fork, knife, teaspoon. He swallowed the saliva in his mouth. My first Australian meal!

Two fried eggs, brown at the edges, lay between pale chips and curled pink bacon. Shreds of lettuce protected a slice of beetroot.

Yossel was circumspect. He avoided looking at the food too closely. He lifted the bacon, looked around quickly, then dropped it under the table. If he couldn't see it, nor could his mother, far away at home. On the boat, he had disposed similarly of other cuts of pig. I must find out the English names of other meats. Australia is covered with sheep. I

Made in Czechoslovakia

must remember to ask for a piece of sheep next time.

He ate everything but the beetroot.

The next day, Yossel began looking for work. He walked up and down the streets, seeking out barber shops. 'I have here all my instruments, see—for cutting, and shaving. Razors, scissors and combs, polished ready for action.' Half in Polish, half in English, he made himself understood. But nobody wanted to employ him. It was January 1938, and women were cutting their men's hair at home, a bowl over the head and snip round the edges. Barbers could not afford to employ assistants.

On the third day, Yossel went to the *Kadimah*. His wallet was growing thin, so he must swallow his pride.

'Is there any work?' he asked the elderly man from the Jewish Welfare Society.

'Work?' said the man sadly. 'Digging ditches I can offer you. Hey! Come now, don't be in such a hurry, sit down. Rest your feet. You're a young man, we'll find something for you. A tradesman, eh? From Warsaw? I'm from Cracow myself. Fifteen years in Australia. It's a good country. But it's hard times everywhere now, hard bitter times.'

Yossel drank some coffee, chatted, and looked at a Yiddish newspaper. No work, but the kindness and company drew him back day after day. On the seventh day, the Welfare Society man took him to Flinders Lane, to a wholesale jeweller. The wholesaler was a small, wizened man, with two fingers missing on his left hand. He barely nodded at Yossel.

'Another one. What are you bringing him here for? Haven't I got troubles enough of my own? Every Jew who arrives in Melbourne, you bring here to me. What do you think I am, a magician?'

The Welfare Society man smiled placatingly.

'You're a man with a big heart, Mr Norman. Something, you'll find for him to do. He's young, strong. A good boy.'

The jeweller peered at Yossel through his rimless spectacles.

'What's your trade, young man?'

'I'm a barber. First class.' Yossel's voice cracked.

'Ha! A barber, eh. Good. Just what I need. You can shave my diamonds, eh!'

If he wasn't so old, I'd hit him. Flatten him. Knock his teeth out.

Mr Norman gave Yossel a job. A salesman. A hawker. He went back to his rooming house, emptied the contents of his barber's case on to the bed, and took the case back to the warehouse. In place of razors and combs he now carried red, blue and yellow brooches. Made in Japan. They sold for a penny at Coles. To make a living, he must sell them for sixpence.

'Catch a tram,' the jeweller said. 'Catch a tram and ride till it stops. Then get off and sell.'

He hadn't cried since he was a boy of ten. That night, sitting on his lumpy mattress, Yossel tasted salt on his lips.

The first week, Yossel caught the No. 15 tram, and sold fifteen brooches. The next week he caught the No. 1, and sold only eleven. He reverted to the No. 15.

Most people said 'No, thanks' and slammed the door. Some women looked at his face, then bought. One woman paid for three brooches. He saw her drop them into a hall vase as she walked back inside. If I had the money, I'd get drunk.

'Try the country,' said the man at the *Kadimah*. 'Money's not so tight out there. Try Geelong.' He absent-mindedly pressed some coins into Yossel's hand.

Yossel travelled down to Geelong by train. There were two nuns in the carriage with him. They tried to engage him in conversation, but his English was still inadequate. As well, he felt awkward in their company. Who ever heard of a Polish Jew chatting to nuns!

Geelong didn't look like the country. There were houses and shops, streets laid out in exactly the same criss-crossed way as in Melbourne. An Aborigine stood on a street corner playing a gum leaf. Occasionally, someone tossed a coin into the hat at his feet. I'm poor too, thought Yossel grimly, and crossed over to the other side.

Be methodical. Do ten houses at a time. After every ten, have a break. Relax. Sit on a bench. Smell the flowers. Now. Begin!

It was the tenth house. The woman who opened the door was large, with strong muscular arms and a full jutting bosom. Her fair hair was plaited and twisted at the nape of her neck. She opened the main door, but left the fly-wire door shut.

'What do you want?'

'Czechoslovakian.' Yossel had discovered that Australian women thought most highly of Czechoslovakian jewellery. They sometimes asked where the brooches were made. 'Czechoslovakian. Very nice.' He began to open his case.

She stared at the tawdry jewellery through the wire door. There was a high colour in her cheeks. Then, with a sudden movement that almost knocked the case out of his hands, she pushed open the wire door.

'Welcome!' She kissed him warmly on both cheeks. 'Come in, come in, don't stand out here.'

Is she a maniac? Have I stumbled into a nest of murderers? Or worse. Are there women rapists in Geelong? Yossel clung to his case and blundered along the passage. Behind him came the woman, urging and encouraging. There must be a back door.

'Josef!' She was calling loudly into the darkness ahead. An accomplice. He would be robbed, his throat cut, his body thrown under the train.

A middle-aged man shuffled towards him. Yossel's eyes had adjusted to the dimness of the passage. The man wasn't very big. Yossel would hit him on the head with his case, then run for it.

'Who is this?'

'A countryman—from Czechoslovakia! A young man all the way from our dear homeland! Isn't it wonderful, a visitor after all these years.'

Yossel understood just enough Czech to follow what she said. He was suddenly grateful that Polish and Czech had words in common. Now what do I do? I'd better tell her that she's made a mistake.

There was no time. First they gave him brandy, then a steaming glass of Russian tea. Biscuits, chocolates. She patted his hand and pinched his cheek.

'Just a boy. Look at him. Just like my sister's boy, Klement. What part of Czecholslovakia are you from?'

It was too late.

'Prague,' said Yossel bravely.

'The most beautiful city in the world! What street?'

Yossel spilt his tea. It gave him a moment to think.

'I Australian now,' he said firmly. 'In Australia, I speak only English.'

They admired his strength of mind. They insisted that he eat a meal with them. The woman bought every one of his brooches.

'Come next week,' they said. 'Come whenever you like.'

Yossel smiled his thanks, and left the house carrying his empty case.

He never visited Geelong again.

FAY ZWICKY

Hostages

I THINK I BEGAN to hate when I was twelve. Consciously, I mean. The war was then in its fourth year, there was no chocolate and my father was still away in Borneo. I barely knew him. Till then I had learnt to admire what my mother believed to be admirable. Striving to please with ascetic rigour, I practised scales and read Greek myths. Morality hinged on hours of piano practice achieved or neglected. I knew no evil. The uncommon neutrality of my existence as a musical child in wartime was secured in a world neither good nor malevolent. My place among men was given. Did I have feelings? I was not ready to admit them for there seemed to be rules governing their revelation which I either could not or would not grasp. Nameless, passionless, and without daring I repressed deepest candour. But *tout comprendre c'est tout pardonner*; what was once self-indulgence is now permissible revelation. Why, then, should shame crimp the edge of my reflection so many years after the event?

It all started with the weekly visit to our house of a German refugee piano teacher, Sophie Lindauer-Grunberg. Poor fat sentimental Sophie, grateful recipient of my mother's pity. I was to be her first Australian pupil.

'But why me?'

'Because she needs help. She has nothing and you, thank God, have everything. She's been a very fine musician in her own country. You have to understand that this is someone who has lost everything. Yes, you can roll your eyes. *Everything*, I said. Something I hope, please God, will never happen to you. So you'll be nice to her and pay attention to what she says. I've told Mr Grover he lives too far away for me to go on taking you to lessons twice a week.'

Suddenly dull and bumbling Mr Grover in his music room smelling of tobacco and hair oil seemed like my last contact with the outside world. I was to be corralled into the tight, airless circle of maternal philanthropy.

The day of my first lesson a hot north wind was tearing at the huge gum in front of the house. Blinds and curtains were drawn against the promised heat. The house stood girded like an island under siege. My younger brother and sister had gone swimming. I watched them go, screwing up my eyes with the beginnings of a headache, envying their laughter and the way they tore sprigs off the lantana plants lining the driveway. I awaited my teacher, a recalcitrant hostage. The rooms were generous and high-ceilinged but I prowled about, tight-lipped, seeking yet more room. A deep nerve of anger throbbed in me and I prayed that she would not come. But she came. Slowly up the brick path in the heat. I watched her from the window, measuring her heavy step with my uneasy breath. Then my mother's voice greeting her in the hallway, high-pitched and over-articulated as if her listener were deaf, a standard affectation of hers with foreign visitors. 'Terrible day ... trouble finding the house ... Helen looking forward so much....' I ran to the bathroom and turned on the tap hard. I just let it run, catching sight of my face in the mirror above the basin.

Could I be called pretty? Brown hair hanging long on either side of high cheekbones, the hint of a powerful nose to come, a chin too long, cold grey eyes, wide mouth, fresh colour. No, not pretty. No heroine either. A wave of self-pity compensated me for what I saw and tears filled my eyes. Why me? Because she has to have pupils. Am I such a prize? No, but a Jew who has everything. 'Be thankful you were born in this wonderful country.' My mother's voice sounded loud in my ears. 'They're making them into lampshades over there.' I had laughed but shrank from the grotesque absurdity of the statement. Why the dramatics? All I remember is the enveloping anger directed at everything my life had been and was. I wanted to be left alone but didn't know how or where to begin. 'She has lost her whole family. Taken away and shot before her eyes. . . .' So? Now she has me.

My mother and Miss Grunberg were talking about me as I stood in the doorway. My own hands were clammy as I moved forward to the outstretched unfamiliar gesture. Hers were small, fat and very white, surprisingly small for such a tall, heavily built woman, like soft snuggling grubs. She herself looked like some swollen, pale grub smiling widely and kindly, a spinster of nearly sixty. Her little eyes gleamed through thick, round spectacles. On the skin beneath her eyes tiny bluish vessels spread their nets.

'So here is *unsere liebe Helene*!'

I raised my eyebrows insolently as the girls did at school after one of my own ill-judged observations. It was essential to the code governing the treatment of victims. But this time I had the upper hand and didn't know how to handle my advantage. The cobbles of Köln and Cracow rang hollow under my boots. The light from the pink shaded lamp fell on my new teacher. The wind blew in sharp gusts outside.

'Helen, this is Miss Grunberg.' My mother with a sharp look in my direction. 'I've been telling her about the work you've done so far with Mr Grover. Miss Grunberg would like you to have another book of studies.'

'Perhaps you will play *ein Stück* for me. Liszt perhaps?' She nodded ponderously at our Bechstein grand that suddenly took on the semblance of some monstrous piece of abstract statuary, out of all proportion to the scale of the room. 'Lord no. I've never done him.' I fell into uncharacteristic breeziness. 'I'm not really in practice. Hardly anything going at the moment and I'm pretty stale on the stuff Grover had me on for the exams.' Deliberately fast, consciously idiomatic, enjoying, yes, *enjoying* the strain of comprehension on my victim's round, perpetually smiling face. 'You can *still* play those Debussy "Arabesques",' said my mother, her neck flushed. 'I put the music on the piano,' and she gave me yet another warning look.

I opened the lid noisily and sat down with elaborate movements, shifting the metronome a few inches to the right, altering the position of the stand, bending to examine my feet fumbling between the pedals. The 'Arabesques' moved perfunctorily. I kept my face impassive, looked rigidly ahead at the music which I didn't see. Even during the section I liked in the second piece, a part where normally I would lean back a little and smile. I had begun to learn how not to please. But the process of self-annihilation involved the destruction of others. *Tout pardonner* did I say?

Miss Grunberg arranged with my mother to return the following week at the same time. 'Why are you behaving like this?' asked my mother, red and angry with me after she had left in a taxi. The young blond driver had tapped his foot noisily on the brick path as Miss Grunberg profusely repeated her gratitude to my mother for the privilege of teaching her talented daughter. Moving rapidly away from them I conversed with him, broadening my vowels like sharks' teeth on the subject of the noon temperature. I was desperate that the coveted outside world and its tranquil normality should recognize that I was in no way linked with the heavy foreign accent involved in demonstrative leave-taking on our front lawn.

'Behaving like what?'

'You know what I mean. You behaved abominably to that poor woman.'

'I played for her, didn't I?' She came closer to me with a vengeful mouth.

'You could call it that. I don't know what's got into you lately. You used to be such a good child. Now you know the answers to everything. A walking miracle! What terrible things have we done, your father and I, that you should behave like a pig to a woman like that? We've given you everything. *Everything!* And because I'm good to an unfortunate refugee who needs help wherever she can find it, you have to behave like that! I'm sorry for you, *really* sorry for you!'

'Spare your sympathy for the poor reffos!' The taxi driver's word burst savagely out of my mouth. She flew at me and slapped me across the face with her outstretched hand.

'One thing I do know,' she was trembling with rage, 'the one thing I'm sure of is that I've been too good to you. We've given you too much. You're spoilt rotten! And *one* day, my girl, one day you too may be old and unwanted and. . . .'

'A lampshade perhaps? So what.' I shook with guilt and fear at the enormity of what I'd said, terrified of the holocaust I'd shaken loose and my mother's twisted mouth.

But the revolution didn't get under way either that day or that year. The heroine lacked (should one say it?) courage. Sealed trains are more comforting than the unknown wastes of the steppes. The following week Miss Grunberg toiled up our front path and I sat down to the new course of Moscheles studies and a movement of a Mozart concerto. *Her* music. Scored heavily in red pencil, the loved and hated language dotted with emotional exclamation marks. Her life's work put out for my ruthless inspection. She moved her chair closer to my stool to alter the position of my right hand. 'Finger *rund*, *Kleine*, always *rund*. Hold always the wrist supple, *liebe Helene*.' I shrank from the alien endearment and her sour breath but curved my fingers, tight and deliberate. Her smell hung over me, a static haze in the dry air. Musty, pungent and stale, the last faint reminder of an airless Munich apartment house. Her dress, of cheap silky fabric, rustled when she moved her heavy body. Breathing laboriously she tried to explain to me what I should do with the Mozart. She couldn't get used to the heat of the new country and was beginning to find walking difficult. But I didn't practise between her visits and gave only spasmodic attention to her gentle directions. I was shutting myself off from words and from music, beginning a long course in alienation. I seldom looked my mother in the eye in those days. I quarrelled bitterly with my sister, ignored my brother.

About six months after my lessons with Miss Grunberg started I was not much further advanced. I spent a lot of time reading in my room or just looking out of the window at the garden which was now bare. Squalls lashed the gumtree and drove the leaves from the weeping elm skittering across the grass. Miss Grunberg now had several pupils amongst the children of the Jewish community and even one or two gentiles from the neighbouring school. She lived in a very poorly furnished flat in a run-down outer suburb. She still travelled to her pupils' homes. Her breathing had become very short in the last few weeks. Inattentive and isolated as I was, I had noticed that she was even paler than usual.

My mother one day told me with some rancour how well the Lapin girl was doing with the piano. 'She never had your talent but what a worker! She's going to give a recital in the Assembly Hall next month.' I merely shrugged. The boots of the conqueror were no picnic. She was welcome to them. 'And while I'm about it, I've decided to tell Miss Grunberg not to come any more. I don't feel there's much point as you seem quite determined to do as little with music as possible. I've done all *I* can. At least she's on her feet now.' On her feet! Oh God! But I replied, 'That's all right with me' in as neutral a voice as I could summon.

But that night I ground my face into the covers of my bed, no longer a place of warmth and security but a burial trench. At the mercy of my dreams appeared Sophie Lindauer-Grunberg, pale as brick dust. Her face wasting, crumbling to ash, blasted by the force of my terrible youth. And, waking in fright, I mourned for the first time my innocent victim and our shared fate.

MORRIS LURIE

My Greatest Ambition

MY GREATEST AMBITION was to be a comic-strip artist, but I grew out of it. People were always patting me on the head and saying, 'He'll grow out of it.' They didn't know what they were talking about. Had any of them ever read a comic? Studied one? *Drawn* one? 'Australia is no place for comics,' they said, and I had to lock myself up in the dining room to get some peace. My mother thought I was studying in there.

I was the only person in my class—probably in the whole school—who wanted to be a comic-strip artist. They were all dreamers. There they sat, the astronomer, the nuclear physicist, the business tycoon (on the Stock Exchange), two mathematicians, three farmers, countless chemists, a handful of doctors, all aged thirteen and all with their heads in the clouds. Dreamers! Idle speculators! A generation of hopeless romantics! It was a Friday night, I recall, when I put the finishing touches to my first full-length, inked-in, original, six-page comic-strip.

I didn't have the faintest idea what to do with it. Actually, doing anything *with* it hadn't ever entered my mind. *Doing* it was enough. Over the weekend I read it through sixty or seventy times, analysed it, studied it, stared at it, finally pronounced it, 'Not too bad,' and then put it up on the top of my wardrobe where my father kept his hats.

And that would have been the end of it, only the next day I happened to mention to Michael Lazarus, who sat next to me at school, that I had drawn a comic-strip, and he happened to mention to me that there was a magazine in Melbourne I could send it to. We were both thrown out of that class for doing too much mentioning out loud, and kept in after school, to write fifty eight-letter words and their meanings in sentences—a common disciplinary action at that time. I remember writing 'ambulate' and saying it was a special way of walking. Do I digress? Then let me say that the first thing I did when I got home was roll my comic up in brown paper, address it, and put it in my schoolbag where I wouldn't forget it in the morning. Some chance of that. Lazarus had introduced an entirely new idea into my head. Publication. I hardly slept all night.

One of the things that kept me tossing and turning was the magazine I was sending my comic to. *Boy* Magazine. I had never bought one in my life, because it had the sneaky policy of printing stories, with only one illustration at the top of the page to get you interested. *Stories?* The school library was full of them, and what a bore they were. Did I want my comic to appear in a magazine which printed stories, where it would be read by the sort of people who were always taking books out of the library and sitting under trees and wearing glasses and squinting and turning pages with licked fingers? An *awful* prospect! At two o'clock in the morning I decided no, I didn't, and at three I did, and at four it was no again, but the last thing I saw before I finally fell asleep was Lazarus's face and he was saying, 'Publication!' and that decided it. Away it went.

Now let me properly introduce my father, a great scoffer. In those pre-television days, he had absolutely nothing to do in the evening but to walk past my room and look in and say, '*Nu?* They sent you the money yet?' Fifty times a night, at least. And when the letter came from *Boy* Magazine, did he change his tune? Not one bit.

'I don't see a cheque,' he said.

'Of *course* there's no cheque,' I said. 'How can there be?

We haven't even discussed it yet. Maybe I'll decide not to sell it to them. Which I will, if their price isn't right.'

'Show me again the letter,' my father said. 'Ha, listen, listen. "We are very interested in your comic and would like you to phone Miss Gordon to make an appointment to see the editor." An appointment? That means they don't want it. If they wanted it, believe me, there'd be a cheque.'

It serves no purpose to put down the rest of this pointless conversation, which included such lines as 'How many comics have *you* sold in your life?' and, 'Who paid for the paper? The ink?' other than to say that I made the phone call to Miss Gordon from a public phone and not from home. I wasn't going to have my father listening to every word.

My voice, when I was thirteen, and standing on tiptoe and talking into a public phone, was, I must admit, unnecessarily loud, but Miss Gordon didn't say anything about it. 'And what day will be most convenient for you, Mr Lurie?' she asked. 'Oh, any day at all!' I shouted. 'Any day will suit me fine!' 'A week from Thursday then?' she asked. 'Perfect!' I yelled, trying to get a piece of paper and a pencil out of my trouser pocket to write it down, and at the same time listening like mad in case Miss Gordon said something else. And she did. 'Ten o'clock?' 'I'll be there!' I shouted, and hung up with a crash.

It hadn't occurred to me to mention to Miss Gordon that I was thirteen and at school and would have to take a day off to come and see the editor. I didn't think these things were relevant to our business. But my mother did. A day missed from school could never be caught up, that was her attitude. My father's attitude you know. A cheque or not a cheque. Was I rich or was I a fool? (No, that's wrong. Was I a poor fool or a rich fool? Yes, that's better.) But my problem was something else. What to wear?

My school suit was out of the question because I wore it

every day and I was sick of it and it just wasn't right for a business appointment. Anyway, it had ink stains round the pocket where my fountain pen leaked (a real fountain, ha ha), and the seat of the trousers shone like a piece of tin. And my Good Suit was a year old and too short in the leg. I tried it on in front of the mirror, just to make sure, and I was right. It was ludicrous. My father offered to lend me one of his suits. He hadn't bought a new suit since 1934. There was enough material in the lapels alone to make three suits and have enough left over for a couple of caps. Not only that, but my father was shorter than me and twice the weight. So I thanked him and said that I had decided to wear my Good Suit after all. I would wear dark socks and the shortness of trousers would hardly be noticed. Also, I would wear my eye-dazzling pure silk corn yellow tie, which, with the proper Windsor knot, would so ruthlessly rivet attention that no one would even look to see if I was wearing shoes.

'A prince,' my father said.

Now, as the day of my appointment drew nearer and nearer, a great question had to be answered, a momentous decision made. For my father had been right. If all they wanted to do was to buy my comic, they would have sent a cheque. So there was something else. A full-time career as a comic-strip artist on the permanent staff of *Boy* Magazine! It had to be that. But that would mean giving up school and was I prepared to do that?

'Yes,' I said with great calmness and great authority to my face in the bathroom mirror. 'Yes.'

There were three days to go.

Then there occurred one of those things that must happen every day in the world of big business, but when you're thirteen it knocks you for a loop. *Boy* Magazine sent me a telegram. It was the first telegram I had ever received in my life, and about the third that had ever come to our house. My mother opened it straight away. She told everyone in our street about it. She phoned uncles, aunts, sisters, brothers, and finally, when I came home from school, she told me.

I was furious. I shouted, 'I told you never under *any* circumstances to open my mail!'

'But a telegram,' my mother said.

'A telegram is mail,' I said. 'And mail is a personal, private thing. Where is it?'

My mother had folded it four times and put it in her purse and her purse in her bag and her bag in her wardrobe which she had locked. She stood by my side and watched me while I read it.

'*Nu?*' she said.

'It's nothing,' I said.

And it wasn't. Miss Gordon had suddenly discovered that the editor was going to be out of town on my appointment day, and would I kindly phone and make another appointment?

I did, standing on tiptoe and shouting as before.

The offices of *Boy* Magazine were practically in the country, twelve train stations out of town. Trains, when I was thirteen, terrified me, and still do. Wearing my Good Suit and my corn yellow tie and my father's best black socks and a great scoop of oil in my hair, I kept jumping up from my seat and looking out of the window to see if we were getting near a station and then sitting down again and trying to relax. Twelve stations, eleven stations, ten. Nine to go, eight, seven. Or was it six? What was the name of the last one? What if I went too far? What was the time? By the time I arrived at the right station, I was in a fine state of nerves.

The offices of *Boy* Magazine were easy to find. They were part of an enormous building that looked like a factory, and were not at all imposing or impressive, as I had imagined them to be. No neon, no massive areas of plate glass, no exotic plants growing in white gravel. (I had a picture of myself walking to work every morning through a garden of exotic plants growing in white gravel, cacti, ferns, pushing open a massive glass door under a neon sign and smiling at a receptionist with a pipe in my mouth.) I pushed open an ordinary door and stepped into an ordinary foyer and told an ordinary lady sitting at an ordinary desk who I was.

'And?' she said.

'I have an appointment to see the editor of *Boy* Magazine,' I said.

'Oh,' she said.

'At ten o'clock,' I said. 'I think I'm early.' It was half past nine.

'Just one minute,' she said, and picked up a telephone. While she was talking I looked around the foyer, in which there was nothing to look at, but I don't like eavesdropping on people talking on the phone.

Then she put down the phone and said to me, 'Won't be long. Would you like to take a seat?'

For some reason that caught me unawares and I flashed her a blinding smile and kept standing there, wondering what was going to happen next, and then I realized what she had said and I smiled again and turned around and bumped into a chair and sat down and crossed my legs and looked around and then remembered the shortness of my trousers and quickly uncrossed my legs and sat perfectly straight and still, except for looking at my watch ten times in the next thirty seconds.

I don't know how long I sat there. It was either five minutes or an hour, it's hard to say. The lady at the desk didn't seem to have anything to do, and I didn't like looking at her, but from time to time our eyes met, and I would smile—or was that smile stretched across my face from the second I came in? I used to do things like that when I was thirteen.

Finally a door opened and another lady appeared. She seemed, for some reason, quite surprised when she saw me sitting there, as though I had three eyes or was wearing a red suit, but I must say this for her, she had poise, she pulled herself together very quickly, hardly dropped a stitch, as it were, and holding open the door through which she had come, she said, 'Won't you come this way?' and I did.

I was shown into an office that was filled with men in grey suits. Actually, there were only three of them, but they all stood up when I came in, and the effect was overpowering. I think I might even have taken a half-step back. But my blinding smile stayed firm.

The only name I remember is Randell and maybe I have that wrong. There was a lot of handshaking and smiling and saying of names. And when all that was done, no one seemed to know what to do. We just stood there, all uncomfortably smiling.

Finally, the man whose name might have been Randell said, 'Oh, please, please, sit down,' and everyone did.

'Well,' Mr Randell said. 'You're a young man to be drawing comics, I must say.'

'I've been interested in comics all my life,' I said.

'Well, we like your comic very much,' he said. 'And we'd like to make you an offer for it. Ah, fifteen pounds?'

'I accept,' I said.

I don't think Mr Randell was used to receiving quick decisions, for he then said something that seemed to me enormously ridiculous. 'That's, ah, two pounds ten a page,' he said, and looked at me with his eyes wide open and one eyebrow higher than the other.

'Yes, that's right,' I said. 'Six two-and-a-halfs are fifteen. Exactly.'

That made his eyes open even wider, and suddenly he shut them altogether and looked down at the floor. One of the other men coughed. No one seemed to know what to do. I leaned back in my chair and crossed my legs and just generally smiled at everyone. I knew what was coming. A job. And I knew what I was going to say then, too.

And then Mr Randell collected himself, as though he had just thought of something very important (what an actor, I thought) and he said, 'Oh, there is one other thing, though. Jim, do we have Mr Lurie's comic here?'

'Right here,' said Jim, and whipped it out from under a pile of things on a desk.

'Some of the, ah, spelling,' Mr Randell said.

'Oh?' I said.

'Well, yes, there are, ah, certain things,' he said, turning over the pages of my comic, 'not, ah, *big* mistakes, but, here, see? You've spelt it as "jungel" which is not, ah, common usage.'

'You're absolutely right,' I said, flashing out my fountain pen all ready to make the correction.

'Oh, no no no,' Mr Randell said. 'Don't you worry about it. We'll, ah, make the corrections. If you approve, that is.'

'Of course,' I said.

'We'll, ah, post you our cheque for, ah, fifteen pounds,' he said. 'In the mail,' he added, rather lamely, it seemed to me.

'Oh, there's no great hurry about that,' I said. 'Any old time at all will do.'

'Yes,' he said.

Then we fell into another of these silences with which this appointment seemed to be plagued. Mr Randell scratched his neck. A truck just outside the window started with a roar and then began to whine and grind. It's reversing, I thought. My face felt stiff from smiling, but somehow I couldn't let it go.

Then the man whose name was Jim said, 'This is your first comic-strip, Mr Lurie?'

'Yes,' I said. My reply snapped across the room like a bullet. I was a little bit embarrassed at its suddenness, but, after all, wasn't this what I had come to talk about?

'It's very professional,' he said. 'Would you like to see one of our comic-strips?'

'Certainly,' I said.

He reached down behind the desk and brought out one page of a comic they were running at the moment (I had seen it in the shop when I'd gone to check up on *Boy* Magazine's address), *The Adventures of Ned Kelly*.

Now, Ned Kelly is all right, but what I like about comics is that they create a world of their own, like, say, *Dick Tracy*, a totally fictitious environment, which any clear-thinking person knows doesn't really exist, and Ned Kelly, well, that was real, it really happened. It wasn't a true comic-strip. It was just history in pictures.

But naturally I didn't say any of this to Jim. All I did was lean forward and pretend to study the linework and the inking in and the lettering, which were just so-so, and when I thought I'd done that long enough, I leaned back in my chair and said, 'It's very good.'

'Jim,' said Mr Randell, who hadn't spoken a word during all this, 'maybe you'd like to take Mr Lurie around and show him the presses. We print *Boy* Magazine right here,' he said. 'Would you like to see how a magazine is produced?'

'Yes,' I said, but the word sounded flat and awful to me. I hated, at thirteen, being shown around things. I still do. How A Great Newspaper Is Produced. How Bottles Are Made. Why Cheese Has Holes And How We Put Them In.

And the rest of it, the job, the core of the matter? But everyone was standing up and Mr Randell's hand was stretched out to shake mine and Jim was saying, 'Follow me,' and it was all over.

My Greatest Ambition

Now I'm not going to take you through a tour of this factory, the way I was, eating an ice-cream which Jim had sent a boy out to buy for me. It lasted for hours. I climbed up where Jim told me to climb up. I looked where he pointed. I nodded when he explained some involved and highly secret process to me. 'We use glue, not staples,' he explained to me. 'Why? Well, it's an economic consideration. Look here,' and I looked there, and licked my ice-cream and wondered how much more there was of it and was it worth going to school in the afternoon or should I take the whole day off?

But like all things it came to an end. We were at a side door, not the one I had come in through. 'Well, nice to meet you,' Jim said, and shook my hand. 'Find your way back to the station OK? You came by train? It's easy, just follow your nose,' and I rode home on the train not caring a damn about how many stations I was going through, not looking out of the window, not even aware of the shortness of the trousers of my ridiculous Good Suit.

Yes, my comic-strip appeared and my friends read it and I was a hero for a day at school. My father held the cheque up to the light and said we'd know in a few days if it was any good. My mother didn't say much to me but I heard her on the phone explaining to all her friends what a clever son she had. Clever? That's one word I've never had any time for.

I didn't tell a soul, not even Michael Lazarus, about that awful tour of the factory. I played it very coolly. And a week after my comic-strip came out in print, I sat down and drew another comic story and wrapped it up and sent it to them, and this time, I determined, I would do all my business over the phone. With that nice Miss Gordon.

Weeks passed, nearly a whole month. No reply. And then, with a sickening crash, the postman dumped my new comic into our letterbox and flew on his merry way down the street, blowing his whistle and riding his bicycle over everyone's lawns.

There was a letter enclosed with my comic. It said that, unfortunately, *Boy* Magazine was discontinuing publication, and although they enjoyed my comic 'enormously', they regretted that they had no option but to return it.

My father had a field day over the whole business but no, no, what's the point of going over all that? Anyhow, I had decided (I told myself) that I didn't want to be a comic-strip artist after all. There was no future in it. It was risky and unsure. It was here today and gone tomorrow. The thing to be was a serious painter, and I set about it at once, spreading new boxes of water colours and tubes of paint all over the dining room table and using every saucer in the house to mix paint. But somehow, right from the start, I knew it was no good. The only thing that was ever real to me I had 'grown out of'. I had become, like everyone else, a dreamer.

LEN FOX

Bailey's Pine

THE TOP BRANCHES of the towering Norfolk pine shuddered as though they knew they had to fall. There were sounds of axe-blows and shouts, and then there was silence for a while, as though the men working below had paused to give the tall tree a few more hours of life.

Across the street, on the front verandah of the oldish square brick home with the carefully tended garden and the high pittosporum hedge, Phil Barnett had been sitting for a long time, listening to the noise and watching the convulsions that every now and then shook the upper limbs of Bailey's pine.

A small wiry man in his seventieth year, he had been sitting as though in a daze, thoughts passing through his mind without expressing themselves in words, thoughts that seemed more like feelings or dreams. At times he had, without fully realizing it, been identifying himself with the tree, feeling the axe-blows and responding to the shudderings of the branches. At times his sensations had gone back in a vague dreamlike way to his early life, to the Jewish home in the eastern suburbs, to the warmth of his family, the tenderness of his mother, the noisy affection of his brothers and sister. They were all dead now, and it seemed far away, and he seemed alone.

Suddenly he realized that his wife Helen was talking to him. She had opened the door and was asking should she pour the tea as usual; it was three minutes to eleven, the set time for the morning cup of tea. The time was never varied, but Helen always came to ask him, always at three minutes to the hour.

Yes, he replied, as he always had; he would come inside. And then he found himself saying: 'Could you bring it outside? I think I'll stay here.'

'Very good,' she answered, as though there was nothing unusual in what he had said. But she stood there a fraction longer than usual, thinking to herself that simple as his request was, it was like a revolution, like the world turning upside down. The felling of the tree must mean a lot to him. She wondered what he was thinking as he watched its death. But she did not even consider asking him; she had learnt in their thirty years of married life that he was not a man who spoke about his thoughts, that he was not a man who liked to be questioned.

Often she had wondered what sort of a man he was, and how she had ever come to marry this man so much older, so different, who at times seemed so hard—or was he merely inarticulate, with a tenderness beneath and a longing to communicate but somehow ... ? Whatever it was, she had learned to accept it, and to respect his uprightness, his belief in doing the right thing, his loyalty to family and friends, his devotion to the children, his moments of warmth. She was fifty-five now, and had learned to accept life. Not passively, because mingled in her character was an Irish rebelliousness; but stronger than this was a deep love of everything around her, from poems and plays and books and paintings to birds and beasts and flowers and people—people above all, men and women and children and their sayings and doings and strangenesses.

She made the tea, and as she took the tray out to the verandah, looked across to Bailey's pine, remembering how ever since they had first come to this south-eastern suburb of Melbourne the tree had towered over Bailey's paddock with its wild shrubs and rambling sheds, its cows and hens, its old house hidden among trees—the whole place an anachronism, a relic of older times that had lingered on in the midst of spreading suburbia. The pine, neighbours said, had been a tall tree at the turn of the century, forty years ago.

Her husband must feel deeply about it. She herself would miss the tree; it had been part of her life for thirty years. But she had learnt that change was a part of life. Her whole life had been change. The careless childhood with the Irish mother and the North of England rationalist father, the sudden move to the din and dull routine of the workshop, the lightning courtship with the man who was so much older, the excitement of the new home merging into the ordered routine of family life, the joy of her first child. And then—she could hardly bear to think of it even now—the crushing blow when the child had suddenly and inexplicably died. It had seemed like the end of the world, the end of everything—and yet the numbness and the agony had at last faded.

Life had come flooding in again, bringing her children and friends and happiness, sweeping her along till she had learned to hold her head high again, to become one with the life around her, meeting its changes and challenges as friends came and went and children grew up, as she herself grew older.

Life was change. And if Bailey's pine had to fall, its place would be taken by homes and flats and families and children. But to Phil it would be different. Under his hardness there was a sensitivity. She would like to know what he was thinking. They had finished their tea. She picked up the tray and went inside, leaving him in the winter cold which still persisted though the sun was shining. Leaving him silent on the verandah.

Across the street there was noise again, and although he could not see because of the hedge, he knew the men must be preparing another attack. Soon Bailey's pine would fall.

His thoughts went back—clearer and more detailed now—to when he had first come out here to buy the block of land and build his home. Bailey's pine had seemed like an elderly patriarch even then, towering over a region that had a strong attraction for him, with its many paddocks among the houses, its neat little streets that spoke of order and civilization but also its wide roads that meandered out to the south-east to open paddocks, to farms and market gardens, to vistas of the far blue Dandenongs and further south the curving beaches of Port Phillip Bay. His brothers had lived all their lives in inner suburbs, and had hired gardeners to care for their gardens, but he had been different. He had a feeling for the land, for the soil; he had a love of pottering around in the garden; and also he had a feeling for a region, for knowing its geography, its streets and roads. Many a weekend had seen him cycling to the east or the south-east, exploring, learning the main roads and the short-cuts, stopping at times to gaze on the paddocks ablaze with yellow cape-weed flowers—and finding again and again that if he looked back towards where he had come from, he could see on the skyline, distinguishable by its tall shape and the neighbouring church spire, Bailey's pine.

In later years, after his eldest son Lionel had joined an accountancy firm and settled out at Clayton, he had cycled out there often, and it had become a regular routine for him to stop on the brow of the little hill before Clayton, and to gaze back at the pine on the horizon. It had become a sign and a symbol that the world was an ordered world, and that he had a place in it.

Now, as the noises opposite grew louder, his wife came and sat beside him. The top branches of the pine again began to shudder, and it almost seemed to him as though they were groaning in pain. Then there was silence, and the

Bailey's Pine

branches were still. It is too strong, a voice inside him seemed to say. They will never fell it. Then there was a strange noise; the tree shook violently, then fell, slowly at first, then with a tremendous clamour and crash that seemed to shake the whole earth and to leave him stunned and speechless.

Helen stood up. The felling had affected her more than she had expected. She wanted to talk, or to weep, or to do something. But she didn't know what to do, what to say. She turned and went inside.

Phil continued to sit there, feeling dazed, his thoughts vague and dreamlike as they had been earlier, wandering back to his childhood days.

The warmth of his mother's presence again, the nearness of his elder brothers, his love for the only sister, for Naomi, Naomi the beautiful, the wilful, the musical, the playful. The Jewishness that seemed a warmth around them, a shelter that protected them even though their father had died, a cloak and protection and yet at the same time a burden that imposed endless tasks on their mother and on themselves.

A family closeness that had gradually changed—he had never understood exactly how and why, for his elder brothers had done the thinking and struggling and he had followed—into a sense of broadening exploration of the outside world and a realization that they too were part of the outside world, a world where the exciting thing was to be a man among other men, where Jewishness or non-Jewishness, and other divisions of religion or race or culture, faded into the past as people advanced into a new human world.

He had accepted it all without question. There had been no need to make a violent break from the orthodox positions; the orthodoxies had simply become unimportant and faded away. It had been made easier not only by the stand of his brothers, but also by Naomi returning from her visit to the musical centres of Europe to talk of Enlightenment and Internationalism. To his down-to-earth mind it had seemed somewhat unreal and visionary, yet it had helped him feel the world was a good place that would reward any man who respected his fellow men and who did right.

Vaguely he saw that period now as happy—a period whose promise had blossomed in his marriage, his home, his garden, his children. And yet together with this was the knowledge of the many ways in which his happiness had turned sour, causing the deep anger that was in him, silent, seldom expressed, yet always there.

Sitting there on the verandah he felt this anger, and the incidents that had given birth to it, only in a broad, general way. He did not want to go over the details. If he had, he would have thought of the dullness of his life in the big office, the lack of promotion that had fed the seeds of self-doubt within, the searing knowledge that this was because the man who should have promoted him was a relative, a man so upright that he would not do so for fear of charges of nepotism. The silliness of it did not make the hurt less, and perhaps it hurt all the more because of the feeling within him, never put into words, that if he had been in his relative's place he might have done the same thing.

The war. It had not worried him much at first. He liked to read and to discuss, but he was not a deep thinker; to him the war was simply a matter of militarist nations existing and every now and then causing trouble. When one of his brothers used the phrase 'sickness of Western civilization', he put it out of his mind. It had been a terrible shock to him that day to go to Naomi's and hear her criticize the war and those who supported it in a way that seemed to him unpatriotic and unforgivable. He stormed out of the house in anger, and had never spoken to her in a friendly way again. When, some years later, the message had come that she was ill, he felt a maelstrom of emotion in which tenderness finally conquered, but he had delayed going to see her. The next day they told him she had died.

There had been other family quarrels. And even his own children, growing up, rebelling, defying him. Even Lionel at times. All of them except the youngest, Paul, who had done everything his father could have expected of him. Till suddenly he had come home one afternoon to say—as calmly as if he had been telling them he had bought a new tennis racquet—that he had joined the Communist Party and had given up his job. At first they had hardly spoken to each other, and Paul had gone to live elsewhere. Later he came back, and the two were able to get along together, but it hadn't been the same. Now he was living away from home again. And the way the war was going. . . .

The second world war. The first had been bad enough. But this time, with the bad news over the last few days. Belgium, Holland, France. . . . Could it be? Could everything go? He looked across to where Bailey's pine had stood for so many years. There was only empty sky there now.

For the rest of the day he was silent. He went for a long walk, and felt a little calmer. At night he took a stiff whisky before going to bed, where he lay restlessly for a long time before dozing off to a troubled sleep. Helen lay beside him, listening to his heavy breathing, till she too sank into unconsciousness.

She woke with a start to hear the doorbell ringing violently, ringing in the dead of the night. She was in a daze; before going to bed she had been reading of the relentless German advance in Western Europe, and the crazy idea was in her head that Hitler's armies had advanced round the world and right up the street to her front door. Then Phil awoke with a half-stifled groan and a noisy protest, and she was in her dressing-gown and opening the door.

The two men on the doorstep loomed so large and ominous that for a second she thought they might be criminals come to burgle the house; then one of them was saying politely that they had a warrant. 'Paul Barnett, he is your son?' No, she felt, Paul couldn't be in that much trouble, they couldn't have come to arrest him she muttered. 'You know he doesn't live here any longer?' One of the men had begun to step into the hall, but as she asked the question he stopped, and the two men looked at each other open-mouthed. Suddenly, instead of feeling small and helpless in the face of something powerful and unknown, she felt in command of the situation.

'Come in,' she found herself saying. 'I'll show you the room where Paul slept.' She led them down the hall and opened the door. 'His books are still there.' They went eagerly to the bookcase, and peered at the titles. In the top shelves were still Paul's boyhood books. *Coral Island*, *The Gorilla Hunters*, *Life of Nelson*, his books on cricket and wrestling. Lower down were Meredith and Shelley, Barrie and Shaw, Zola, Steinbeck, Lawrence, *We of the Never Never*, Shaw Neilson.

He had taken most of his political books with him, but there were still some Left Book Club editions there. One of the men took a handful of these from the shelves, and inspected them uneasily.

'What's gone wrong?' It was Phil coming down the hall, clutching his dressing-gown round him and looking pale and old. The men introduced themselves, speaking softly and politely, almost apologetically. 'Come and sit down, Phil,' she said. 'It won't take long. They're just looking at a few books. I'll put the kettle on and make a cup of tea.' She led him to the dining room, to his armchair.

Sitting there he felt a wave of burning anger against Paul. Why, why, why? Everything had been going so well; the future was so bright for him. And then—. Why? Gradually his anger subsided, and he sat there without thinking, without feeling.

'We're sorry, Mr Barnett.' It was one of the men who had come into the room, with the other man and Helen behind him. 'But there has been some talk of money coming into the country from Russia.'

Money from Russia? What could that have to do with him or his family? He looked up amazed, unable to find words. 'Look,' Helen was saying, 'perhaps you'd like to see something in our spare room.' She led them to the spare room at the back of the house, opening the door to take the men inside and then shutting it again. Hanging on a hook behind the door was an old pair of grey trousers. 'You see those patches on the seat of these trousers?' Helen showed them the carefully sewn patches, and turned. 'You see the patches, and the patches on top of the patches?' They stared. What was she getting at? 'Well, those are Paul's old trousers,' she said. 'Does that look like Russian gold?'

Back in the dining room, the men looked uncomfortable and sheepish, and Phil felt his anger growing again. No longer against Paul, but against these blundering men, or rather against something that they represented, something he could not define. . . . And to his own surprise, he found that he was speaking, that he was confronting these men—he who had always been inarticulate in his anger, so that he had been all his life a man of cold silence. Now he found himself speaking.

'My son has never hurt anyone. All his life he has done what he considered right. He may have been mistaken in what he thought was right; his ideas may have seemed wrong to you; they may have seemed wrong to me. But has he ever deserved this; has he ever deserved that men come in the middle of the night, that they . . . ? My son is no criminal.'

They stood there looking at him silently, and one of them said, 'We are only doing our job, Mr Barnett.'

After they had gone, he felt so weak that he doubted

whether he would be able to walk as far as the bedroom. 'I'm glad you spoke up, Phil,' his wife said. They stood looking at each other, neither knowing what to say. At last she spoke.

'Paul will be all right,' she said.

'Yes, yes,' he replied. 'He'll be all right.'

But when finally he found himself in bed again, he knew that you couldn't say of anyone in this world that he would be all right. He knew that for the first time that day he had found the ability to speak his anger; he knew too, though he could hardly have expressed it in words, that for the first time he had admitted fully to himself something that for most of his life he had been trying to hide. He had had to admit at last that life was not a neat and orderly thing, with punishments for the wicked and rewards for the good, but that it held unknown forces and powers that came storming suddenly into men's lives, uprooting, smashing, destroying, killing, taking away the things men hold most dear.

And all a man could do was to sometimes make a stand for what seemed right, to speak out even if one's voice were drowned in the storm.

He drifted slowly into a troubled sleep, in which he was trying to approach his sister Naomi, who sometimes changed into his wife Helen, or back again to Naomi. But whether it was Helen or Naomi, he could not reach her, could not find the words to say to her. The words that he tried to say were plucked from his mouth and torn away by the raging gale, and flung up high to where the topmost branches of Bailey's pine were tossing madly in the storm, shuddering and crying as though they knew they had to die.

HARRY MARKS

The Fat Girl

O, THAT THIS too too solid flesh would melt, Evie sighed despairingly. Through her dress she grabbed a fistful of flab where it overflowed her girdle, and held it tight till she squirmed.

Hamlet bored her silly. She had only to think of him to grow drowsy. Better than the sleeping pills her mother took. She'd often been tempted to say, take Hamlet to bed with you, Mum . . . you'll go out like a light.

What could Ophelia have possibly seen in him? There was some point in drowning yourself for love of a Bob Dylan or a Peter Fonda, but Hamlet, that grotty individual, never! Ophelia was well shot of him. Pity school kids weren't.

She would have forgotten Hamlet as completely as yesterday's lunch if it hadn't been for that line, that damn, bloody line. Even now, a year and a half later, she recalled with bitterness the day she had flounced from the classroom vowing never to return. Heard again the shrieks of derision that woke her. Saw with frightening vividness forty-two pairs of smirking eyes . . . no, forty-three, Miss Milligan's too . . . with their burning mockery.

'Well, I'm waiting.'

Waiting? Waiting, Miss Milligan? Waiting for what?

'Evie, you haven't heard a word. Stand up and tell the class what I've just read.'

Sensing disaster, 'I—I don't know.'

'Then repeat it after me: "O, that this too too solid flesh would melt."'

And in the uproar that followed she tearfully spoke the

line that Shakespeare, in a flash of visionary perception, had written about her, Evie Atkins, standing there, fourteen and a half stone of quivering misery. She hated them all, even those she thought were her friends, wishing the floor might open and devour her, but forcing her way between the desks, her flanks pushing against her tormentors, who reeled back in surprise. With Miss Milligan breathlessly catching her in the passage, saying 'Come back, I'm sorry, please forgive me, I don't know what came over me!' and tearing herself from the woman's grasp crying 'No, no, no, you're right, I'm a big fat pig and I wish I was dead.'

But she couldn't go back. She couldn't face them again. Not after that.

Evie flopped on to the seat at the edge of the high-rise building's play area, delving into the rolled newspaper to fuel the furnace of her appetite with a handful of hot chips. Some children ran past, full of the excitement of the moment, darting this way and that, tigging around her as though she wasn't there. Pulling her feet in to avoid tripping the youngsters, she saw them not unkindly as gazelles sporting around a grazing hippopotamus.

She opened her bag and took out a crumpled, folded sheet of paper. She had read it a dozen times but she went through it again.

> Dear Madam, We acknowledge receipt of your ten dollars and detailed description of yourself, your life, hopes and mind's-eye picture of your future partner. These have now been fed to the computer which, after digesting the facts, has advised us to contact you once more for additional information. According to the computer's calculations, the details as supplied by you are insufficient for it to assess your physical characteristics against the most suitable of our more than forty thousand carefully carded, prospective suitors.

> On re-checking the form you filled in for us, we find, Miss Atkins, that you have omitted to supply the following:
> (a) bust measurement
> (b) waist measurement
> (c) hip measurement.
> We regret the delay this must necessarily involve but, as you will readily understand, such dimensions are essential if the computer is to accurately locate your ideal mate. Kindly reply by return mail.

A week had passed. Of course she hadn't filled in those details. How could she? She had hoped the computer might overlook them. Hell, that was the last thing she wanted, someone as fat as herself. But who would have her, faced with the facts? All this love and passion going begging, she thought disgustedly, shoving the letter away and shaking the chips to loosen the few which had stuck together now that they were almost gone.

You up there. Yes, you! Don't think I can't see you, because I can. That goes for you too, whoever you are on the eighth. As for you, Mrs Smith, I know you're there. You're always there. Come on out from behind those curtains.

Go on. All of you. Take a good look. It's free. You'd be better off, the lot of you, seeing to your husbands' tea before they come home from the pub and start walloping you.

The shadow of the building had been creeping unnoticed towards her. Suddenly it pounced, and she was cold. So was the last small chip she located in the salt which she'd tipped on to the palm of her hand. Then she screwed up the paper, tossed it in the bin with the 'Don't rubbish Australia' sign and started towards the great stone heap that rose like a phallic symbol from the body of the earth.

Whichever way you looked at it, Evie and her mother had come up in the world. The twenty-seventh floor was as close to heaven, Evie reckoned, as either of them was likely to get.

Ravenous dogs had descended on the district. Hunting in packs. On the day. At the hour. As was foretold. Their steel jaws tearing mercilessly at the houses in Morey Street, empty and somehow, shed of their purpose, pathetically defenceless. Morey Street, where Evie had lived almost as long as she could remember. Then Barnes Street with its little shops where you paid a few cents more rather than trudge all the way to the supermarket. Past Fingleton Lane and the old Chinese joss house that was historical some said and should certainly be spared. Through as far as Potter Street's dusty strip of park and the creaking swings which were silent only when the last protesting child was sent to bed. The bulldozers of the Housing Commission, savaging the tiny weatherboard houses, row upon shoulder-tight row of them, shabby and cared for alike, owned, rented, loved, hated. Destroying the past in the glorious name of Progress.

Hopes lay in the rubble. And memories. The whole of the human comedy had been played out in these houses by generations of characters, the roles handed down from parents to progeny with little, if any, re-writing. But those who were there at the final curtain stepped out of their predetermined parts to do what none had done before. To write to the newspapers. Attend meetings. Petition the local M.P. And when all failed, called in the reporters who for days whipped up sympathy with stories and pictures of pensioners, widows and deserted wives, till a stock market swindle, a murder and a politician charged with speeding took precedence.

Some, when the dreaded time came, clung to the fence-posts crying what's to become of us, until forced with their belongings on to the footpath. All agreed it would never be the same again. The Housing Commission had allotted them places in the high-rise flats they were building strategically across the face of the city. Sure, they've found us a place, someone said. And it seemed at least to sum up the thoughts of the old among them. They're shoving us into holes in the wall, and you'll see, that's where most of us will finish up, permanently, before long.

Not that the house had been anything to write home about. It needed a man. To hold it together with a few nails. You couldn't keep it clean, although they never gave up trying. They swept the front porch the morning they left, a last defiant gesture towards the powers-that-be who make the decisions that change people's lives, whose beastly machines, only hours later, would be ripping it down, achieving in minutes what time and tempest had threatened on many an occasion.

Shoes left by the bed had grown mould overnight. And the bathroom wall was plastered with pin-ups of film stars, reinforced over the years, Clark Gable being laid over Hedy Lamarr, with Elvis Presley on top of them again, until the pictures themselves formed a wall of protection against the winds that tried to take a short cut through the house.

Evie, who quietly wondered what all the fuss had been about, preferred the flat. Her mother had hated it from the first day. It wasn't the house she missed, but her friends. There she knew everyone, and people accepted you for what you were, without having to put on a false face. Not like here, where one had the feeling of being watched. At 16 Morey Street it was always open house.

Out of the past Evie remembered waking, thinking it must be about midnight and she'd just dozed off. Then the milkie's horse came clopping along the street, bottles dancing in the crates, and still there'd be laughing, joking and sometimes singing.

That was when her mother worked regular hours, at the chocolate factory, day shift because she wanted to be home when Evie got in from school.

Once, Evie recalled, a man stumbled into her room with beer and glasses, mumbling 'Come on, love, wakie wakie, you're missin' all the fun; c'mon, sit up and have a drink with Uncle Fred.' She didn't know what made her do it. Perhaps finding him standing over her, a hulking shape against the light. Or coming too quickly out of a dream. But she screamed so loudly she frightened herself, and started screaming again.

'Sssssh, ssssh' he muttered in confusion, reaching out to quieten her as Evie's mother ran in, switched the light on, stopped astonished and with a shrill 'You bastard!' threw herself at him, striking again and again until it seemed all strength must go from her. 'Cradle snatcher' she cried. 'Bloody cradle snatcher.'

Beer spattered the floral bedspread, and blood too, when he thudded across the bed, a tree falling in the forest, the glasses crunching in his hands. His face was smeared red from the broken glass, where he'd tried to shield himself, blubbering 'I didn't mean nothing by it, Belle. As God's me judge.'

She had watched her mother bathe his face and bandage his hands. He put his arms round her, but she said 'No, not in front of you-know-who.' Then someone said 'Let's have another drink all round to show there's no hard feelings.' They poured her a shandy, which she forced down, not wishing to appear unsociable and feeling in some way responsible for what had happened.

They'd had their fights and disagreements, and Evie remembered when they didn't speak for a fortnight. But she was her mother. Evie needed her, wanted her. Even on the unwritten, unspoken conditions her mother laid down. For Evie had known for longer than she cared to admit that her mother needed her as much as she needed a hole in the head.

There I go, Evie inwardly chided. At it again. Being hard on her, and I shouldn't. God knows what she's been through. That bloody, bloody man. I'd gladly wring his neck. I don't care what she did. Or whether she did anything at all. He had no right to go off and leave her. Never knowing where he was or who he was shacked up with.

He was a good looking man, this much she knew. That was his trouble, her mother added. He knew it. Evie would have liked to see a picture of him. There wasn't one. They were all torn up. Still, you can't wipe a man from your mind by destroying all trace of him, and Evie, who conceded it was a profitless pastime, felt she couldn't be blamed for thinking of him occasionally, of hating and loving him alternately. Especially when she was younger. Playing at wondering what he was doing and thinking and whether he was feeling sorry for what he'd done. Wondering if he was lonely and missing them, but too proud to say, or admit he'd made a mistake.

Back in Morey Street, windows weren't for light or fresh air. They were for leaning out of. Talking from. But in the flat Evie loved to sit with the window up and the rain on her face, watching the great flashes illumine the sky. Like having a box seat to hear God conduct a symphony. And all the time her mother yelling, 'Come away, come away do you hear?'

The view from her window was something, she knew, most people would pay to see. Although she hadn't been in an aeroplane she imagined it must be like this. She could see clear across the bay, even further when the mists lifted, to the oil refinery and beyond. And at night the car lights flickering for miles.

Life at the top, however, had its drawbacks. The water, particularly on Friday nights, that trailed to a trickle by the time it reached their bath tub. The lights dimming when the electricity was overloaded. The cracks that opened the walls.

The one in the lavatory they'd stuffed with toilet paper, a commodity which seemed unsuited for the lounge. Birds smashing themselves against the building. The smells that lived and grew old in the building's orifices. Oh well, Evie decided, it's a Housing Commission place after all. Beggars can't be choosers. But she wished ... how she wished there was a better way of getting to the twenty-seventh without having to take the lift.

She had said as much to one of the boys in despatch at the factory, a surfie type with blond bleached hair with whom she had slept in her dreams. 'Whatcha worrying about?' he'd laughed, 'You could always use a winch.' She'd laughed, too. Uneasily, to cover her confusion. And he had pinched her bottom, quite adventuresomely hard, which made her wince with pain and excitement. So she'd given a playful slap of reproof to show him she wasn't that sort of girl (wishing she was, wishing he would give her the chance to be) and forgot what he had said. Until later, rubbing the spot, she was disgusted with herself for having provided the opportunity for him to ridicule her. If there was one thing she was sick to death of, it was people telling her the truth about herself. As if she didn't know. As if she needed to be reminded.

At least she was thankful she wasn't claustrophobic. Like poor sick little old Mrs Bailey, whose husband was killed at Gallipoli. It broke Evie up to see the frail handful of a woman hanging on to the banister, her knees buckling, the breath wheezing out of her in broken gasps. 'Listen,' coaxed Evie, 'I don't like the lift any more than you do, but will you try it with me, just once, for my sake?'

'No ... no. I'll be all right in a minute,' Mrs Bailey said. 'You run along, there's a dear. Leave me be. I'm in no hurry. I always do it in stages.'

Evie had offered to go and complain for her. Tell them at the office they'd have to do something. But the old woman

The Fat Girl

wouldn't agree. 'You mustn't,' she cried, 'that's the worst thing you could do. Oh, you mean well, bless your heart, you're the only one that bothers, but don't. Please. Then they'd really have it in for me. I don't want to get a reputation as a troublemaker. You know what they're like. Once you're in their bad books.... I wouldn't want to lose my pension.'

That's what I dread, Evie thought. Being old and sick and alone. And the way I'm going, it's on the cards.

She had seen a few of the forgotten remnants in those tumbledown houses behind Morey Street and wondered when the houses went whether the inhabitants just curled up and died. Living in cupboards, what else could you call those rooms with barely enough space for a bed and a suitcase. The only times they seemed to stir was when the ladies came from Meals on Wheels, and promptly opened the windows which were shut again the moment they left. Or when the old people wrapped themselves in a blanket and tottered down to the bottom of the yard. Goodness knows how they managed in winter, or were too ill to get out of bed, and no one to help. Though she had seen the Salvos there. And a hearse once or twice.

You'd think I'd learn from seeing what it does to Mrs Bailey. But anything was preferable, she decided, to using that lift. So she'd had a go herself. Walking up.

She didn't remember reaching the fifth floor, but the journey from third to fourth had seemed like the last telling stretch to the summit of Everest. Her knees were trembling so much she couldn't stop them. It was on the fifth, however, that she collapsed and banged her head.

She came to on the floor of Mrs Guthrie's lounge with a rug over her and her throbbing head on a cushion. Several women were having a cup of tea to settle their nerves and one was replacing the damp face washer on Evie's forehead. 'Oh, you did give us a turn,' she told her. 'At first we thought you were dead. If you don't mind me saying so, dear, you really shouldn't wear such a tight corset.'

Evie hadn't tried again. But that lift! It had the stale smell of a railway carriage in which a hundred surreptitious winds had been broken.

Her mother had said, and Evie knew she spoke from experience, never get into a lift, this one particularly, alone with a man. Even a man you know. The ones you know are often the worst. That's all very well, Evie told her mother, it's not so easily arranged. And since it wouldn't do to make a sudden dash when some unsuspecting male got into the lift, both Evie and her mother carried wrenches. In their handbags.

'But Mum,' she'd countered, 'there wouldn't be time to get it out.' 'Get it out?' her mother yelled, 'Use your head, girl. Just swipe him with your bag and ask questions later.'

Several times her mother had readied herself to use her secret weapon. Only once had it happened. A man jumped at her from out of the dark as she was walking home. A beefy six-footer, high with old sweat and new liquor. Well, the bigger they are the harder they fall. 'Struth, lady,' the young constable marvelled, looking at her with admiration, 'I wouldn't care to go ten rounds with you. What did you hit him with, a ton of bricks?'

Anyone who thinks the artistic talent of this city is reserved for public conveniences hasn't seen our lift, thought Evie, as the door slid across and she passed from fresh to foul. An empty lift, for which she was thankful. It's a travelling art gallery, she mused, new shows every day, the backyard Michelangelos a step ahead of the caretaker who had learned to accept the routine of scratching, scraping and rubbing-out as part of his daily chores.

Some of the sketches of nude women showed a somewhat distorted knowledge of the female form, while the prolific drawings of male equipment were, in Evie's opinion, either the result of wishful thinking or the fruits of pretty vivid imaginations.

Now and again among the filthy words she'd see a saying like, 'Candy is dandy but sex won't rot your teeth', which made her smile. Or, 'May the dove of peace crap on Nixon's head', which made her wonder. Some of it, jokes aside, was sick. Sick, sick, such as tonight. And her stomach turned as she read, scrawled on the lift wall in large erratic letters, 'HitLeR WaS riGHt, KILL tHe BlOOdY jEws'.

Her eyes brimmed. How long had it been there? How many had seen it? And more to the point, how many agreed? She didn't know if there were any Jewish families in the flats. The people on the fifteenth, they were swarthy enough, but were just as likely to be Greeks or Italians for all she knew.

Compared with this the other doodlings and daubs were nothing but childish prattle. Oh, she cried, the worms are really eating at some poor devil's brains. The sad, mixed up, unhappy sod. But what made her mad, and her ears were burning, a sign that she was boiling mad, was that instinct told her this wasn't merely for passing eyes. Whoever did this, *knew*. It could only be directed at one person, her mother, who hadn't admitted to being Jewish since the day her father disowned her when she told him she was marrying out. But someone, somehow, knew. Or maybe, the possibility wasn't absurd ... maybe, thought Evie, it's me they're after. They think that because Mum is, I'm Jewish too. Little they know, we're as kosher as ham and eggs, that I've never seen inside a synagogue and I'm never likely to, that I'm ... nothing.

She'd need a rubber. A piece of sandpaper would do. Anything to get it off. I'm not leaving this lift, she vowed, until I've cut that cancer off the wall. Nine. Ten. The lift's lights spoke silently.

Evie opened her bag, tempted to whack the wall with

her wrench. Instead she took her new lipstick, her Summer Sunset, and smothered that message of hate until all that remained in her hand was the case.

She had hardly recovered her breath before the lift stopped. On the eighteenth floor. And she was joined by an unsmiling woman whose face was as harsh and deeply lined as a dried-up river bed. Mrs Clough, empty cup in hand, going up to the twenty-ninth to borrow some sugar from her former neighbour, Mrs Flannery.

Her practised eye caught the closing of Evie's bag. There must have been something in the way Evie did it and the way she looked, flushed and distressed. The woman gazed from Evie to the great pink splotch and back to Evie, the ticker tape of her mind spewing out messages. The door opened at the twenty-seventh and without so much as a nod Evie fled, straight to the kitchen where she made herself an enormous sandwich with as many bits and overs as she could find in the refrigerator. This consumed she sliced herself a thick slab of cake and, feeling a little better, began to think of what to cook for tea.

Australia–Israel

For centuries on Passover Eve, Jewish people, in their own homes, have commemorated the flight from Egypt with a meal at which bitter herbs, unleavened bread (*matzo*) and wine are taken and prayers, blessings and psalms are sung. This is the *Seder*. (The Last Supper was a *Seder* meal and service.) The formal *Seder* concludes with the symbolic words: 'Next year in Jerusalem'. Since the establishment of the state of Israel the symbol 'Jerusalem' takes on wider meanings. For some people it is a choice to be made; should they, Americans, Australians, English, Russians... migrate again? For nearly all modern Jews the very existence of Israel adds to old symbols extra dimensions whether of pride, hope, determination or, sometimes, disappointment. The two stories which end this book express some facets of this symbolism.

NANCY KEESING

Middle Eastern Questions

WHETHER OR NOT he had guessed she would never know, and since 1974 when it happened, and through the wars in Lebanon, the question grew in significance and quality of distress.

The ordered taxi was slow in coming. She waited, fuming, not because she would be late since, these days, she always ordered a cab for a good half-hour earlier than ought to be necessary, but impatient at inefficiency. Impatient with herself, too, because she felt it should be possible to put to some use the time one wasted in waiting, but was always too restless to do anything other than prowl. If she was ready for an expected taxi, visitor or arrival of that sort she couldn't even force herself to read.

She set her suitcases outside the front door, then returned to the house to check, compulsively, that doors and windows were all locked, the stove switched off. She stood by a window facing up the leafy lane and peered through heavy shrubs in the next-door garden towards the road. There was no sign of a cab.

She opened the door of the hall cupboard and stood at its long mirror, adjusting a scarf, worn like a cravat inside the collar of her green tweed coat. A single hair floated above the well-sprayed surface of thick, still reddish hair; she patted it down and, when it drifted free again, tweaked it out. She decided that she really didn't look to be nearly fifty, and then, with dissatisfaction, that she did. Angry at looking nearly fifty she closed the door and strode with consciously lithe, long strides—because the walk gives away one's age, and she dreaded the careful, fostered gait of the elderly—to the garden path, and saw a glitter of garish yellow duco through trees. It had arrived. No. It overshot the entrance of the narrow lane, and had to reverse while she dashed back to pull shut and check the door behind her, and carry the suitcase down steps to the gate.

Exasperated, she now wished that, after all, the taxi had not come. Then she would have been forced to drive herself to the airport, which might have been preferable despite the awkwardness of having to carry luggage from parking station to terminal lounge. But at least she would have avoided the inevitability of yet another taxi driver's marvellous excuses.

This one pulled up, glanced at the suitcases, and jumped out of the car to open the boot. A stocky, swarthy man, as short as she was tall, and as crouched as she straight; and quite appallingly cheerful. 'My God,' she thought, 'a monkey.'

'My-a God,' he cried, as she settled herself on the front seat beside him, which she forced herself to do, as a rule, because she so loathed the conversations of drivers, consequently feeling guilty and aware of intellectual snobbishness as one of her besetting sins, 'My-a God, I nearly do not find you. Nice quiet little lyne though. On the radio, they tell me Map 46, F7. They-a wrong. Always I check my own map. Here,' he thrust a dog-eared volume towards her as he reversed up the lane, 'you-a look for yourself.' So pleased with himself that it was impossible to express annoyance at the delay.

She pretended to scrutinize the map, and agreed that 'they' were wrong. All the 'theys' who are always wrong, and all the garrulous taxi drivers who are always right. Know-alls about everything under the sun. Half an hour of the company of this simian. To prove himself a conversationalist, he switched off his two-way radio.

'You want-a overseas terminal?' he asked.

'No, domestic, ANA.' If he expected her to explain two large, much and internationally labelled suitcases, she did not intend to oblige.

'Ah,' he sighed, and turned to smile fetchingly, displaying nut brown, and gleaming golden teeth. 'And I think to myself: this-a lovely lydy and her nice ports, she goes overseas, so lucky.'

Three choices now: impossible silence; ridiculous explanations of reasons for, and duration of, visit to Melbourne, or predictable enquiry.

Despising banality she asked:

'Which country do you come from?' Glancing at his fleshy, rounded nose and full lips, she awaited one of the several possible answers that would be as predictable as her question. Wonderful if he should answer as the enquiry deserved with inventive Greenland or Alaska. He said:

'Lebanon, lydy. But twenty-three years I been in Austrylia.'

'Have you ever been back home for a visit?'

Oh yes. Yes indeed. He has. Only last year he spent six months in Beirut, staying with his mother.

'How lovely. She was well?' How odiously gracious-lady could one sound?

'Well!' She feared, groundlessly, that he would take his hands from the wheel but he was a careful driver with none of the swoops and sudden sickening dashes of so many of his colleagues. Nor was he in competition with everything else on the road. Nor critical of any other car, truck or bike. The golden smile sufficed. She continued to look at his hands, though. Spiky black hairs bristled as far as the first joints of his stubby fingers. The yellowish nails, she noticed, were cut straight and kept very clean.

'Well! She-a well all right. Like a young girl. Like one-a my sisters. She-a beautiful. She-a thin. She-a black hair. Beautiful.' His rasping voice was warm.

Her questions now elicited five brothers and six sisters, all remaining in Lebanon, and that he was the only one of his family to migrate. Also that he had never married.

'Freedom. I like-a freedom. Why I give up-a freedom? You tell me!' She cannot. Nor what he is free for. To travel in Australia, perhaps? No! When he first arrived he had to work, for two years, on an engineering project in the country and he hated living there, though the work was not bad.

'But then I come for Sydney. Big city. Nice big city. I always lived in a city. Beirut, she was my home town. I now live-a Sydney twenty-three years.'

'A beautiful city,' she said, meaning Sydney.

'Was beautiful. Not now.' He said, meaning Beirut. 'Could be beautiful now, but—pah—the big powers, big countries, big politics, no one knows what goes on. No one. . . .' But he is a taxi driver, so he knows, and his passenger will be made to know.

Desperately she tried to think of some topic to turn the conversation and could not, so she offered him a cigarette which he took with a 'thank you lydy' and lit when the next red light halted traffic. She also lit a cigarette—the nearest available substitute for shared salt.

'No one knows,' he blew smoke savagely, 'not in Austrylia or anywhere else.'

This is the point, she thought, where I really ought to tell him. It is somehow unfair, and even indecent, to allow him to go on. If I don't, or can't, tell him, then I must change the subject. But how? To what? Too late.

'I tell you. Last year, last September, near where I live-a Beirut with my mother, the Israels' planes, they bomb a school. Seventy-four little children playing in yard. Mostly killed. Like-a that school there,' but he didn't take his hand from the wheel to point it out, and she glanced from the wrong side of the car to a row of 1920ish brick cottages, neatly kept with tiny gardens, painted wooden porches and shiny little windows like pursed lips.

'Frightful,' she said.

'Why those Israels do that?' His voice was aggrieved but not aggressive. 'I tell you. You ask America. You ask Russia. Ask those big countries. Why those big countries not leave everyone else alone? Why those Englands take Palestine and say-a that Abba Eban: you-a Premier and that yankee Golda Meir: you-a Prime Minister? And I tell you. No one knows-a nothing. Nothing is what they tell us. Listen. Every day that six months in Beirut, I get-a *Sydney Morning Herald* sent-a me air mail. And I tell you there-a nothing told in this country about seventy-four little children at all.'

His face was expressionless, his eyes fixed on traffic.

'Why-a we not told? They not want us-a know. Why those Israels do that? Big politics. Jewses and Arabs good friends-a thousand years, eh? Brothers, eh?'

She really ought to tell him, but said something weak like: 'Oh yes.'

All her life she had disliked being close to squat, swarthy people with greasy, large-pored skin, rounded features and dark, oppressed eyes. All her life had resisted the unreasoning, unreasonable, unsuitable prejudice. Once, as a girl, she'd allowed a man like that to take her out a few times. He was a nice fellow, intelligent and good. But it was no use. When they danced together the very feel of him made her shudder; his black, oily hair at the level of her chin was torture; squeamish horror choked her throat at the pressure of his reticent, fat fingers on her back.

She feared and despised these reactions. She held passionate beliefs—that appearance counted for much less than character and ability, that race should count for nothing. Irrational repugnance aside, she would have married anyone. She always felt wretched when belief and passion were so easily dispelled by arcane and unwished-for emotions. She also perceived these dreaded and dreadful emotions as another side of her own vanity, her pride in being slim and tall and vigorous and straight-spined.

During their silence the driver glared morosely at a container truck inching the narrow road ahead. He made no stupid attempts to overtake it. He was a patient, excellent driver. She should think herself fortunate.

The truck turned off at a corner. The Lebanese accelerated and said, matter-of-factly:

'In Beirut last year, every Sunday, I spend ten dollars. Not a rich man, but I spend ten dollars, and I carry-a big bag to one of those Palestine camps. You know how-a children live there? In rags. In ten inches-a mud. I take food. I take-a chips. I-a not mind for adults, you know. But children—I crazy about children. Beautiful children, so happy-a see me every Sunday.'

It came into her mind to say that, free as he said he liked to be, he wore chains, like everyone else. Instead she replied:

'How very good of you.'

'Look, I tell you. Arab countries, we got all-a oil. America short-a oil. We stop oil-a America. America stop. Just so. Stop. So, one day, we have to do that.'

She contemplated asking about that oil. About the inequalities of wealth in Middle Eastern countries. About sheiks with millions, and refugees who were no longer refugees, in stinking mud and rags. About his ten dollars every Sunday.

But it was impossible to pursue those questions unless she could, in return, offer her own disclosure.

One safe question, though.

'You speak French too, I suppose?'

'French, Arabic, English. In-a Lebanon school you-a learn them all. Now. When I-a school, only Arabic and French. I learn English in-a war. We like Austrylians in-a war. Lot-a Austrylians in Beirut. Nice blokes. Americans—pah! Lot-a Americans in Beirut. You know, no one speak-a them damn Yanks. No one. But Austrylians—in our home, all-a time. So nice, so friendly, so you-as-good-as-me-mate. You know?'

'And that is why you came to Australia?'

'So now I speak English all-a time. In Austrylia. This last month, I don't like even-a think French. My brother-in-law makes me very sad. Six weeks ago, in Paris, he die. He go-a Paris for a medical conference. He-a doctor. Only twenty-eight, and he drop dead. He wore himself out. Looking after those seventy-four children, he burst his heart.'

'How frightful.' How banal.

'So now,' he straightened himself in his seat, 'I speak English only. All-a time.' After a very brief silence he said:

'I tell you. I had a very good friend. Ever since I came-a Sydney. Austrylian lydy. Old woman, you'd say; name-a Shirl. Every Sunday a dinner at her house. Her son my good friend too. And what you think? In her will, she give me that house. Her son live in-a country and now I live in that house. Big plyce. Nice yard—big. Kids next door-a me kick-a football in my yard. Welcome, any time. You know what. Those kids are Jewses. Their father, that Jew, my good friend. We talk. I tell him what I tell you, but we good friends. His wife, when they come-a my house, she cleans it sometimes like-a mirror and I say, now I got-a house like-a mirror, not like my house at all.'

He laughs.

'Do you cook for yourself?' They were close to the airport now. Three minutes of food talk should see them safely arrived.

'Nah! Not cook. Good cafés. But I tell you what, now.' Remorseless.

'Last week in my cab I pick up-a lydy. Lydy like you. Lovely fair hair. Nice dress. Nice house. She want to know what country I come from, and I tell her and she says she is a Jew and she says, how Arabs be so wicked-a God's choosen people? On-a on she goes. I say-a her: "Lydy, Arabs and Jewses are brothers, I-a not hate Jewses." But she goes on-a on about them Israels. I-a not supposed-a answer her, you know? Taxi rules, see. Not-a say anything back. By cripes, I got-a hold my mouth. On-a on. God's choosen! You know? When we get-a Bellevue Hill to the address she wants, I so angry I-a shake. I let-a open-a own door and then I say: "You know why people hate Jewses? Because-a Jewses like you!" What you think-a that, lydy?'

She thought he was absolutely right. Perhaps absolutely percipient. Now, entering the entrance of the airport, she should at least and at last tell him that she was, herself, a Jew. But he had drawn up at the Terminal and was making a great business of reading the meter. So she told him nothing, but added a generous tip, for which he thanked her warmly. He jumped out of the cab to lift the two heavy suitcases from the boot, and set them carefully, side by side, on the pavement. She looked down at his bushy black hair, his hunched shoulders. On his feet he seemed older than when he crouched over the steering wheel.

'Thanks very much,' she said.

'Thank *you*, lydy,' he answered gravely. She met his sombre, nearly black, gaze.

Whether or not he had guessed she would never know.

MORRIS LURIE

Messiah in Fatherland

No BUSES, no trains. I ran through the streets of Haifa, looking for a cab. My bag banged against my leg. My jacket flapped. Every shop was closed. I saw no people, not one. My footsteps rang in the deserted streets, hollow and immense, a magnification of my pounding breath. Four hours. I ran. Maybe in the next street, the next. I heard it before I saw it, a cab turning into the street, and behind it—miracles! doubly blessed!—another. Neither had passengers. I shouted, I waved. The first driver shook his head. The second looked at me astounded. I stared dumb-founded as they disappeared down the street, I ran on.

I ran up a hill. I saw a cab parked by a corner. I ran, insanely, heart beating to burst. The driver was asleep behind the wheel. I shook him awake. 'Jerusalem,' I said. 'I'm in a hurry. I have to get to a *Seder*.' I reached for the back door.

He was a fat man, with a snub nose. He wore a cracked leather jacket, just a singlet underneath. Curly hairs crawled on a pink chest. He looked at me with small eyes.

'English?' he said.

I nodded.

'OK,' he said. 'Sixty pounds.'

My hand fell away from the door. I stared at him, mouth open. This didn't seem to worry him. He scratched his chest, his small eyes looking at me thoughtfully, but friendly, smiling.

'What kind of money you got?' he said. 'Not English?'

'Dollars,' I said. 'American dollars. USA.'

'OK.' He continued to scratch his chest. 'Dollars is good. Get in.'

'How much?' I said. 'I'm not paying—'

'Hundred American dollars,' he said. 'Good price. Cheap. Get in.' He switched on the engine.

'A hundred dollars? To Jerusalem? Forget it.'

'OK, eighty,' he said.

'Twenty.'

'Get in,' he said. 'Sixty.'

'Twenty.'

He smiled. 'Fifty?' he said.

'*Twenty.*'

'OK, forty. Come on.' He had talked to me enough. His smile dropped away. He put the car into gear. I got into the back.

I don't know what kind of car it was, a Packard, a Dodge, anyhow, American. Post War, but only just. Outside, it was battered and rusty beyond belief, hardly an inch without a dent or a scratch, and indescribably dirty, mud-splattered, thick with dust, but inside it was comfortable. In fact, it was lush, a limousine. Wide soft leather seats. Vast space. When I stretched out my legs I didn't touch the front seat. It was like being inside a moving room. I lit a cigarette. We went through the streets of Haifa. We didn't seem to be going very fast. I looked at my watch. Half an hour had gone. My heart jumped.

'Listen, can you go a bit faster?' I said. 'I have to get to a *Seder*.'

'Sure,' he said. 'This is a good car. Very strong.'

Three and a half hours. How far was it to Jerusalem? It looked like nothing on a map. I tried not to think about time. I would get there. Relax. The car picked up speed. We were out of Haifa now, through the outskirts, an open road. The road ran straight, a line to the horizon. There was not another car on it. The Mediterranean shone blue on the right. It flashed with sun.

I lit another cigarette, staring out of the window, trying to see everything, trying to print it on my brain, to keep it forever, the hills, the trees, the look of the land. Where was it different? How was it different from anywhere else? That hill? That clump of trees? I searched the landscape for specialness, for significance, for difference, my eyes leaping from one side of the road to the other.

Because it *was* different. My father had laid the telegraph line here, from Haifa to Tel Aviv. It had all been desert then. There was no water. He had slept in the desert. He had carried a gun. There were four of them. They slept two to a tent. At night they heard howling. Savage dogs. Wolves. My father had laughed. He wasn't frightened. Nothing frightened him. He fired his gun into the sky. He was a joker, a prankster, a *yut*. One night he slipped a thick rope under his tent friend's sheet. The friend leapt from his bed in terror. 'Snakes!' he shouted. My father roared. Another night he pasted paper on his friend's spectacles, woke him with a whisper. 'Arabs,' he hissed. 'Bandits.' His friend clapped on his spectacles. 'Help!' he cried. 'I can't see! I'm blind!' My father rolled with laughter, his face red to bursting, tears streaming down from his eyes. What a joke. What a good joke. He had told me these stories, these and others, to belittle me—Look at me when I was young! Look at you! A *pisher*! What do you know about being alive? I sat in silence before his boastful laughter, his taunts. I had nothing to match his stories, his life. I sat, humiliated, small and shamed. But now, my eyes flying across this landscape where he had walked, worked, laughed, played jokes, slept on the hard earth, fired his gun jubilantly into the night sky, they were no longer taunts, belittlements. They were flags, and I planted them firmly, proudly on the top of each hill as we rushed past.

My father, my father.

But he didn't like me. He ignored me. He hated me. I heard his insults, his sneers, his mockery. *The Genius. The Prince. Pisher. Dreck.* Everything I did he said was clumsy, stupid, and when I did nothing it was even worse. And then he sat down at the kitchen table with his knives, his screwdriver, his pliers, and began to 'fix' things, as he called it, the toaster, the iron, the kitchen clock, his thick fingers grappling and slipping, my mother alarmed, a hand to her heart. 'Sam!' she called. 'Sam! What are you doing?' 'Ah, be quiet!' he snapped. 'Can't you see I'm fixing here?' He broke the toaster, the iron, the kitchen clock. Whatever he touched fell to pieces. And then he turned on me. 'Get out of here!' he shouted. 'What are you sitting here for, go and do something!' And I would slink out.

I smiled. I laughed. I was excited. I couldn't sit still. I wound down the window to flip out my cigarette. Wind rushed in, taking away my breath. I gulped air, beaming, I laughed out loud. I saw the driver watching me in the rear vision mirror. I didn't care. Our eyes touched. He winked. I winked back.

'It's a good car, yes?' he shouted over his shoulder.

'Beautiful!' I shouted back. 'Very good!'

'America,' he said, slapping the wheel. 'Strong.'

I wound the window back up. Relax, I told myself. Relax. But how? I felt in my jacket for my address book, took it out. I flipped quickly through the pages. There it was. Chaim Axelrod. My father's brother. My uncle. What if he's moved, I thought, seized with sudden panic, what if he doesn't live there any more? I had copied the address from a letter. I had sent a cable, and then a letter to this address, when my father had died. No reply.

Relax, relax. Someone will know.

But I don't even know what he looks like!

I remembered a photograph of a girl holding a rabbit, another one of a young man with a revolver. Who were they? Cousins? An old woman sitting under a tree. An aunt? There were so many photographs, so many faces, aunts, cousins, family friends—was my uncle there? Had I ever seen his face? My father used to show them to me, and before I had even properly looked, snatch them away, his family, not mine. He was jealous of them. He guarded them. They were all he had. 'What would you know?' he said to me. Snatch, gone.

But he did tell me some things, or they slipped out, impossible for him to contain. He had to tell. I tried to remember, tried to think. Chaim, Uncle Chaim. What did I know of him? Was he older, younger than my father? He was something, I think, in the government. He wrote books. Ah! Yes! And I saw them arriving, one a year, small books with bright red covers, always the same, year by year slowly growing on the bottom shelf in the front room, like mercury in a barometer. He wrote in Hebrew. *Ivrit*. I saw my father proudly holding up the latest one, showing it to me, letting me hold it, and then snatching it from my hands. 'Huh, *gelernte mensch*?' he said. 'Can you read it?' He showed his brother's books to everyone who came into the house, anyone, boasting, his chest flung out, pointing to the name on the cover, on the title page. I saw my father's thick finger, the nail rimmed with black, stabbing his brother's name.

And did he read them? I lit a cigarette. No. I couldn't remember my father ever reading his brother's books. He didn't read books. He never read. Well, sometimes a Western, which he got from the lending library around the corner. I remembered the thick pages, thumbed so much they were like felt, I saw my father sitting with one, his mouth half open, blinking fast, and then suddenly throwing the book to the floor. 'Rubbish!' he shouted. '*Dreck!* It's always the same thing. Can't they write something new? Anyhow, I think I read this one before. Big deal.' He kicked the book with his foot. He didn't like books. He was suspicious of them. He felt they were trying to pull the wool over his eyes, baffle him with their so-called cleverness. Cleverness! How he hated cleverness. 'Smart' was one of his most cutting words. I was 'smart'. 'What have you got there?' he'd growl at me, when I was reading a book. 'Ah, Mr Smart?' Before I could speak, he'd snatch it from my hands. A quick flick through the pages. '*Dreck!*' He'd fling it down. But he wasn't finished. 'What are you reading that *dreck* for?' he'd torment me. 'If you want to read, read Chekhov! Tolstoy! Dostoyevsky! The Russians, that's literature! Not this *dreck*!' I bought the Russians, I bought Chekhov, Tolstoy, Gogol, Dostoyevsky, Lermentov, Pushkin, at first to please him, but then for themselves, for me. He came in. He snatched from my hand. 'What's this *dreck*, smart boy?' 'Dostoyevsky,' I said. That stopped him for a moment. His mouth fell open. He blinked. 'Uh?' he said. He flicked through the pages, frowning, thoughtful, his eyelids a blur, his brow ruffled, the pages flying in his hands like a live bird trying to escape. Thoughts raced openly across his face. I had beaten him. I had won. But only for a moment. He was searching. Ah! He had found a loophole, a breach. He charged in. 'But this is in English!' he roared. 'What does it mean in English? Nothing! Idiot! You have to read it in the original! In Russian! In Russian it's poetry! In English, you know what it is in English, huh, smart boy? In English it's *dreck*!'

I remembered how angry this used to make me, how I could never win, the rules were his, but now I smiled, I saw the joke. Had my father read Chekhov, Gogol, Dostoyevsky, any of them, in Russian? Of course not. He couldn't read Russian. He couldn't even speak it. All he knew in Russian were some swear words, some shouts, some curses. I heard him shouting them. I smiled, drawing hard on my cigarette. And then suddenly I panicked again, forgot all about my father. The sun was setting. The light was fading from the sky. The country to left and right was growing dark. I shot another look at my watch. We weren't going to make it. We weren't even at Tel Aviv yet.

Relax, relax.

I tried to think of other things. I saw myself knocking on my uncle's door. The *Seder* had just begun. I saw glittering candlesticks, a spreading tablecloth white as a fall of new snow, crystal goblets dancing with wine. 'Yes?' It was my uncle at the door, kindly man with white hair. I saw his puzzled eyes. Who is this calling at such a time? I introduced myself. 'I'm Sam's son,' I said. 'I have just arrived from Australia.' There would be a look of astonishment, amazement, and then a smile, a beam, a shout of joy. The door would fly open. And in I would sweep, like the Messiah, Elijah the Prophet, into my uncle's flat.

My heart leapt. I thought at once of Popov.

Popov!

There is a part in the ceremony of the *Seder*—about halfway, just after the meal—when a glass of wine is filled to the brim and the youngest member of the family is sent to open the front door. This was always my job. The wine is for Messiah, Elijah the Prophet. In he will sweep, when the time is right, into every Jewish home in the world, with one gulp drink down his glass of wine, and at once peace will reign on earth. The dead will arise. All men will be brothers. The lion will lie down with the lamb. Year after year I opened the door and there was never anyone. And then there was Popov.

I was fourteen years old. Popov stood on the doormat in his lumpy clothes, shuffling his awkward feet to and fro like a bashful suitor. He wore a shiny black suit, too wide in the trousers, too tight around the waist. His hair was flat with water (later it would rise like a rooster's comb). The peaks of his shirt collar pointed left and right, two unruly horns. His tie was crooked, the knot pulled too hard. He smiled, showing his metal teeth in the front. I retreated. Popov advanced. He came shyly into the room where we sat. My mother uttered a cry. Her hand flew to her mouth. She was frightened of him, as I was. 'My wife has left me,' mumbled Popov. 'I have nowhere to go.' He sat down awkwardly at the table. The chair creaked. He weighed two hundred pounds, more. He overflowed it on both sides. He steadied himself with his arms on the table. His hands were enormous, thick with black hair, a fearsome pelt. It sprang down his fingers. On one, tight into the flesh, a gold ring flashed. The light from our candles turned the thick glass in his spectacles to milk. 'You are the only one, *chaver*,' he said to my father, 'the only one left.' My father began to chant. Popov moved his thick lips. At first no sound came out, and then a deep rumble emerged, so low you could hardly make out the words. I stared at him in terror, in awe.

He had been a businessman, practically a millionaire, some said, but now all that was gone. His factory had burnt down. A partner had swindled him. There was trouble with income tax, with the police. Also his health was no good. He had pains around the heart, in his back, his feet. His eyesight was failing. He couldn't sleep. His bladder screamed all night long. My mother served the meal. Popov crumbled *matzo* nervously with a heavy hand. 'Eat,' my father said. Popov ate. 'I am broken in half with sorrow,' he said. He stuffed in chicken. He gulped wine. His face grew red. Sweat stood out on his brow. He lifted up his spectacles, those milky discs, wiped tears from his swollen eyes.

He had finished. 'Very nice,' he said to my mother. He was happy now. He leaned across the table to pinch my cheek. I ducked. Popov laughed, showing his metal teeth.

He poured another glass of wine, and one for my father. 'Sam,' my mother said. 'Be quiet,' my father said. 'It's *Pesach*.' My father drank down his wine. 'Come on,' he said to Popov, holding out the bottle. 'You're too slow.'

Then my father banged the table with his fist and began to sing the songs that follow the meal. He had never sung so loudly before. Popov, at first mumbling, growling, began to sing loudly too. He rocked on his creaking chair. He stamped his heavy boots. They sang together, faster and faster. They raced like two trains. They drank more wine, glass after glass. Popov tore open the collar of his shirt, forced down his tie. My father did the same. Popov was wet with sweat. My father's face shone like wax.

They sang, '*La Shona Huboh! B' Yerroosholuyim!*'

In the year to come we will be in Jerusalem. When the *Seder* was over and my mother was in the kitchen washing the dishes, Popov sat with my father in the front room and they talked about their days in Palestine. In English, in Yiddish, and then in *Ivrit*, only in *Ivrit*. 'We'll go back, *chaver*,' Popov said. 'There's no life here. We'll go back. You and me. Next year we'll dance in the streets of Jerusalem. Huh? You and me. We'll live again.'

In the streets of Tel Aviv I saw only our car, flashing black in the windows of shops, a phantom, a shadow, a rushing ghost. There were no people. The sky was darkening. Full night was not far away. I didn't dare look at my watch.

We turned inland, away from the sea. I saw lights shining in windows, bright rectangles hanging in the dark. Then fields, trees. And then nothing, blackness. It was night. We were going to be too late.

I tapped the driver on the shoulder. 'You know this address?' I asked him. He took the book from my hand. I crouched behind him. He squinted as he drove. Then he handed it back.

'We'll ask someone,' he said.
'You don't know it?'
'Don't worry, don't worry. It's all OK.'

It was after eight o'clock. The *Seder* would have begun. When I wound down the window to throw out a cigarette, the air was cold. I wound it quickly back. The road began to climb. We went around a bend. I saw lights on a hill.

'Is that it?' I shouted. 'Is that Jerusalem?'
'Half,' he said. 'Another half.'

I stared at the address in my hand. What if we couldn't find it? What if he'd moved? What if no one knew where he was?

We drove into Jerusalem just after nine o'clock. A cold wind was blowing. The streets glistened. It had recently rained, and looked as though it soon would again. Black clouds scudded across the moon. I saw three men walking along a street. 'Stop!' I shouted to the driver. I leapt from the car. I showed them the address. I read it out to them. They shrugged, not interested. One of them sneered. They walked away as though I didn't exist.

'Bastards!' I shouted after them. 'Just keep going,' I told the driver. 'Drive around. We'll find it.'

We drove slowly up and down streets. I craned to read signs. There were no people to ask. We went around and around.

'Try up there!' I shouted.
'We've been up there already.'
'Are you sure? Try it again.'

The driver pulled over to the side of the road.
'What are you doing?'

'I think it's better I leave you here,' he said. 'On foot you'll find it quicker. You'll be OK. You can knock on a door.'

'I'm not paying you!' I shouted. 'Try up there!'
'OK, OK,' he said. He looked tired. He had zipped his

jacket up to his throat. 'Up there,' he said.

He drove slowly, as though resigned to driving like this forever. I saw a woman. 'Stop!' I shouted to the driver. I was out of the car before it had properly stopped. I ran up to the woman. I showed her the address. She pointed up a hill.

'I've already been up that street,' the driver said. 'I think even twice.'

'Maybe we missed it. Maybe it's only a little street. *Please!*'

It was there. A block of grey flats. I gave the driver his forty dollars, and then—'Here! Thank you! *Gut yomtov!*'—another ten, grabbed my bag, was off, running. It was nearly ten o'clock.

The first two doors said Ashkenazy and Slonim. I ran up stairs.

Pincus, I read on the third door, heart pounding. I read the name on the fourth and turned to run up more stairs before I realized what it was. I turned back. I stopped. I closed my eyes, dizzy with running, panting for breath. I gulped air, trying to calm down. I was in a sweat.

I pressed the bell.

I heard footsteps, or maybe it was my heart. I stared at the door, trying to prepare my expression. A smile? Or should I look serious, reserved? I should have brought something, I suddenly thought, a gift. A bottle of whisky, something, anything. I felt all at once empty-handed, standing before the door. My face grew hot. The Messiah? Elijah the Prophet sweeping in in a cloud of glory? Oh, fool, fool. I didn't know these people. What were they to me, I to them? Why was I here? Why had I come? I stood before the door, small and belittled, a fool, a burning fool.

I heard the sound of a lock being drawn. A click. The door opened a few inches. It was a woman, a short woman, with a halo of frizzy grey hair. 'Yes?' she said. I took a step forward. 'Yes?' she said again. She opened the door wider, throwing out more light. She peered out at me. Now I could see her clearer, her eyes. My aunt. This must be my aunt. I opened my mouth to speak but before I could say a word her eyes went suddenly wide, a hand flew up to her mouth, and then she screamed.

I had brought back to Israel my father's face.

BIOGRAPHICAL NOTES

LILIAN BARNEA. Born in Poland and educated in England. She has lived in Israel and America. She came to Australia in 1966 and lives in Melbourne. She is married and has one daughter.

She likes to read and to write. At present she is working on her second novel, towards the writing of which she has been awarded a grant by the Literature Board of the Australia Council.

HERZ BERGNER (1907–1970). Born Radinmo, Poland, to a family of writers and painters. He emigrated to Melbourne in 1937 with his wife. From 1928 he published short stories in leading Yiddish periodicals in Europe, Israel, Australia and the United States.

His novels in lude *Tsvishn Himel un Vaser* (*Between Sky and Sea*, translated by Judah Waten, Australian Literature Society Gold Medal) which deals with a boatload of Jewish refugees; and *Likht um Shotn* (1960; *Light and Shadow*, translation published in 1963) describing the struggle of a Jewish family for acceptance in an Australian community. Bergner's short stories, especially those in his volume *Vu der Emes Shteyt Ayn* (*Where the Truth Lies*, 1966), realistically mirror Jewish life in Melbourne and focus on the Jewish immigrants who arrived in Australia after World War II.

LYSBETH COHEN. Born in Sydney. Her mother was English, her father of a family established in Australia since 1890. Educated Sydney Girls' High School; University of Sydney. She is married to Dr Douglas Cohen; and has one daughter and one son.

She has had short stories and factual articles published in Australian and overseas magazines; she also writes radio talks and plays, and a regular feature column in *Australian Jewish Times*. Her published books include *Dr Margaret Harper, Rachel Forster Hospital: The First Fifty Years,* and *Coronary Wife* (by 'Lysbeth Rose').

JUNE FACTOR. Born in Lodz, Poland; came to Australia as an infant, now living in Melbourne. Educated at schools in Melbourne and the University of Melbourne, graduating in Arts and Education. She worked as a secondary school teacher and is now a lecturer in English at the Institute of Early Childhood Development.

She learned to read and write Yiddish, and consequently has had access to a wonderfully rich literature; she acknowledges the influence of Scholem Aleichem.

Her publications include a short story 'The Wedding' which has been widely anthologized; and stories for children and radio scripts.

LEN FOX. Born 1905 in Melbourne. On his father's side, a member of a Jewish family whose Australian members include the artist E. Phillips Fox and the literary critic A. A. Phillips. He became a teacher; spent 1933–34 in Europe; worked in the Movement Against War and Fascism, writing a number of pamphlets including *Australia and the Jews* (1939), one of the first Australian publications specifically opposing anti-Semitism.

He came to Sydney in 1940 and became a journalist on *Progress*, *Tribune*, and later the miners' publication *Common Cause*, of which he was editor until his retirement in 1970. He has been a Vice-President of the Aboriginal-Australian Fellowship and of the Fellowship of Australian Writers.

He is married to the writer Mona Brand.

His publications include short stories, one of which won the Grenfell Henry Lawson Festival prize in 1965, *Monopoly*, *Vietnam Neighbours* (poems), *E. Phillips Fox, Notes and Recollections*, *Eureka and its Flag*, *Depression Down Under* (editor in collaboration with other writers).

PINCHAS GOLDHAR (1901–1947). Born at Lodz in Poland and, after coming to Australia in 1926, lived in Melbourne. He wrote a number of short stories and essays in Yiddish and edited Australia's first Yiddish newspaper, the *Yiddishe Nayes*. He translated many Australian works into Yiddish including stories by Henry Lawson, Vance Palmer, Katharine Susannah Prichard, Frank Dalby Davison and Dowell O'Reilly.

He found the situation of Australian Jewry depressing and he thought decaying, and his writing was intended to describe

and, if possible, strengthen Australian Jewish life.
His published books include *Zerzeilungen Fun Australie*.

NANCY KEESING. Born in 1923 in Sydney to parents whose familes have been established in New Zealand since 1843 and in Australia since 1851. Educated Sydney Church of England Girls' Grammar School; Frensham School, Mittagong; University of Sydney, Diploma in Social Studies. She is married to Dr A. M. (Mark) Hertzberg; and has one daughter and one son.

Her work includes poetry, short stories, factual articles, criticism, and book reviews published in most leading Australian magazines and newspapers, and radio scripts for ABC. She is represented in numerous anthologies. Her published books number over twenty, among which are four volumes of poetry including *Hails and Farewells*; six collections of Australian folk verse in collaboration with Douglas Stewart including *Australian Bush Ballads, Old Bush Songs, Favourite Bush Ballads*; literary criticism including *Australian Postwar Novelists*; two books for children including *The Golden Dream*; an autobiographical memoir *Garden Island People*; numerous anthologies including *History of the Australian Gold Rushes* (with introduction, annotation and notes); and *The White Chrysanthemum: Changing Images of Australian Motherhood* (1977).

JOHN GEORGE LANG (1816–1864). The first native-born Australian writer of fiction was born at Parramatta, grandson of John Harris, a Jewish convict who arrived in Sydney in 1788 with the First Fleet. Lang was educated at William Cape's school in Sydney, was a foundation pupil of Sydney College (the precursor of Sydney Grammar School) and read for the Bar in England. In 1842 he left Australia for India where he became a celebrated barrister and proprietor of an English-language newspaper.

His published books include two about Australian life, *The Forger's Wife* (a novel, 1855), and *Botany Bay* (short stories, 1859).

MORRIS LURIE. Born Melbourne 1938. Married, 'Glorious English wife, two spotless children'. He lived abroad for eight years, chiefly in England, but also in Greece, Copenhagen and Tangier.

His stories have been published in major Australian, British and American magazines, broadcast on the BBC, and they have been widely anthologized and translated. His children's books have been televised on BBC TV and broadcast on ABC radio. He has written a screenplay which is about to be produced. His published books include three novels: *Rappaport*, *The London Jungle Adventures of Charlie Hope*, and *Rappaport's Revenge*; two books for children: *The Twenty-Seventh Annual African Hippopotamus Race*, and *Arlo the Dandy Lion*; two collections of short stories: *Happy Times*, and *Inside the Wardrobe*; and two books of pieces: *The English in Heat*, and *Hack Work*.

HARRY MARKS (1923–1977). Born in Melbourne in 1923, a fourth generation Australian. He saw active service during World War II, spent a year in England, but otherwise spent all his life in Melbourne. He married and had two children.

He edited *Concern* and *Australian New Writing*. At the time of his death he was immediate past President of the Fellowship of Australian Writers (Victorian Branch), and President of the Athenaeum.

His publications include numerous articles and radio scripts and six or seven short stories; a novel, *The Heart Is Where the Hurt Is*; and *I Can Jump Oceans*, a biography of Alan Marshall which won the 1977 Weickart Award.

DAVID MARTIN. Born in Budapest in 1915, educated in Germany. He left Germany in 1935. He has lived and worked in Holland, Israel (on a *kibbutz*), Britain and India. He is married to Richenda and has one son.

His poetry, short stories, factual and autobiographical articles have been published in leading Australian and overseas magazines and newspapers. His published books include many novels, among which are *Tiger Bay*, *The Young Wife*, *The Hero of Too*, *The King Between*, *Where a Man Belongs*; poetry: *Poems 1938–58*; a radio verse play: *Spiegel the Cat*; books for children: *Frank and Francesca*, *On the Road to Sydney*, *The Chinese Boy*, *The Cabby's Daughter*, *Mister P. and His Remarkable Flight*, *The Devilish Mystery of the Flying Mum*, and, with Richenda Martin, *Katie*.

Biographical Notes

NATHAN SPIELVOGEL (1874–1956). Born and educated in Ballarat at the Dana Street State School where, later, he was headmaster for many years. He founded the Ballarat Historical Society.

His short stories, verse, essays and historical articles were published in many Australian journals and magazines including the *Bulletin*, the *Lone Hand* and the *Ballarat Courier*. His published books include *A Gumsucker on the Tramp, The Cocky Farmer, Old Eko's Note Book, The History of Ballarat* and *Selected Short Stories*.

JUDAH WATEN. Born in Odessa, Russia 1911. In infancy he migrated to Western Australia with his parents. Educated Christian Brothers College, Perth, and the University High School, Melbourne. He has worked in England and travelled widely in Australia, India, Europe and the U.S.S.R. His many jobs have included state school teacher, itinerant cook, journalist, and railway porter. Married to Hyrell, one daughter.

His short stories and factual articles appear in a wide range of Australian and overseas magazines. He also writes book reviews. His work is widely anthologized and widely translated. His published books include his novels: *The Unbending, Shares in Murder, Time of Conflict, Distant Land, Season of Youth* and *So Far No Further*; a volume of short stories: *Alien Son*; and a children's book: *Bottle-O!*

FAY ZWICKY. Born in Melbourne in 1933. Educated in Melbourne and at the University of Melbourne where she began to publish poetry and short stories. Married with two children, she is Senior Tutor in English at the University of Western Australia.

Her work is published widely in literary journals and anthologies. She has published a book of poetry, *Isaac Babel's Fiddle*.